MURDER AT THE POLO CLUB

CLEOPATRA FOX MYSTERY, BOOK 7

C.J. ARCHER

WWW.CJARCHER.COM

CHAPTER 1

LONDON, JUNE 1900

Flossy and Floyd waited in the foyer of the Mayfair Hotel with as little patience as five-year-olds before an outing to the circus. The reason for their restlessness was different, however, even though all three of us were heading off to the polo together. In Flossy's case, it was because she didn't want to be late and our mode of transport was supposed to collect us fifteen minutes ago. In Floyd's case, it was because he was full of excitable energy in anticipation of riding in an automobile borrowed from a guest.

Flossy tugged her brother's watch out of his waistcoat pocket and flipped open the case. "We'll miss all the pre-match entertainment."

Floyd snatched the watch from her and tucked it back into his pocket. "I told you before, we'll get there on time. Now stop whining. You'll spoil the experience." He glanced over her head as Frank opened the door for two guests entering the hotel. "Anything?"

"No sight yet, sir."

Floyd strode past the doorman and gazed along Piccadilly in the direction from which the automobile should arrive, given it was housed in the hotel's stables. He then checked the other direction before returning to the foyer. Frank had held the door open the entire time without complaint, although his smile tightened as his employer's son passed him again. Knowing Frank was a curmudgeonly sort, I was surprised he managed to hold the smile for as long as he did.

Not that Floyd noticed. "Perhaps the mechanic discovered a problem when he started it."

"I knew we should have gone by horse and carriage." Flossy tucked her closed parasol under her arm and pulled a fan from her bag. "Horseless carriages are too unreliable."

"You enjoyed the ride last time."

She fanned herself more vigorously than was necessary, given it was pleasant inside the hotel. "We were driven around a circuit by the manufacturer's driver that day. We had no destination and no schedule." She closed the fan with a snap and poked her brother with it. "Go and see why it's taking the driver so long."

"Mechanic, not driver."

"But he'll be driving us, won't he?"

"Yes, but he's called a mechanic, not a driver."

"Why?"

"I don't know. It's just what they prefer to be called. I suppose it's because they're more than a mere driver. They fix engines when required, too. They're also called automobiles by those in the industry, not horseless carriages."

"Whatever the contraptions are called, if they didn't break down so often in the first place, mechanical skills wouldn't be required."

Floyd rolled his eyes. "Cleo, tell her the driver of an automobile is called a mechanic before she insults the fellow."

I'd been beginning to wonder if my cousins remembered I was waiting with them. They'd seemed so preoccupied with the arrival of the vehicle, or lack thereof. "I like the word the French use. *Chauffeur.*"

Floyd nodded, but Flossy dismissed the suggestion with a shake of her head. "It'll never catch on outside of France. The English prefer English words and English things."

"Like the food our *chef de cuisine* serves in our restaurant?" Floyd asked with a smirk, knowing very well that Mrs. Poole's dishes had a decidedly French influence.

Flossy sighed dramatically. "Where *is* he? All our friends will be wondering where we are."

"Don't worry, we'll still arrive on time. The automobile will go much faster than a horse once we're out of London."

"That's if it ever gets here at all." Her shoulders rounded, as if the thought weighed her down. "It'll be a disaster if we can't get to the polo today."

"There'll be other matches," I told her. "I'm sure Floyd's friends will invite us again."

"But it's the final of the Champion Cup! Everyone who matters will be there *today*, not next Saturday or the one after. *Today*, Cleo. There's a rumor the Prince of Wales will attend."

Only members and their invited guests could gain entry to the exclusive Elms Polo Club. Guest vouchers were highly sought after at the best of times, but they were rarer than rubies on the day the final cup match was to be played.

Flossy's shoulders drooped even further. "We need to be there, Cleo. After being snubbed by the Duchess of Kirklees, we simply *must* be at the polo. The success of my season depends upon it."

"It's not as if we will be at a loose end the night of her ball."

"Lady Trefusis's ball is hardly in the same league as the Duchess of Kirklees's." She gave me a look that implied I ought to know better.

I did know better. Flossy made sure of that. She reminded me on several occasions that an invitation to the duchess's ball was first prize and an invitation to Lady Trefusis's was the consolation. The only people in attendance at the latter would be those who didn't get invited to the former. In Flossy's mind, the snub was a disaster.

The success, or not, of her social season was in the hands of whichever lady was hosting the latest ball, dinner, party, breakfast, afternoon tea, exhibition, concert or other event. The polo was a welcome variation on the usual round that I'd endured of late. It wasn't that I found socializing tiring but, rather, *tiresome*. I craved stimulation of a different kind. The two weeks since the end of my investigation into the murder of a businessman at a dockside tavern had dragged, even though I'd been busy every day doing the rounds with my cousin and aunt. I was looking forward to spending the day watching a sport I'd never seen before. I enjoyed learning new things.

"I don't know why we didn't get an invitation to the duchess's ball this year," Flossy went on. "We went last year."

"I'm afraid it's most likely my fault," I said. "I hear she's old-fashioned, and the fact that I'm the bluestocking daughter of a Cambridge academic doesn't sit well with ladies like her."

Ever since my aunt's social circle learned I was better educated than their sons, some had given us a wide berth. Fortunately, those who did weren't close friends, so it mattered little to Flossy and Aunt Lilian, and not at all to me. Missing out on the duchess's ball was different, however. It cut Flossy deeply.

She looked pained by my apology. It hadn't occurred to her that I was to blame. She stumbled over herself to assure me that wasn't the case. "Don't be silly, Cleo, it's not you. That business was forgotten weeks ago. No, no, I'm quite sure it was simply a matter of numbers. Too many ladies and not enough gentlemen. Don't you agree, Floyd?"

"For once, my sister is right," Floyd said with too much bluster to be convincing. "It's either because of the numbers, or the fact that our family are in trade. You said so yourself— she's an old-fashioned snob."

It was kind of him to try, but we all knew that wasn't the reason, since they'd been invited to the ball last year. Aunt Lilian's father—my maternal grandfather—may have been in trade, but he'd been wealthy and, these days, wealth mattered. It helped that Uncle Ronald was the son of minor nobility, so his wife's connections were overlooked, as was the fact he owned a hotel. Well, they were *usually* overlooked.

The conversation had taken an awkward turn, one that had the three of us seeking a distraction. Flossy flapped her fan in an attempt to hide her embarrassment, while Floyd strode outside again to look for the automobile. I was about to send one of the porters to the stables to see what was holding up the mechanic when Peter entered the foyer from the direction of the senior staff offices. He craned his neck to peer over the heads of the guests milling about and, spotting us, made his way towards us, smiling and greeting guests as he went.

The smile slipped when he joined us. "I've been sent by Mr. Hobart to tell you that your driver has been delayed."

"Mechanic, not driver," Flossy said.

Frank opened the door again and Floyd returned to the foyer. Peter repeated the announcement for his sake. "The automobile will be here as soon as Mr. Hobart resolves the dispute between the, er, mechanic and the coachmen and grooms. Hopefully that won't be long." He didn't look entirely confident, however.

"What dispute?" Floyd asked.

"The grooms and coachmen say the smell of the automobile is unbearable and that it should be stabled elsewhere."

"They're complaining about the smell?" Floyd scoffed. "They work with horses all day!"

"The noise also makes the horses jittery. I'm sure Mr. Hobart will resolve the issue quickly and without fuss."

Not even Mr. Hobart's diplomatic efforts could resolve it in a brief space of time, if at all. Lord Dunmere, a guest at the hotel, had arrived in his automobile two days ago. The only place to house it had been in the hotel stables in the nearby mews. He was the first of our guests to bring his own automobile, but I doubted he would be the last. The vehicles were becoming quite popular with those who could afford them. Although few were seen in London, I suspected it was only a matter of time before the streets were clogged with them, pushing out the slower, more cumbersome horse-drawn carriages. It didn't bode well for the future livelihoods of coachmen and grooms.

"Bloody hell," Floyd muttered. "I'll sort it out." He walked off, his purposeful strides getting him to the door before Frank.

Frank attempted to atone for his laxness by doffing his cap and wishing Floyd a "very pleasant day at the polo."

Floyd ignored him. Flossy followed her brother out, while I turned to Peter.

"I'd better go, too. Thank you for passing on the message."

"My pleasure, Miss Fox. You can exit the back way if you want to get there faster."

"It's all right, I'll go with my cousins."

I slipped past Frank, still holding open the door, albeit with a scowl on his face for me instead of the smile he sported for my cousins. He never bothered to butter me up like he did them. I preferred his real grumpiness to his false courtesy, anyway.

"You look a little warm, Frank. Perhaps you should go inside and rest in the staff parlor for a while."

He bristled. "I can manage. Don't go replacing me with a machine yet." Clearly he sided with the coachman and grooms when it came to the question of progress.

"No machine could replace you, Frank. It could never capture your attitude."

He puffed out his chest. "Thank you, Miss Fox."

I trotted to catch up to Flossy, some distance behind Floyd. We passed the hotel's new restaurant, opened a mere two weeks ago with a triumphant dinner. It had been a roaring success ever since. The reservation book was full until the end of July.

Just past the restaurant was the arched entrance to the mews that contained stables and coach houses, some of which belonged to the Mayfair Hotel. Unlike most London hotels, the Mayfair had its own stables where it kept two carriages and four horses for the use of our family and special guests. Where other luxury London hotels were purpose-built, the Mayfair had once been a private mansion home. After my uncle inherited it, he poured my aunt's money into renovations after their marriage. The building's past as a home afforded the benefit of the equine accommodations. Accommodation that was now doubling as a stable for Lord Dunmere's motor vehicle.

The voices of the mechanic and coachman filled the narrow passage of the mews as they rose to be heard over each other. Mr. Hobart looked small as he stood between them, his hands up in an attempt to calm tempers.

"What am I supposed to do?" the mechanic shouted.

"I don't care," the coachman shouted back. "Take it away, anywhere but here!"

Mr. Hobart's response was drowned out by the mechanic's. "I already told you. I've got permission—"

"And I told *you*, I don't care! Take it away!"

"What do you think I'm trying to do? I've got passengers to collect from the hotel."

"I meant, take it away and don't come back!"

The mechanic crossed his arms over his chest. "No."

The coachman followed suit. He stood in front of the wide coach house entrance. The automobile was parked inside. The mechanic must have driven it in while the coachman was absent.

One of the horses in the adjoining stables whinnied. The coachman stabbed a finger in its direction. "See! The horses hate it."

"The engine's not even running."

"They can smell the oil. It disturbs them. Tell him, Mr. Hobart."

The mechanic looked at Mr. Hobart for the first time. "Who are you?"

"The manager of the Mayfair Hotel," Mr. Hobart said evenly. "I assume you are Lord Dunmere's mechanic."

The mechanic touched the brim of his cap in greeting. "That I am, sir. Can you tell this horse-brained idiot that I have permission to stable his lordship's vehicle here?"

Before Mr. Hobart could answer, Floyd spoke. "It's true, he does. Cobbit, step aside. Let the mechanic take out the automobile."

"But sir!"

"Hobart will relay your complaint to my father and a resolution will be found. But right now, we have a polo match to get to. Step aside."

The coachman's ruddy cheeks turned even redder and, for a moment, I thought he'd disobey Floyd. But he spun on his heel and headed into the stables, his fists clenched tightly at his sides. He brushed past the two young grooms flanking the door who exchanged glances before following.

The mechanic reached for long linen coats hanging from hooks inside the stables and handed one to each of us along with goggles. A few minutes later, I could see why the coat, goggles and thick veils we'd been advised to wear were necessary. We would have been covered in oil smuts by the time we reached the Elms Polo Club if we'd not worn suitable outerwear.

The drive out of London was slow as horse-drawn vehicles held us up, but once we left the city behind, I could see why travel by automobile was all the rage with those who could afford one. It was positively the best way to drive on country roads. We passed horse-drawn carriages with ease, and even the wind whipping at our faces ceased to bother me after a while. As we picked up speed, Floyd let out a *whoop* from the front seat.

In the back seat of the Peugeot, with a picnic basket stocked by the hotel's kitchen staff between us, Flossy and I exchanged grins.

"She can reach speeds of up to twenty miles an hour!" the mechanic shouted at us over the noise of the engine.

"Marvelous," Floyd shouted back. "May I have a go at driving?"

"Sorry, sir, not without his lordship's permission." The mechanic turned the handlebar rising out of the floor. The vehicle responded by turning the corner, albeit a little too quickly. Floyd ended up almost in the mechanic's lap, but with the basket wedged tightly between us, Flossy and I had nowhere to go and managed to stay seated on our respective sides.

Flossy clamped a hand to her hat, although it was held firmly in place thanks to the veil secured beneath her chin. "Isn't this thrilling, Cleo? What a shame it can't go faster."

Until they built an automobile with doors and a roof to stop me being thrown onto the road if it overturned, the pace was fast enough for me.

We arrived at the Elms in a little over twenty minutes. Floyd was the envy of several of his friends who witnessed our arrival. The mechanic obliged their curiosity by answering their questions about the vehicle, while Flossy and I dispensed with our protective outerwear.

When the men had finished ogling the glossy black paintwork and shiny brass lamps, Flossy directed her brother to collect the picnic basket. We headed through the gate and found a position on the lush lawn under one of the eponymous elms in front of the palatial Georgian-style clubhouse. The lawn rolled gently to the edge of a lake where small sailboats drifted lazily past. Some of the younger gentlemen participated in boat races to show off their skill, and several ladies indulged them by watching on from the shore, broad hats shielding their eyes but not their smiles. Everyone was in a sunny mood to match the fine weather.

The Elms Polo Club was as much a social club as a polo playing one, so naturally Flossy and several other girls of marriageable age were on the hunt for eligible bachelors. One of those girls was my friend and a guest at the Mayfair Hotel, Miss Clare Hessing. She spotted us and waved, but did not leave her mother's side beneath the large umbrella they shared with two other ladies. Miss Hessing seemed happy. Considering she was in the company of her mother, that was unusual indeed. I suspected it had more to do with the fact that she would be able to rendezvous with her paramour, Mr. Liddicoat, at some point today. He would be here somewhere. His cousin was the captain of one of the teams playing for the Champion Cup.

It would be difficult for the lovers to find each other among the sea of picnickers spread across the lawn, but the crowd would also provide coverage. With Mrs. Hessing planted on her chair for the day, they could do as they pleased without worrying the matriarch was scrutinizing her daughter's every move.

At the end of our last investigation, I'd suggested she use the services of Armitage and Associates to look into Mr. Liddicoat, but I didn't know whether she'd hired Harry Armitage. As curious as I was to find out, I stayed away from his Soho office. Staying away from Harry when we weren't investigating was the best for everyone, including me. Especially me.

I grew drowsy after our picnic of pies, jam tarts, salads, sandwiches and ginger beer. The hotel's cooks had packed more than the three of us could possibly eat and drink, which Floyd's friends found most agreeable as they finished off what we left. The soporific combination of the warm air and a full stomach would have sent me to sleep if it wasn't for the loud angry voices coming from the clubhouse steps.

Heads turned to watch the two men arguing, but we were too far away to hear what they said. Either they thought no one noticed or they didn't care. Both wore the riding outfits of players, although in different team colors. The one on the higher step towered over the other, two steps down, but the fellow wasn't intimidated and held his ground.

"What handsome specimens," Flossy murmured.

"How can you see their faces from here?" I asked.

"I can tell by their physiques. Look at those broad shoulders, Cleo. And those riding breeches are hugging their thighs in a most pleasing way. Hopefully they'll turn around soon so we can see their b—"

"Flossy!"

"I was going to say *backs*, but now I know where *your* mind is wandering to." She giggled and ignored her brother's raised brows as he questioned what she found so amusing.

"I wonder what that's about," I said, nodding at the two men. "Who are they?"

"The captains from the teams competing today," Floyd said. "The taller one in the light blue jersey is the captain of the Elms team, Rufus Broadman, and the other man is Vernon Rigg-Lyon from the Polo and Gun Club. Today's his last match. He's retiring. They're fierce rivals both on and off the field, apparently." His smirk implied there was an interesting story behind their rivalry.

Before I could ask, the argument escalated. They pointed aggressively at one another, then Mr. Rigg-Lyon pushed Mr. Broadman. Mr. Broadman tripped up the step behind him but regained his balance without falling. He retaliated by shoving the other man in the chest.

Mr. Rigg-Lyon fell backward onto his rear. The only thing that was injured was his pride, however. He refused the assistance of a third man who'd hurried up to them, arriving too late to be of any use. The newcomer must have said something to both men as the two captains suddenly looked towards the crowd who were paying them more attention than their picnics.

The two captains parted, striding off in opposite directions, leaving the third man on his own. He tugged on his cuff before lowering his head and returning to the picnicking onlookers. It was Mr. Liddicoat, the cousin of Rufus Broadman and paramour of Miss Hessing.

She sat with her head also bowed on the rug near her

mother's feet, her hands twisting together in her lap. Mrs. Hessing pinched her lips as she gossiped with her friends, no doubt voicing her displeasure at seeing her daughter's paramour's cousin in a physical altercation. Poor Mr. Liddicoat, the victim of guilt by association. I hoped it didn't color her opinion of him too greatly.

With the match due to start shortly, Flossy and I retreated to the pavilion, a grandstand overlooking the field with a terrace promenade out the front and tearooms on the ground level. It was far too crowded to stay inside, so we abandoned the idea of taking tea and found a spot in the stand to watch the match. She tried to explain the rules of polo to me, but it became clear that she was no expert when she couldn't answer even simple questions.

When Floyd joined us with his three friends, I soon learned that the sport of kings was something only the very wealthy could afford to participate in. Horses were bred and trained specifically for the purpose. The animals were magnificent, with their muscular flanks pushing them to incredible— and dangerous—speeds, although Floyd was convinced they could go faster. The horses had steady nerves, too, as others drew close, and riders swung their mallets.

The players were even more magnificent, none more so than the two captains. They were as commanding as generals as they directed their teammates, and as fearless as warriors as they drove their mounts to their limit. It was Mr. Rigg-Lyon who came out on top in such contests, however. Much to Mr. Broadman's frustration, he couldn't keep up. His team lost two to nil.

Afterwards, the riders shook hands. All except Mr. Broadman and Mr. Rigg-Lyon. They exchanged glares but not a single word. So much for polo being a gentleman's sport.

Mr. Broadman's animosity was nowhere in sight when he gave his speech congratulating the winning team. He even smiled graciously when Mr. Rigg-Lyon thanked the Elms team for playing well and in good spirit.

"Lastly, I want to thank my good friend, Barnaby Hardwick, the best vice-captain a fellow can have," Mr. Rigg-Lyon finished. "We all wish him and his magnificent horse, Leopard, well on their retirement. The sport will miss them enormously." He waited for the round of cheers to fade, before adding, "As to the expected announcement about my own retirement, I want you all to be the first to know that I've decided to play on with my loyal mount, Panther. We've both got a few good years left in us, and we can't possibly retire now that we have the Champion Cup to defend!"

Barnaby Hardwick's jaw dropped. He stared at his captain, standing beside him. He was the only one of the team not to pat Rigg-Lyon on the back.

Cheers erupted around me as Mr. Rigg-Lyon held the cup aloft in triumph. Many of the women in the crowd applauded enthusiastically as they tried to catch his attention from behind the wooden fence. Only one was allowed onto the field with the players, however. A red-haired woman approached him, smiling. She placed her hands to his chest and he leaned down to plant a kiss on her cheek. She spoke in his ear, her smile having vanished. His own smile tightened before he turned away.

"His wife," Floyd said to me as we continued to applaud. "She's French."

"He's married? That must be a disappointment for half the crowd here today."

"Even more of a disappointment if they knew the position of his mistress is also taken."

I looked sharply at him and he grinned back.

"Have I shocked you, Cousin?"

"Not at all," I said smoothly.

Floyd chuckled. "The pinkness of your cheeks must be due to the heat then."

"Entirely." He would never speak to Flossy with such wicked candor, but it no longer surprised me that he treated me like one of his male friends. I knew more of his secrets than his sister did, and I'd helped him out of some difficult situations. I also appreciated and enjoyed this easy acceptance he had of me. Our relationship was unique to us and that made it special.

I watched as Mrs. Rigg-Lyon looped her arm through her husband's and clutched him tightly. It was to no avail, however. He extricated himself and turned his back to her to speak to one of his teammates.

"Does she know about the mistress?" I asked Floyd.

"I'm not sure."

"How do *you* know?"

"It's common knowledge. Rigg-Lyon is a popular fellow with the lads."

"Young men do like their sporting heroes," I muttered.

He didn't hear me. He was too busy cheering along with the rest as Mr. Rigg-Lyon and Mr. Hardwick raised the large silver cup in triumph again.

The players of the losing Elms team were the first to depart, leading their horses back to the stables beyond the mounting yard. Before he entered the building, Mr. Broadman kicked over a barrel. One of the grooms rushed to right it before taking the horse's reins and leading it inside. The players all headed to another group of buildings closer to the clubhouse.

The Polo and Gun Club team soaked up the celebrations for a little longer before they also left. Mr. Hardwick strode ahead of the others, his back stiff. Mr. Rigg-Lyon called out to him to wait, but the vice-captain ignored him.

Spectators lingered for a while, enjoying the sunshine and good company. Once refreshments dwindled, the crowd began to thin. We collected our picnic basket and headed to the area set aside for vehicles. With our coats and goggles in place and the picnic basket on the back seat between Flossy and me, we were all set to go. Unfortunately, the automobile wouldn't co-operate. The engine hissed then spluttered before going silent.

The mechanic opened the engine compartment's doors at the rear of the Peugeot and quickly stepped back as steam billowed out. He thrust his gloved hands on his hips. Going by the frown on his brow, it was clearly going to take a while to fix the problem.

Flossy and I left him and Floyd to their mechanical problem. We strolled across the lawn to the lake, enjoying the club's gardens without the crowds. As busy as the place had been earlier, it was now quite empty except for a handful of ground staff stamping down the divots on the playing surface.

I was contemplating dipping my toes in the water when we heard a shout.

"Help! Somebody help!" The voice was a man's and it appeared to be coming from the stables.

I picked up my skirts and ran.

"Cleo!" Flossy cried. "Wait! It could be dangerous. Leave it to the men."

I ran towards Mr. Broadman, who was furiously waving a hand above his head to attract attention. In his other hand, he held a polo mallet.

It was stained with blood.

I reached him at the same time as one of the grooms. "Sir? What's the matter? Is it Hercules?" A look of panic came over him, but it was nothing compared to Mr. Broadman's ashen face.

Mr. Broadman pointed the mallet into the stables. "He's dead."

"Hercules?" The groom pushed past him.

"Vernon Rigg-Lyon."

The groom stopped just inside the door. "Sir?"

A middle-aged man strode towards us just as Flossy caught up. "I heard shouting. What is it? Broadman? Something wrong?"

Mr. Broadman swallowed heavily. "He's dead. Rigg-Lyon. In the back."

The newcomer charged past him, the groom on his heels. I followed.

"Cleo!" Flossy cried. "You shouldn't go in there."

"Stay here if you don't want to come in," I said over my shoulder.

I plunged into the depths of the stables, passing horses contentedly munching on feed in their stalls. I glanced back to see that Flossy hadn't followed. She stood in the doorway, the sun silhouetting her figure.

I found the two men in an end stall, empty except for the body of Vernon Rigg-Lyon. The men I'd followed were on their haunches, checking the body for signs of life. But I could see without testing for a pulse that he was dead. The captain of the Polo and Gun Club team lay sprawled awkwardly on the straw-covered floor. There was a lot of blood. It matted his hair and streaked the back of his team jersey and the straw.

The older gentleman shook his head. "He's gone."

The groom stood, his back to us, and rested a hand against the wall. He lowered his head and sucked in several breaths.

The gentleman rose to his feet. "Broadman, what in God's name happened here?" Then his gaze dropped to the blood-stained mallet, still clutched in Mr. Broadman's white-knuckled grip.

Mr. Broadman's somewhat vacant stare cast down. His fingers sprang apart, and he dropped the mallet. He stumbled backwards, hands in the air. "It wasn't me! I swear to you, I didn't do it!"

The gentleman straightened his shoulders and finally addressed me. "Miss, send someone to fetch the police. Tell them we have a suspect in custody."

CHAPTER 2

I could hear Mr. Broadman protesting his innocence as I instructed Flossy to ask someone at the club-house to telephone the police. She hesitated, and I suspected she was about to insist I leave with her, but one glance at my face changed her mind. She hurried away and I returned inside.

"He was already dead when I came in! I swear to you." Mr. Broadman could run off and none of us would be able to stop him. He was athletic whereas the groom had a slight limp and the middle-aged gentleman and I were very unlikely to be as quick. "I entered the stall, saw the body and picked up the mallet."

"Why?" the gentleman demanded.

"I don't know." Mr. Broadman tugged on his tie to loosen it. "Good God, Major. Surely you know me well enough to know I wouldn't kill a man. Not even him."

The major's bushy gray moustache moved as he pursed his lips.

"He didn't do it," I said. "Not unless he was in the stables earlier."

All three men looked at me.

"Miss, you shouldn't be in here." The man known as Major moved to block my view of the gruesome sight. His tone wasn't protective, however. It was condescending. "This isn't a scene young ladies should witness."

"Let her speak," Mr. Broadman said. "Go on, Miss…?"

"Cleopatra Fox."

"Why do you know I'm innocent?"

"The blood has dried, so he died earlier. I assume you are telling the truth and did just arrive here, because your hair is a little damp and you're wearing a suit, not the uniform you wore when playing. You've just come from the changing rooms, haven't you?"

He nodded with no small measure of relief. "Yes. It's true. You can ask one of the attendants."

"Why were you back here?" the major asked. "Hercules is in one of the stalls near the front."

"I wanted to speak to one of the grooms, but none were about." He frowned at the groom. The young man studied his feet. "I checked every stall. When I got to this one, I found…" He closed his eyes. "God, it's awful."

"Where had the grooms gone?" I asked.

"To the tack and equipment room," the groom said. "We've all been in there for at least the last forty minutes."

"Surely someone should be seeing to the horses."

"They have everything they need, miss. I made sure of that before I left. I'd never leave any of them before they were settled."

"Bert knows his business," the major assured me.

Mr. Broadman nodded. "I know you care for the animals, Bert."

The groom looked relieved to be believed.

"Cleo? Are you still in there?" Flossy entered the stables but remained near the door. A handful of staff streamed past her, all talking at once.

The major approached them, hands in the air. "No further. This is a crime scene."

The distraction allowed me the opportunity to inspect the body and the stall. Vernon Rigg-Lyon seemed to have fallen where he'd been struck. A spray of blood covered the straw approximately two feet from the body. Some of the blood may have ended up on the killer after such a violent attack. The victim still wore his playing uniform which meant he hadn't gone to the changing rooms with the rest. He'd come here after the grooms left. Why?

I glanced behind me to check that no one was looking my way, then quickly inspected the body. I hazarded a very brief glance at his face, but that was quite enough. His features had frozen into an expression of surprise. A chill skittered down my spine.

I drew in a fortifying breath. Thankfully the smell of horse overrode the smell of death.

I looked again. The blow had struck Mr. Rigg-Lyon on the back of the head; he either hadn't seen his assailant or he'd turned his back to them before he was struck. There was nothing in the stall except straw, so it was unlikely he was attending to anything. So why was he there? Was he meeting someone? His killer?

I was about to stand when a hint of color against his beige breeches caught my eye. It was the corner of a coral-colored ribbon, about the length of my hand.

"Miss Fox? Are you all right?"

I tucked the ribbon back into the victim's pocket before standing and facing the major. His bushy brows were drawn together like tufts of gray wool, but it was from concern not irritation.

He held out his arm to me. "Allow me to escort you away. This must be very distressing for you."

I accepted his assistance. "Thank you. That's very kind, Major...?"

"Leavey, of the 12th Lancers. I'm club manager."

"Oh? So you're in charge of the entire operation."

"I've been the manager for four years."

"I suspect you've been very busy today. There would have been staff meetings before and after the match."

"Before, yes, but I've been in my office going over a few things since the presentation. I was just leaving the clubhouse when I heard Mr. Broadman's shout." From the way he eyed Mr. Broadman, I suspected he didn't like him or didn't trust him.

I had a lot of questions but didn't have the opportunity to ask any of them. Flossy was waving at me from the door, trying to get my attention. She and the other onlookers were blocked from entering by two staff members. Suddenly Mr. Liddicoat burst through.

He rushed towards us. "Rufus, are you all right? What's going on?"

"Someone bashed Rigg-Lyon's head in with his mallet. I found the body."

"Good God! That's dreadful. You need a stiff drink. Come into the clubhouse."

"He can't leave," the major bellowed.

Mr. Liddicoat jumped. He adjusted his glasses to get a better look at the major. "He's not a suspect, surely."

"He was the first to discover the body and was holding the murder weapon. He also had a very public disagreement with Rigg-Lyon before the match." From the stern look the major gave Mr. Broadman, it was clear the public nature of the incident displeased him.

Mr. Broadman laughed off the accusation, but given the gravity of the situation, his attempt at levity fell flat. "That was nothing more than a healthy rivalry fueled by nervous energy. It provided atmosphere—a spectacle, if you will. The crowd lapped it up. Anyway, Miss Fox already declared me innocent. The blood is dry. He died some time ago, when I was in the shower." He beckoned to one of the staff members. "Sid. Come in. Tell them I was in the changing room for at least thirty minutes or so before I left."

An elderly attendant with a stoop shuffled towards us. He squinted up at the major. "That's correct, sir. It was a great honor to assist Mr. Broadman today."

The major brushed him off. "Very well, thank you, Sid. I'm sure the police will have more questions for you."

"There you are, then," Mr. Liddicoat said as the attendant shuffled away. "It can't have been Rufus."

"Nor was it one of my staff," the major said.

From what I could see of the large group gathering outside the stables, he couldn't possibly know every staff member personally, let alone know them well enough to make such a declaration.

"There were hundreds of people here today," Mr. Broadman said. "It could have been any of them."

I shook my head. "The grooms were in here immediately after the match and would have noticed someone who didn't belong in the stables, or even if one of their own attacked Mr. Rigg-Lyon."

"It wasn't one of us!" Bert piped up. "We left here at three-fifty."

"Then it was committed in the time between the grooms leaving the stables for the tack room and some time before Mr. Broadman arrived. I'm not sure how long it takes for blood to dry in weather like this, but I suspect a pool that size would take at least twenty or thirty minutes." I removed my watch from my bag and checked the time. "The murder was committed after three-fifty, when the grooms left, and no later than ten-past-four, which is approximately twenty minutes before Mr. Broadman shouted; long enough for the blood to dry."

"A twenty-minute window for which I have an alibi." Mr. Broadman pointed to Sid, standing beside the groom.

We all turned towards the door where someone was shouting to be let through. Mr. Hardwick, the retiring vice-captain of the winning team, entered the stables. His breathing was ragged and his brow shiny. "Someone said Vernon is dead." He peered past us. "Is it true?"

The major clasped Mr. Hardwick's arm. "He's been murdered."

Mr. Hardwick covered his mouth with his hand. He stared wide-eyed at the major and shook his head over and over.

"Is Mrs. Rigg-Lyon still here?"

"She didn't want to wait and went home straight after the presentation." Mr. Hardwick winced as a painful thought struck him. "I'll call on her now. It's going to be dreadful."

"Go inside and have a snifter of brandy first. I'll join you when the police get here." Major Leavey made a shooing motion. "In fact, I think everyone should get out. I'll stand guard to make sure the scene isn't disturbed. Broadman, take Hardwick inside. You there!" he shouted at the staff. "Back to work. This isn't a show."

I joined Mr. Liddicoat as we followed Bert, Mr. Hardwick and Mr. Broadman out of the stables. The groom stopped at one of the stalls to check on a black horse. I recognized it as the one the victim rode in the match. It paced the floor and tossed its head, snorting loudly.

Bert opened the stall door. "Easy, Panther." He tried to get close enough to stroke the horse, but Panther was too restless. "It's all right, boy. It'll be all right."

"Poor thing," Mr. Liddicoat said as we continued. "He must know. They say animals sense these things."

Mr. Hardwick ran his hand through his hair and muttered, "I can't believe it. Who would do such a thing?"

Mr. Broadman handed him a handkerchief since Mr. Hardwick wore no jacket or hat. Mr. Hardwick used it to wipe his brow.

"I can't believe it either," Mr. Liddicoat said to me. "Were you nearby, Miss Fox? Is that how you got here so quickly?"

"I wasn't far away. And you? Did you hear your cousin's shout?"

He nodded but seemed distracted. He suddenly stopped. "I saw someone in the vicinity during that window of opportunity. I remember him, because he didn't seem to be staff, a player or a spectator. He wore a long coat, you see, and a bowler hat rather than a boater. Who wears a long coat in this weather, Miss Fox?"

Someone who didn't want to be identified.

Someone who didn't want their clothing covered in blood when they bludgeoned a man to death.

"Were there any distinguishing features? His height? Gait?"

"The coat was brown and there were black patches on the elbow."

Floyd had joined Flossy and they both waited for me. Flossy took my hand when I reached them. "Are you all right, Cleo? Did you see him?"

Sometimes a little white lie is better for everyone. "I stayed well away."

She eyed me skeptically.

"The automobile is ready," Floyd announced.

"Just a moment." I'd spotted Sid, the elderly changing room attendant, walking slowly away from the stables on his own. Everyone else was ahead of him, so I could ask him a question without being overheard.

I approached him and introduced myself, even going so

far as to say I was a private detective. His only reaction was to remove his cap and scratch his balding head.

"Are you the only attendant in the changing rooms?" I asked.

"Aye, miss."

"That's eight players whose needs you must see to."

"Seven. Mr. Rigg-Lyon wasn't there."

I glanced towards the back of the stables. "Even so, seeing to the needs of all seven must keep you busy."

"It does, miss."

"So you fetch towels, prepare their clothes and help them dress. Anything else?"

"I collect their uniforms while they shower and take them to the laundry."

"Is the laundry attached to the changing room?"

"No, miss, it's on the other side of the courtyard."

I suspected the door to the changing room wouldn't be visible from the laundry. He wouldn't notice anyone leave then return a few minutes later, covered in blood.

I thanked him and rejoined Flossy and Floyd, waiting patiently for me.

"Any idea who did it yet?" Floyd asked as we walked.

"She's not investigating," Flossy said. "She doesn't have time. We have a full week of social engagements coming up."

Floyd snorted. "You underestimate our cousin."

I glanced over my shoulder towards the stables where the major stood in the doorway, guarding it. He wouldn't let me back inside now, even if I begged. As frustrating as it was to leave, I had no reason to stay. No one had hired me to investigate. With a sigh, I continued to the automobile.

The mechanic sat in the driver's seat with the engine purring nicely. "Hop in, folks. I'll have you back at the hotel in no time."

Floyd held out his hand to assist me up to the back seat. His fingers closed tightly around mine to get my attention. "At least this investigation will have nothing to do with Armitage. I know Father allowed you to investigate together, but I think if he'd known how often you were in Armitage's company, he wouldn't have allowed it in the first place. I still can't believe he did, considering—" He cut himself off.

"Considering what?"

"Considering how well you get along."

I tried to tug my hand away, but he held on.

"Don't push your luck, Cleo."

"You seem to think I'm going to try to solve the murder."

"Aren't you?"

I was about to tell him that his concerns were unfounded. Even if I did investigate, there was no reason to involve Harry. But a carriage pulled to a stop alongside us before I could respond. Three uniformed policemen spilled out of the cabin, followed by a detective in plain clothes. They paid us no mind, not even bothering to ask us for our names and a statement. Harry's father, a former Scotland Yard detective, would never have been so lax.

* * *

FRANK STIFLED a cough as the automobile drove off, leaving a trail of fumes in its wake. A shake of his fist would not have been out of place when accompanied with the glare he gave it, but he kept a professional composure and changed the glare to a welcoming smile.

"Good afternoon, Miss Bainbridge, Miss Fox, Mr. Bainbridge. How was the polo?"

"The captain of one of the teams died," I said.

"Bloody hell." Realizing he was still on duty and my cousins were within earshot, he quickly apologized for his language. "Did he fall off his horse?"

"He was murdered with his own mallet in the stables."

"Murdered!"

Flossy flapped her fan in front of her face. "I'm going upstairs to lie down. It's been a tiring day. Cleo, are you coming?"

"Soon," I said.

"I wouldn't stay down here too long, if I were you. It's going to take you a while to clean up."

"Why?"

"Come along, Sis." Floyd took her arm and they headed for the lift. The wicked gleam in his eye made me curious, but I quickly forgot about them as Frank peppered me with ques-

23

tions. Seeing us talking in earnest, Goliath, the hotel's porter, and Peter approached. I told them everything I knew about the murder.

"Are you going to take on the case?" Goliath asked.

"There is no case," I said. "No one has hired me to investigate."

"That hasn't stopped you before."

Frank tapped the side of his nose. "A client will come out of the woodwork, Miss Fox, don't you worry. I have a good feeling about this one."

Goliath arched his brow at him. "A good feeling about a murder? I knew you were odd, Frank, but I didn't think you bloodthirsty."

"I'm not. Idiot."

"Me, an idiot?" Goliath snorted. "I'm not the one who thought automobiles would never catch on when we saw our first one a couple of years back. There are more now than ever. Miss Fox even rode in one today."

Frank gestured at my face. "And look at what it did to her! No lady will want to ride in those bloody contraptions after the initial curiosity dies down."

I rounded on him. "What did it do to me?"

Goliath thrust out his hand to Frank. "Want to have a wager on it?"

Frank rolled his eyes. "How will we determine a winner? Count the number of vehicles that pass by?"

Goliath shrugged his hulking shoulders. "Why not? I reckon Victor will want in on this bet. He agrees with me. Motorized vehicles will increase in number, not decrease."

Frank made a scoffing sound in his throat. "Not here at the hotel, they won't. Sir Ronald won't replace the carriages with those unreliable machines."

"He does what the guests want, and if the guests want to be collected from the station in a hotel motor vehicle rather than a horse-drawn one, then he'll buy one."

"I heard he told Cobbit he won't."

"He just said that to shut the old codger up. Cobbit's negative about everything, even more so if it means he needs to learn a new skill."

"I like the fellow," Frank said defensively.

"That says everything a person needs to know about both of you."

I cleared my throat. "Will someone tell me what's wrong with the way I look? Do I have smuts in my hair? My hat moved in the wind, dislodging the veil." I touched my hair and discovered it had come out of its arrangement.

"You look as pretty as always," Peter said quickly.

"Frank?" I prompted. Of the three men, he was the only one who'd give me an honest answer.

"Harmony's going to need to be at her best to get you ready for dinner," he said.

Peter glared at him, but Frank didn't care. He spotted a gentleman walking towards the door and hurried to reach it before him. He smiled at the man as he passed then followed him outside.

"Ignore him," Peter said to me. "He's been in a mood since speaking to Cobbit earlier. Apparently the two of them have decided that automobiles represent everything that's wrong with this country. They're thinking of going on strike if Sir Ronald decides to replace one of the carriages."

"Surely things aren't that dire."

"You know what Frank's like," Goliath said. "He hates change. Cobbit is just as bad. Put the two of them in the same room and it's one complaint after another. They feed off each other's negativity."

Frank opened the door and beckoned to Goliath. "Two new guests just arrived. You'll need a trolley."

Goliath went to fetch a luggage trolley while Peter smiled and greeted the new arrivals as they passed us on their way to the check-in desk. He then turned to me.

"Harmony was looking for you."

"Shouldn't she be resting at the residence hall?" Her cleaning duties would have finished at two and she wouldn't be starting her rounds as personal maid for another hour.

"She wanted to hear how your day went. I think she's bored."

I'd come to the same conclusion about Harmony. Ever since her role as assistant to Floyd ended, and she'd returned to her duties as maid, she seemed listless. She never complained, but I could see the dissatisfaction in her eyes.

They no longer lit up when we ate breakfast together in the mornings. Cleaning rooms wasn't enough stimulation for her. She'd liked being involved in the opening of the new restaurant. She'd been good at it, too. Floyd had made a few key decisions, and had been influential in getting the right people to attend opening night, but Harmony had organized it all.

I found her on the sofa in my suite, reading a book I'd borrowed from the hotel library. Her feet were tucked up under her and she was absent-mindedly twisting a curl of hair around her finger.

"You'll never guess what happened at the polo today," I said as I unpinned my hat.

She put her feet on the floor and closed the book. "A horse attacked your hair."

I sat beside her and touched my hair. "No."

"You fell over and got dirt on your cheek." She rubbed my cheek then inspected the smudge on her thumb. She sniffed it. "It's not dirt."

"It's probably oil from the automobile smuts. I'll clean up in a moment. But first, listen to this. There was a murder in the club's stables."

She sat up straight. "Good grief! Are you a witness?"

"I was second on the scene after the fellow who discovered the body."

"Then you are in a unique position." She retrieved a pencil and notepad from the desk and returned to the sofa. "Tell me everything."

By the time I needed to get ready for dinner, we had two full pages of notes, questions, and information about the victim and potential suspects. Talking it over with Harmony helped consolidate my scattered thoughts and decide what to do next. While I hadn't declared it in so many words, I knew I would investigate. Starting in the morning, I would find out all I could about Vernon Rigg-Lyon.

I was unable to escape talk of the murder that evening. It was the topic of conversation at dinner, particularly after our fellow diners discovered we were at the polo.

Aunt Lilian and Uncle Ronald had invited several American guests to dine with us in an attempt to garner favor with the wealthy travelers. Some were coming to the end of their stay in England and he wanted to ensure they would return to the Mayfair Hotel next year. The personal touch from the city's last remaining family-owned luxury hotel was the Mayfair's best attribute and he was aware of that more than anyone. To make them feel special, he'd asked Mrs. Poole to add several American dishes to the menu. Alongside canvasback ducks, terrapin, clams, oysters, and green corn were seasonal vegetables, all accompanied by her own unique sauces and seasonings.

I was disappointed to find I wasn't seated with Miss Hessing. My aunt had chosen the traditional arrangement of alternating the sexes which placed me between two men, only one of whom was under thirty. The other was his uncle, a contemporary of Mrs. Hessing. After the requisite exchange of pleasantries, he turned to her on his other side and found himself stuck for the remainder of the evening. I was left with his nephew, Marshall Miller. Fortunately, the younger Mr. Miller was rather pleasing to look at with his dark hair and warm brown eyes. *Un*fortunately, we got off on the wrong foot.

"The Mayfair is spectacular," he said in his American drawl. "I hear it was once your uncle's manor house and he converted it to a hotel after he married your aunt."

My heart sank. He was interested in me only because of my connection to the hotel and the Bainbridge family. The *wealthy* Bainbridge family, distantly related to nobility.

"I wish I lived in a luxury hotel," he went on.

My disappointment at being seen as nothing more than an object in the Bainbridge orbit meant my next words were bitter ones. It was a poor excuse, however, and I regretted them the moment they were out of my mouth. "Why? Don't you already have your laundry done for you, room service at your beck and call, maids to clean for you, and a fine menu at your disposal every evening?"

His lips parted and a strangled noise escaped. He recovered quickly, however, and laughed. "You mistake me for my uncle. I simply meant you're fortunate to meet a variety of people from all over the world. I suspect every day is different to the one before it."

My heart sank even further. "I'm sorry. That was rude of me. I was..." I couldn't think how to get out of it with my dignity intact. I really ought to have learned my lesson about not jumping to conclusions by now, but it seemed I hadn't. I'd made a dreadful mess.

"You were too distracted by my handsome face?" he teased. He tilted his chin and turned to the side. "They say my profile is my best feature. Although that could be because the straight-on view is hideous."

It was a relief to learn I hadn't offended him, and that he was offering me a dignified way out. "Who is this 'they' you speak of, and do they know they need glasses?"

He grinned. "They're work colleagues at my uncle's office. They're the only people I associate with back home. I'm too busy to have friends and my cousins are all dribbling idiots. They're aged under four, though, so there's hope for them yet."

I laughed. "It's good of your uncle to bring you with him on holiday."

"We're not on vacation. He's here for business, and I'm here as his assistant."

"Then you won't have time to see the sights."

"Very few, I'm afraid. My uncle wants to see Buckingham Palace, and I want to go to the museum, but we don't have much free time between meetings." He leaned back in the chair, looking relaxed yet confident in a way that only men comfortable in their own physicality did. He reminded me of Harry. "There is talk of extending our stay if business goes well."

I raised my glass of wine in salute. "Then I hope it does. There's quite a lot to see in London."

He smiled warmly. "I may need a tour guide."

"Then I'll loan you my *Baedeker*."

He laughed. It was so infectious that I couldn't help joining in. When he finally sobered, he settled that luxurious gaze on me. "I didn't know Englishwomen were so funny. We've always been led to believe you're aloof."

"And we've always been told American men are forward."

He saluted me with his glass. "Here's to dispelling cultural myths."

We both sipped.

I enjoyed my evening and forgot all about the murder until I spotted Miss Hessing watching her jellied dessert wobble when she poked it with her spoon. Although the Hessings had left the Elms before the murder, she must have heard that Mr. Liddicoat's cousin discovered the body and worried for her paramour.

I made a point of speaking to her after dinner as we crossed the hotel foyer together. "Mr. Liddicoat was a rock for his cousin today when the club manager accused him of murder."

She must have heard the details already as she showed no surprise. "He's so thoughtful. His cousin was fortunate he hadn't left yet." She wrung her gloved hands together. Something else was on her mind.

"There's no reason for the police to arrest Mr. Broadman," I assured her. "I told the club manager he couldn't have done it." Although at that time, I hadn't known the attendant left the changing rooms for a few minutes. Long enough for Mr. Broadman to slip out and murder someone in the nearby stables.

"That was good of you, Miss Fox. Very good indeed. But that's not what's troubling me. Indeed, my worry has nothing to do with the murder." She glanced at her mother's back, walking ahead of us with the aid of her stick. "After my mother learned that Mr. Liddicoat was courting me, she was furious. She said he was a fortune hunter, only after me for my money. *Her* money."

"I recall. It was an upsetting time."

"It still is upsetting me. She hasn't forbidden me to see him, but she hasn't backed down, either. Every time I ask her what to do, she tells me to wait, that she'll advise me in due course. We're in limbo, Miss Fox, unsure whether to defy her or do as she asks in the hope she'll soon relent."

Mrs. Hessing must have hired Harry after all and be waiting for his verdict. "No news is good news," I assured her. Hopefully the murder investigation wouldn't delay Mrs. Hessing's decision further.

Mrs. Hessing stopped at the lift as John the operator held the door open. She stamped the end of her walking stick on the tiled floor. "Clare! Come along. Miss Fox, you can squeeze in, too, you're such a little thing."

"Don't wait for me," I said. "I want to speak to my cousin."

Floyd stopped when he realized I meant him. He waited for me at the base of the staircase. "What do you want to speak to me about?"

I watched the lift door close. "Nothing. I needed an excuse not to go up in that slow contraption with a crowd of people all breathing over one another."

"You mean you wanted to avoid a conversation with Mrs. Hessing."

"Don't put words in my mouth." We headed up the stairs together. "You're not going to play billiards with the other men?" I glanced back to the foyer where some of the gentlemen from dinner were chatting. Others had already gone into the smoking room or billiards room. Mr. Miller must have been among them as I couldn't see him.

"Soon. So...I see you and that American got along at dinner. I thought you might."

"Why?"

"Women seem to like him, and you're a woman."

"Nice to know I conform to stereotype," I said wryly. "But you were right. I enjoyed his company."

He smiled smugly. "Good. Keep it up."

"Keep what up?"

"Encouraging him."

I stopped and turned on him. "Floyd, you're matchmaking! You know my thoughts on marriage."

He shot me a wicked grin over his shoulder as he continued climbing the stairs. "Nobody mentioned marriage. On your mind, is it?"

I gathered up my skirts and raced after him. "Floyd, don't. If you encourage him, I won't be responsible for hurt feelings when he discovers I'm not interested in courtship. That'll be your fault."

He finally stopped and waited for me to catch up. "I'm just saying that he seems like a better match for you, that's all. Let fate decide what happens next."

"A better match for me?" I echoed. "Better than whom?"

He continued on, taking two steps at a time. I couldn't keep up even if I tried. I knew the answer anyway. He meant Mr. Miller was a more suitable match for me than Harry.

I'd told Floyd numerous times that I had no intention of marrying anyone, yet he didn't seem to believe me. I liked Harry very much, but marriage wasn't for me. I'd seen enough married couples to know that it wasn't what I wanted for my future. One of these days, Floyd and the others would realize I was serious. Until then, I would have to put up with their matchmaking attempts.

I had no intention of discussing the murder investigation with Harry. There was no client and therefore no payment. We worked well together, but he couldn't afford to spend time on something that would cost money, not earn it.

That all changed the following morning when Mr. Hobart said Harry had called and asked me to visit him at his Soho office.

CHAPTER 3

The door to Harry's office stood open, a sure sign that he knew I'd respond to his summons the moment I received his message. With coffee cups from the Roma Café in hand, and a parasol tucked under my arm, I was grateful he knew me so well.

I set the cups down on the desk beside a brass candlestick telephone. "What a smart addition to the office. It looks very professional."

Harry reached for one of the cups. "It was installed yesterday. The call I placed to Uncle Alfred was the first. Thanks for coming. Did any of your family see you leave the hotel?"

"No, but it's all right if they do. Uncle Ronald hasn't retracted his permission allowing me to investigate with you." While his permission had come as a surprise, I'd realized it had been given because I'd told him Harry was courting someone. He'd seemed to think that put an end to any interest we may have in one another. I hadn't told him Harry and Miss Morris had since parted ways. Nor would I. I didn't want him changing his mind.

"Good. Good. Have you been well, Cleo?" He sipped, watching me over the rim of the cup with his velvety eyes. The moment may have been brief, but my pulse quickened nevertheless. My body's reaction to his attention never ceased to amaze me. It unnerved me, too.

"Yes, thank you. You?"

"Yes. Keeping busy."

We both sipped our coffees.

The awkward exchange wasn't unusual for us. Whenever we saw one another after time apart our conversations always started the same way. It seemed to take a while before we became comfortable in each other's presence again. A murder helped to break the ice.

"How is your investigation into Mr. Liddicoat coming along?" I asked.

"That's what I wanted to speak to you about." He set down the cup and picked up a slim folder, removing two sheets of paper. "I'd written my report and was ready to give it to Mrs. Hessing when she came to see me late yesterday. She told me about the murder and tasked me with looking into it."

I sighed. "She wants to know if Mr. Broadman is the murderer, because if he is, his cousin won't be a suitable match for her daughter."

He opened the folder and removed two sheets of paper. "This is the sum total of information I have on Liddicoat. As you can see, it amounts to very little. He comes from a good family. There are no prior engagements, no scandals, and no suggestion of anything problematic associated with his name or that of his close acquaintances."

"Until now, with Mr. Broadman stumbling across the dead body."

"While holding the bloody mallet, I believe." The raise of his brows indicated he wasn't quite sure of the facts. "Since you were there, I wanted to hear your opinion. Do you think he did it?"

"I'd hate to jump to conclusions again, so I can't say either way."

"You're still smarting about getting me dismissed from the hotel? Cleo, it's long forgotten. Don't worry about it."

"Actually, I was talking about something that happened last night at dinner. I was very rude to the American guest seated beside me because I thought he was disparaging me. Once he explained, it was all right between us, but it was a good reminder that I should never assume. I must only deal with facts and evidence, not assumptions or instinct."

"Your instincts are usually very good. Perhaps the American *was* insulting you but backpedaled after you admonished him. What sort of man is he?"

"He's a gentleman who works for his wealthy uncle. We got along very well once I apologized." I smiled, remembering Mr. Miller's little joke that had helped clear the air. "He turned out to be charming and funny."

Harry flicked his hand over Mr. Liddicoat's file as if dusting it off. I thought him preoccupied with the task until he said, "When does he leave?"

"It depends on the outcome of his uncle's business here."

"So you could be seeing a lot of him."

"We might bump into each other around the hotel."

Was Harry jealous? It was difficult to tell when he wouldn't meet my gaze. Part of me hoped so. But mostly I thought how we needed to set aside the feelings stirred by our one and only kiss if we were to remain friends and investigation partners.

I didn't have an opportunity to contemplate it further because he asked me to recount everything I'd seen and heard at the polo club, specifically the parts that involved Mr. Broadman.

"Before the match, I saw Mr. Broadman and Mr. Rigg-Lyon arguing. Indeed, everyone saw. They were too far from us to hear, however. Mr. Liddicoat intervened and they stopped. When asked, Mr. Broadman claimed it was simply a little pre-match tension." Harry's faith in my instincts led me to add the next part. "It seemed heated to me so I think it was about something more."

"And the bloody mallet? Was he really holding it?"

"Yes, but the blood was dry, as was the blood on and near the body."

"You got close enough to see the body?"

"Of course."

"What gentleman would allow a lady near such a gruesome sight?"

"The sort of gentleman who was looking the other way and doesn't know me very well."

He chuckled.

"Given that the blood was dry, and that the grooms

vacated the stables once the horses were settled, I calculated there was a twenty-minute window of opportunity for the murder to occur. Mr. Broadman claims he was in the changing room during that time, and an attendant confirmed it, but the attendant was also absent for a short period."

"So Broadman doesn't have a solid alibi," he said as he wrote on his notepad. "What's he like as a person?"

"Quite the opposite in character to Mr. Liddicoat. He's confident and athletic, well-liked by everyone. Both he and the victim are what some call a man's man. Lesser men seem to idolize them."

"So he's physically capable of wielding a polo mallet."

"They're not heavy. You've never seen one?"

"Polo wasn't a popular sport where I grew up," he said wryly.

I wasn't sure if he was referring to the girls' school where he lived while his birth mother taught there, the boys' orphanage where he lived after she died, the slums where he lived after he ran away, or in Ealing, where his adoptive parents still resided. It was probably all of them. Polo, like automobile driving, was an activity for the wealthy.

"Yesterday was my first match," I said. "The mallets the players use have a surprisingly small head at the end of a long stick. Even a child could have wielded it. He was hit from behind." I indicated the spot on the back of my head, at the very top of my spine and the base of the skull.

"A direct hit there doesn't have to be very hard to be fatal, it just has to be accurate. We can't rule out a woman."

"Speaking of women, the rumors are that Vernon Rigg-Lyon was something of a philanderer. Floyd says he had a mistress."

"Does the wife know?"

"Floyd suggested everyone knew."

"Sometimes the spouse is the last to find out."

"True, but surely she would suspect."

Harry wrote down Mrs. Rigg-Lyon's name underneath Rufus Broadman's. "Did Floyd tell you who the mistress was?"

"Drat. I forgot to ask."

Harry tapped his pencil on the notepad as he thought.

"Stand up, Cleo." He indicated I should join him on the other side of the desk. He grasped my shoulders and squared up to me. "They must have met, argued..." He turned me around. "Then Rigg-Lyon faced away. The murderer picked up the mallet and struck him." His cool fingers lightly touched the nape of my neck above my lace collar.

Tingles washed over my skin, leaving gooseflesh in their wake.

He cleared his throat and sat again. "Who else was there when you arrived on the scene?"

I returned to the other side of the desk with a sigh. "Nobody. Flossy and I were first after Mr. Broadman. A few moments later, one of the grooms came. Bert. Also the club manager, Major Leavey, formerly of the 12th Lancers. He claims to have been working in his office during the time of the murder. I assumed he would be seeing to the players or chatting to special guests after an important match, not retreating to his office." I shrugged. "Then Mr. Liddicoat arrived."

"Why was he still there?"

"Waiting to speak to his cousin, I suppose. He claimed to have seen a man wearing a brown coat in the vicinity. Given the warm day, the coat seemed out of place. The prevailing opinion when I left was that Brown Coat was the killer. Shortly after Mr. Liddicoat's arrival, the vice-captain of the Polo and Gun Club team entered the stables. He was very upset to learn of Mr. Rigg-Lyon's death and claimed they were good friends as well as teammates. Barnaby Hardwick is his name."

He wrote that down. "Claimed? You think they weren't close?"

"I have no reason to doubt him, but..." I shook my head.

Harry looked up, frowning. "Go on."

"I don't think it has any bearing on the case."

"Tell me anyway."

"All right. In his victory speech, Vernon Rigg-Lyon said he wasn't going to retire, after all, but Hardwick was. The change of heart seemed to come as a surprise to the vice-captain. He looked angry."

"Anger seems like an over-the-top reaction," he said as he made notes beside Mr. Hardwick's name.

"When he arrived in the stables, he wasn't wearing a hat or jacket. Perhaps he removed them because they were splattered with blood."

"Or perhaps he removed a brown coat that was splattered with blood," he said as he wrote. "Anything else from the day's events that could be a clue?"

"No. Wait, yes, there is something else. I found a ribbon in the victim's pocket."

One side of his mouth lifted with his smirk. "Those gentlemen really were distracted when you got near the body. Did the ribbon match any worn by the ladies watching the match?"

I arched my brows at him. "There must have been five hundred people there, half of whom were women either wearing ribbons in their hair, on their hats or somewhere on their dress."

"Point taken. I didn't know the polo attracted so many." He pulled the telephone closer. "I'm going to call Detective Forrester to see what the police have."

"That's if he'll talk to you. He might not even be assigned to the case."

"He's not."

"You've already discussed this with your father, haven't you? And he telephoned Detective Forrester last night."

He nodded. "Forrester told me he'll look into it and to telephone him this morning." He lifted the receiver and spoke to the operator. Once connected to Scotland Yard, he asked for Detective Forrester.

I listened to Harry's half of the conversation and gathered something was amiss when he repeated the question about the ribbon, twice.

"There was no ribbon," he said after he hung the receiver on the hook.

"Yes, there was. I pulled it out of Rigg-Lyon's pocket."

"Did you put it back?"

"Of course!"

"It wasn't there when the police searched. The report

noted that the pocket of his riding breeches was empty. It's unlikely they removed evidence."

"The major must have removed it. He remained behind to guard the scene of the crime until the police arrived. Why would he take it?"

Harry stood. "That's what we need to find out."

"We're going to just ask him?"

"Why not?" He plucked his hat from the stand and slapped it on his head. "I believe you saw the ribbon, but the police might assume you made a mistake and dismiss it. My father says not to trust the assigned detective. Forrester claims the investigation is focused on finding the taxicab driver who collected Brown Coat from the venue."

"That could take some time." It may not produce a result, either. The brown coat may never have left the estate, or it may have been stuffed in a bag before the wearer climbed into a vehicle. Or he or she may not have left in a cab at all.

We returned the coffee cups to Luigi's café and took a hansom to the Elms Polo Club. It seemed to take forever to get out of the London traffic and then it felt slow on the open road after traveling in Lord Dunmere's automobile last time.

"Do you have another engagement?" Harry asked when I checked my watch for the second time.

I slipped it back into my pocket. I'd worn a plain russet-colored jacket and matching skirt over a simple cream blouse for practicality. I suspected it would be warm again and the cotton fabric was lightweight. The outfit had few embellishments, so as not to attract attention if we needed to poke around the club or speak to staff. The modest black boater with a ribbon of the same color as my outfit was chosen for the same reason. It was understated compared to the hats worn by most fashionable ladies.

"Nothing until afternoon tea," I told Harry. "I suppose I'm just impatient. Yesterday we traveled at twenty miles an hour in Lord Dunmere's automobile."

"He finally bought one? Last year when he stayed at the Mayfair, he told me he was thinking about it. What did he buy in the end?"

"A black one."

"I meant who is the manufacturer?"

"A French company by the name of Peugeot. It seated all four of us quite comfortably, although it was a little tight in the back seat with a picnic basket between Flossy and me. Lord Dunmere's mechanic drove us."

He tapped a finger on his knee in thought. "I wonder if Dunmere will let me ride in it. We got along well and had some good conversations about automobiles and engines. He's quite knowledgeable."

"You can only ask. He's staying for a few more days before heading off to the seaside. Be warned that if you do go to the hotel's stables to look at it, Cobbit is dead against it. He says automobiles upset the horses. I know he's just worried about them putting him out of work, but he's stirring up trouble amongst the staff. Frank is on his side."

"One day, horse-drawn vehicles *will* be obsolete. I sympathize with Cobbit."

"Sympathy will get him nowhere. He and the other coachmen and grooms need to retrain or risk becoming redundant. I'm worried for them. If Cobbit digs in his heels, he'll be out of work in a few years."

Harry sighed. "If there's one thing I remember about Cobbit, it's that he's stubborn."

We arrived at the entrance to the Elms Polo Club to find the gates closed. I suspected it was to keep the newspaper men out. Journalists and photographers stood out the front, chatting. Our arrival caused a small flurry of activity as they threw questions at us, but soon backed away when Harry told them we had nothing to do with the club or the murder.

I glared at the gates, hands on hips, while Harry inspected the padlock. "How shall we get in?" I asked.

"The fence won't be this high all the way around. It'll be highest at the front entrance."

"How do you know?"

"Because fencing is expensive and this is a sizeable estate. This fence looks quite new, so they probably replaced it recently, making it high near the entrance to deter trespassers looking for an easy way in." He indicated a faint trail marked in the grass to our right. "Let's follow that and see if the fence is more climbable further around."

He was partially right. The fence didn't become lower, but

it was replaced by a tall hedge of yew trees. Most of it was too dense to climb through, but we found a section where one tree was dying, its foliage sparser than the rest.

Harry removed his hat and climbed through, paving the way for me by snapping off brittle twigs as he went. I plunged in after him and emerged on the other side. He removed a twig from my hat and flicked it onto the grass. I reached up and plucked a leaf from his hair. The strands were silky to touch.

He smiled. I smiled back. Then we set off for the stables. We'd decided to begin there before going in search of Major Leavey. If someone threw us out, at least we would have finished looking around.

There were some outdoor staff at work in the gardens but, otherwise, the grounds were empty. The lack of staff could be explained by it being Sunday.

We paused inside the stable block, blinking as our eyes adjusted to the dimmer light after the bright sunshine. Unlike the more ostentatious clubhouse, the stables were the heart of what must have once been a private estate. The thick walls looked as though they'd been there for hundreds of years and would survive for hundreds more, witnessing the birth and death of many horses, and now the death of a famous polo player.

Two grooms were at work in the stalls, one of whom was Bert. I counted six horses, including Hercules, Mr. Broadman's mount. These must be the only ones permanently stabled at the club.

Bert looked up from his task of mucking out one of the stalls as we passed. When he spotted me, he almost dropped the rake. "Miss Fox!" His voice was a high squeak and his face paled. It made the blemishes stand out more. I'd not taken much notice of him yesterday, but now I began to wonder if he'd gone pale from guilt. He'd certainly looked upset when he saw the body of Vernon Rigg-Lyon.

But I wasn't being fair. Seeing a dead body for the first time is a distressing business for anyone. I smiled warmly, which seemed to calm his nerves somewhat.

"Good morning, Bert. This is Mr. Armitage from Armitage

and Associates, a private detective agency. He's investigating the murder and wanted to look at the crime scene."

He picked up the rake. "Does the major know you're here?"

"We're on our way to meet him."

Bert followed us to the last stall. The bloodied straw had been cleared away, but it was otherwise the same. I described the position of the body to Harry.

"What do you know about the victim?" he asked Bert.

"Nothing!"

"Nothing?"

"No more than anyone else. People liked him. He was popular with the other players and the public." There was a glaring omission in that statement.

"Did *you* like him?" I asked.

He shrugged. "I s'pose."

"You hated him," came a voice from the next stall.

I followed it and peered over the low door into the stall where a young groom was inspecting a horse's hoof. The animal lazily turned its head to look at us, then turned away again to munch on the feed in the trough.

"And you are?" Harry prompted.

"Robbie." Robbie set the hoof down and straightened. He wiped his hand on his overalls, then emerged from the stall to join us.

"Why do you say Bert hated Mr. Rigg-Lyon?" I asked.

"Not just me!" Bert cried, one hand in the air. The other still clutched the rake. "All us grooms hated him. He wasn't kind to his horse, and if someone ain't kind to their horse, then they ain't a good human."

It seemed an excellent means by which to judge a person's character.

"They were just possessions to him," Robbie went on. "Something to own, like a chair or watch. But horses have character, like people."

"In what way was he not kind to his horse?" I pressed. "Panther's his name, isn't it? Was Mr. Rigg-Lyon cruel to him?"

Robbie looked at Bert, but Bert studied the floor. "Go on,

Bert. You took care of Panther every time he played here. You tell 'em what Rigg-Lyon was like."

Bert looked to the exit as if he'd rather be anywhere but here, answering our questions. "It was nothing specific. He just rode the poor thing to exhaustion, that's all."

"That's all?" Robbie clicked his tongue and rolled his eyes. "Panther is quick into his stride and has a rare turn of speed. Real magnificent, he is."

"I saw the match yesterday," I told him. "Panther was faster than all the other horses, it's true. The opposition's mounts couldn't keep up. Panther and Mr. Hardwick's horse, too, were lightning fast."

"Not just that, but Panther can start at a touch."

"I don't understand the problem," Harry said.

"Rigg-Lyon pushed him so hard out on the field that Panther always came back near-exhaustion. Almost as soon as we got his saddle off, he'd be restless and wouldn't settle. Then he'd get tired. His muscles twitched like he had an electric shock through him, and he wouldn't let Bert near him. He even kicked you last week, didn't he, Bert?"

"It was nothing," Bert muttered.

I'd noticed Bert's limp yesterday. I'd also noticed Panther's restlessness and put it down to sensing death in the stables.

"His feeding habits changed, too," Robbie went on. "Sometimes we couldn't give him enough, and other times he wouldn't eat a thing."

"Was Rigg-Lyon cruel to Panther in any other way?" Harry asked.

"No," Bert said.

Robbie agreed that he'd never witnessed him harm the animal. "I just got this strange feeling when I saw him with Panther and the other horses on their team."

"That's not cruelty," Bert pointed out. "That's just not caring."

Robbie shrugged as if they were the same to him.

"Stop stirring up trouble, Rob. The man's dead. Let him rest in peace."

We left the stables and made our way to the clubhouse. Bert followed us as far as the stable door then watched us until we reached the steps. Once we were sure he'd returned inside the stables, we diverted our course and headed around the back to the other outbuildings surrounding a large paved courtyard. The laundry was on the opposite side of the changing room and was the only building currently in use. We asked the laundresses how long the elderly attendant had been there yesterday after the match and all agreed it was about ten minutes as he attempted to remove a grass stain from Mr. Broadman's breeches. The trough where he worked faced away from the windows opening onto the courtyard, so he couldn't possibly have seen anyone leave the changing room opposite.

Any of the players had time to slip out, murder Vernon Rigg-Lyon in the nearby stables, and return unnoticed.

We inspected the empty changing rooms next. There were six partitioned shower stalls, all open at the front. Only the man in the first shower could have left without the others noticing he was gone. The rest would have to walk past at least one other.

I was about to follow Harry out of the changing room when I spotted a small hole in the tiled wall of one of the stalls. I checked the other stalls, and there were tiny holes in each of them. They were so small, they'd be easily missed if I hadn't been giving the stall a thorough inspection. I placed my eye to it and could clearly see the stables beyond.

I showed Harry. "The club has a Peeping Tom problem."

"Or Peeping Tabitha," he said as he peered through the hole.

"Harry Armitage, are you implying that ladies would stoop to ogling naked men?"

He straightened, smirking. "Only the athletic kind."

I laughed. I should be embarrassed by such talk, but Harry's joking made me feel comfortable. Sometimes, I felt like I could talk to him about anything.

Yet at other times, when we discussed more personal matters, my cheeks flamed and I couldn't bear to look at him. It was a strange paradox.

We made our way to the grand mansion that was now the members' clubhouse. Unlike the stable block, the building was probably a mere hundred years old. Yet I suspected it had seen just as much, if not more, scandal and intrigue. The entrance was fit to welcome royalty with its soaring ceilings and sweeping marble staircase that opened up to a wrap-around gallery. Two white marble statues of prancing horses honored famous mounts of former players at the base of the stairs, and large silver trophies in locked glass cabinets gleamed in the light flooding the entrance foyer.

The foyer was empty, except for the man behind the front desk. Harry asked him if the major was in. Being Sunday, it wouldn't be surprising if he wasn't.

The assistant frowned. "How did you get in? The gates are locked."

Harry handed him a business card. "I've been hired to look into the murder."

"The police are looking into it."

"Not very thoroughly. They don't even have a constable posted at the crime scene."

The man studied the card, looking torn. "The major won't want to be disturbed."

I spotted the major's name on a plaque on one of the closed doors leading off from the foyer. "He'll want to speak to us," I said, walking towards it. "It'll look bad for him if he doesn't."

"Miss! Miss, you need to make an appointment."

I knocked and entered on the major's instruction. "Good morning, sir. Do you remember me from yesterday? Miss Fox. We met in the stables under unfortunate circumstances." Before he had a chance to react, I introduced Harry. "We're private detectives hired to look into the murder by an interested party."

"Is it Broadman?" the major asked as he shook Harry's hand. "I suppose he wishes to clear his name once and for all and doesn't trust the police to do it."

Both Harry and I simply smiled.

The assistant had followed and hovered in the doorway. "Sir, I'm sorry, they just barged in."

"It's all right, Watkins." The major dismissed him and invited Harry and I to sit. "Clearing Broadman's name must be a priority now. It looks bad for the club if the captain of our premier team is arrested for murder."

The office looked out over the picturesque lawn and elm trees, not the stables or working areas, so the major wouldn't have seen the murderer enter or leave if he was in here as he claimed. Besides, the window would be behind him if he was seated at the desk. Below the window was a table with several framed photographs of the major with a woman and child. The child changed ages from baby to late teen, but the woman and Major Leavey looked ageless. The stack of paperwork in the tray on his desk was piled high, and two ledgers lay open side by side. His fingers were stained with ink.

"Yesterday you were sure Mr. Broadman was guilty," I said. "Why the change of heart?"

"I was impulsive yesterday. When I saw Broadman with the murder weapon, I naturally assumed he was guilty, particularly after I heard about their argument."

Harry handed him a business card. "Do you know what their argument was about?"

"He says it was merely a little pre-match tension, and I have no reason to doubt him."

"How well did you know Vernon Rigg-Lyon?"

"Reasonably well. The Polo and Gun Club is our closest club, both in terms of distance and competition. He was well-liked, somewhat arrogant but all the good players are. Broadman is the same." He clasped his hands together on the desk. "Very similar character. Perhaps that's why they didn't get along. Two proud, masculine men competing to win at everything won't like it when the other gets more attention."

I knew the type, too, although I wouldn't have called them proud or masculine. Vain and arrogant was more like it.

"There are rumors that Rigg-Lyon kept a mistress," Harry said.

The major glanced at me. "Steady on, sir. There's a lady present."

"I was the one who informed him," I said. "My cousin told me all about it. He moves in similar circles to Mr. Rigg-Lyon and Mr. Broadman."

"Then you know more than me, Miss Fox. I have no time or inclination to sit around and exchange idle gossip." The tone was as sharp as a knife. The look he gave me was even sharper.

"Do you know Mrs. Rigg-Lyon?" Harry asked.

"No."

"Does your wife know her?" I asked.

"No. Why the interest in her? Is she a suspect?"

"Everyone is a suspect," Harry said.

"Except for me and my staff, of course."

"Your staff are not as innocent as you believe. At least one of them is a Peeping Tom. There are holes in each of the shower stalls, at about eye-height."

The gray hedge that was the major's moustache took on a life of its own as it moved with his vehement denials. Harry and I simply sat back until the protests lessened and finally stopped.

Major Leavey wiped the spittle off the ends of his moustache with a handkerchief. "Is that all? I have a lot of work to do."

"One more thing," I said. "I saw a ribbon on the body when I inspected it, but the police claim they didn't find one. Do you know what happened to it?"

"No. Why would I? Perhaps you were mistaken, Miss Fox."

"About a coral-colored ribbon? How could I possibly mistake it for something else?"

"You were overwrought after witnessing such a dreadful sight. Considering your delicate sensibilities—"

"My sensibilities are as robust as any man's. I know I saw a ribbon in Mr. Rigg-Lyon's pocket, Major, and I also know the police didn't find it later when they inspected his clothing."

He picked up his pen and dipped it in the inkwell. "I see that you're looking to blame me, but I can assure you I didn't see it." He wrote some figures in the ledger. "Perhaps it fell out of the pocket during transportation to the morgue. The police seemed incompetent, so it wouldn't surprise me." He lifted his gaze to Harry's. "That's why I'm glad Broadman hired you."

"I didn't say it was he who hired us," Harry said.

The major seemed not to believe us, or perhaps he just didn't care. He returned to writing in his ledger.

We left and closed the office door behind us. "He was

lying about the ribbon," I whispered. "He didn't meet our gazes when he denied seeing it."

Harry nodded as he eyed the assistant, Watkins, at the reception desk. "Follow my lead."

He approached the desk with a professional smile. "The major has given us leave to ask you questions and requests that you answer them truthfully. Were you here in the club-house yesterday between three-fifty and four-ten?"

Watkins looked past us to the major's office door. His frown indicated he didn't believe us, but he must have decided it was in his best interests to answer. Perhaps he wanted the murder solved quickly, too. "I was helping the steward tidy up in the dining room. We're short-staffed and he needed the extra hand. You can ask him if you don't believe me."

"So this desk wasn't manned?" I asked.

"No." His gaze wandered to the major's office door again.

I made a show of following his gaze. Then I leaned in and lowered my voice. "Why was he in his office at that time yesterday? If you're short-staffed, shouldn't he be overseeing things out here? Wouldn't he see off special guests?"

"The major used to have a drink with them in the lounge, through there." He indicated a room near the back of the reception area where I could see a fireplace and comfortable sofas through the open door. "But he doesn't socialize much since returning to work last week. He had some time off after a death in the family. He works in his office most of the time and goes home late."

"Who passed away?" I asked.

"His daughter."

"Oh, that's so tragic. The poor man."

He nodded sadly. "She was only seventeen."

Bereavement certainly explained why he'd become a recluse and workaholic. It did not explain why he'd removed a ribbon from a dead man's body.

CHAPTER 4

"*D*id Floyd tell you Broadman was also a philanderer?" Harry asked me as we traveled in the hansom cab back to London. "He and Rigg-Lyon were alike in a lot of ways."

"You won't put that in your report to Mrs. Hessing, will you?"

"Mrs. Hessing hired me to report on *all* of Liddicoat's connections, particularly family, but that's a step too far, in my view. It's not fair to paint him with the same brush as Broadman simply because they're cousins. Besides, Broadman isn't married, and many young gentlemen keep mistresses at his age. He isn't doing anything wrong."

"That's a relief."

"You like Liddicoat?"

"I hardly know him, but Miss Hessing is fond of him. The gentlemen at parties can be cruel to her, and her mother is just as bad sometimes, so it would be wonderful to see her find happiness."

"Wanting her to be happy is not a good enough reason to like him or trust him. Her mother is right to be cautious and make sure he's not after Miss Hessing for her inheritance. I had to be thorough."

From his distant stare, I could tell something was troubling him. "But?"

"No buts. Not about Liddicoat. I remember how Mrs.

Hessing treated her daughter last year, and it sounds like their relationship hasn't improved. I want Miss Hessing to be happy, too, so she can escape her mother. I really hope I'm right and Liddicoat's not a fortune hunter."

If he was wrong, Miss Hessing would be devastated.

We'd decided to speak to the widow next. Detective Forrester had given Harry her address when they spoke on the telephone earlier. The Rigg-Lyons lived in a handsome townhouse in Marylebone, a rather large residence for a couple without children. I suspected they didn't have children as the only photographs in the drawing room were of the Rigg-Lyons on their wedding day and two other adult couples who I assumed were their parents.

Mrs. Rigg-Lyon didn't want to speak with us at first, but Harry convinced her to spare a few minutes. It wasn't his usual charm that convinced her, however. It was his suggestion that it wouldn't look good if she refused. The implication being she would appear guilty.

Most people wouldn't consider the frail, pale woman perched on the sofa a murderess, but Harry and I knew that appearances could be deceiving. The blow that killed Vernon Rigg-Lyon had been hard enough to draw blood, but the mallet wasn't heavy, and this woman could have wielded it as well as anyone.

She may have looked frail, but there was a strength about her. She showed no signs of grief, and her gaze was direct as she informed us that she had much on her plate. "I must meet with the funeral director, so your brevity is appreciated." She spoke with a light French accent. If I had to guess, I'd say she'd lived in England a number of years but hadn't been raised here.

"You left the Elms Polo Club immediately after the match," Harry began. "Why didn't you wait for your husband?"

"He liked to stay awhile after a match, particularly if his team won. I prefer not to linger."

"Why particularly after a win?"

"Vanity. He enjoys—enjoyed—the attention. Winners are lauded, Mr. Armitage. Losers are not." When she corrected her tense from present to past, her fingers curled into a fist on her lap. "The team often had a celebratory drink afterwards. Wives weren't welcome."

It was the perfect opening to ask one of the questions we needed to, yet Harry hesitated. The subtle slide of his gaze in my direction left me in no doubt it was something he thought would be better coming from a woman.

I cleared my throat as I considered the best way to broach the topic. In the end, I decided to be as direct as her. "Your husband had a certain reputation. I'm sorry, but I have to ask this…were you aware of it?"

I didn't think her back could get any stiffer, but she seemed to become even more rigid. "You shouldn't listen to gossip, Miss Fox."

I waited, hoping the silence would force her to continue.

My tactic was rewarded a moment later. "My husband liked to cultivate an image of himself, one of a confident, successful athlete, a winner at life, work and play. It's natural for the public to fall in love with that image. Men wanted to be like him, and women found him desirable. Some were quite brazen in their admiration. Perhaps that's why the rumors have persisted over the years. You should ask yourselves who is spreading the rumors, and do they have anything to gain by telling *you* that he kept mistresses?"

I was quite sure Floyd had nothing to gain, but it was possible he'd bought the lie because it fit the image Mr. Rigg-Lyon wanted to portray.

I was going to ask her about the ribbon but decided against it. It was very unlikely that it belonged to her. The color was all wrong. Coral didn't suit a redhead. A stylish woman would never choose a color that didn't suit her, and the woman seated opposite me certainly had style. Her black mourning outfit may have made her look ghostly, but it was superbly fitted and well-made with dozens of tiny butterflies embroidered on the bodice in silken black thread. She would have been a fetching woman if she weren't so thin.

"Who do you think murdered him?" Harry asked.

Again, her hand curled into a fist on her lap. "I don't like to point fingers."

"Very well, let me put this to you. Mr. Broadman was the captain of the opposing team. He was also seen arguing before the match with your husband, and he was later found holding the murder weapon."

"Mr. Broadman is like my husband. An athlete who enjoys the attention, who likes to win at all costs, and believes he's the most important man at his club. Major Leavey, club manager at the Elms, would argue that he was more important, but the two don't really get along."

She knew the major? Indeed, she knew him well enough to make a statement like that. He'd lied to us. He'd denied knowing her. Why? Did it have something to do with him removing the ribbon from her husband's body?

"Now, if there's nothing else…"

"One more thing," I said. "Your husband's speech after the match informed everyone that he would not retire, after all. Were you aware of his change of heart?"

"Of course."

"Mr. Hardwick, his vice-captain, was taken by surprise. He seemed angered by the news."

"That's a matter of opinion. As I said, Miss Fox, you shouldn't listen to gossip."

"It's not gossip. I was there and saw his reaction."

She looked at me anew, her gaze taking in my simple clothes, my lack of jewelry and hair ornaments. "Do you work at the Elms?"

"I was the guest of a member."

"I see," she said blandly. "I'm afraid I can't answer your question. My attention was on my husband during the speech, not his teammates. If you want to know why Mr. Hardwick was angry, then you ought to ask him, not me."

"Did they get along in general?" I persisted.

"They were friends. They'd known one another for years." She reached for the bell on the table beside the sofa and rang it. "My housekeeper will see you out."

The housekeeper bustled into the drawing room, her gaze flicking to her mistress. Without being asked, she handed Mrs. Rigg-Lyon a glass of water that had been sitting on another table. Mrs. Rigg-Lyon sipped as the housekeeper escorted us to the front door.

"The major lied," I told Harry as we descended the front steps to the pavement. "He does know her."

"I think Mrs. Rigg-Lyon lied, too," he said. "I think she knew about her husband's affairs and lied so we'd think she had no motive to kill him."

We parted ways in Soho, each of us taking on a task to accomplish before we met up again in the morning. Harry's task was to find out what he could from the police about their progress, and my task was to gather as much gossip about the Rigg-Lyons as I could. Given that my afternoon and evening were filled with social engagements, I would be in the perfect position to undertake my task.

I had a little time before I needed to change for afternoon tea, so I followed Frank into the staff parlor where he was scheduled to take a fifteen-minute break with a cup of tea and a biscuit. Later, any food not consumed at the formal afternoon tea in the large sitting room would be brought in here for the staff but, for now, the biscuit options were limited to gingerbread and shortbread.

Victor and Harmony were already there, along with Goliath and three maids. He excused himself from the young women who watched him go with disappointment. He might not be classically handsome, but his height and broad shoulders made sure he had admirers wherever he went.

Harmony and Victor sat close together, not speaking yet looking comfortable in one another's company. A short while ago, Harmony would go out of her way to make it appear she didn't like him, but Victor had persisted. He'd recognized the signs of her interest and pursued her until she could admit to herself that she liked him, even if she couldn't admit it to the rest of us. Nowadays, he often walked her back to the residence hall where they both lived if he wasn't on duty in the kitchen when she finished work. They talked quietly together in the staff parlor instead of bickering, and she no longer pretended not to watch him when he wasn't looking. It was quite a breakthrough. Harmony could be frosty to those who didn't know her well, and most men were put off by her crispness. Victor's persistence showed how highly he regarded her.

My friend reminded me a little of Mrs. Rigg-Lyon. Both were direct and didn't suffer fools. But the resemblance ended there. Harmony was down to earth, and had a wicked sense of humor that made her good company, whereas Mrs. Rigg-Lyon seemed as rigid in character as she was in appearance. She might be different with her friends, of course, which was something I planned to find out later.

Our little circle was complete when Peter joined us. Since becoming assistant manager, he rarely had free time, but Mr. Hobart often insisted he take a few minutes' respite in the parlor. He gathered up several biscuits, poured himself a cup of tea from the teapot, and eased himself onto a chair with a loud sigh. He dunked the gingerbread into the cup and watched it drip before taking a bite.

I gave them an update on the case and asked for their thoughts. All agreed that the widow most likely knew about the mistresses.

"A woman senses these things," Harmony said.

"That's what Harry claimed."

She narrowed her gaze. "So you're sharing the investigating with him?" She shook her head. "Doesn't he have enough paying work? Why does he have to take yours, too?"

"His current investigation has links to this murder. I can't divulge any more than that, but I can assure you, *he* has a client, whereas I do not."

"Can we do anything to help?" she went on.

"I'll let you know if I think of something."

She looked disappointed to be given nothing to do. She truly must be bored.

"I know the cook at the Polo and Gun," Victor said. "Want me to ask him what Rigg-Lyon was like?"

"That would be excellent," I said. "Thank you, Victor. Ask about Mr. Hardwick, too, and what his relationship was like with the victim. According to Mrs. Rigg-Lyon, they were friends, but he didn't seem to know the victim decided not to retire, so perhaps they'd grown apart."

Victor gave me a lazy salute with a forefinger to his temple.

"I know Hardwick," Frank said. "He used to stay here with his parents when he was a boy."

"And?" I prompted.

He shrugged. "There's nothing to tell. I didn't know him well."

"Where does he stay when he comes to London now?"

"He lives in London. His parents have an estate somewhere in the country; I can't remember where. They never come to the city, anymore. They're horse people. You won't catch them buying one of them noisy death traps."

Goliath rolled his eyes. "Here we go again."

Frank wagged a finger at him. "If they don't run us over, they'll choke us to death with their fumes. Imagine if every horse is replaced by an automobile. The fumes'll be as thick as cream in this city, just you wait and see."

"At least we'll be able to cross the road without stepping in manure."

"It's all right for you lot, you work inside. I'm mostly outside. You saw the state Miss Fox came home in yesterday after riding in Lord Dunmere's contraption. She was a right sight. No offence, Miss Fox."

"I'm so glad you told me not to be offended, Frank. It softens the blow." I reached for a gingerbread, unable to wait for my own afternoon tea. "Is Cobbit still talking about going on strike?"

My question was met with a chorus of groans. "You had to ask," Harmony muttered.

"And why shouldn't he go on strike?" Frank said to no one in particular. "He's got a right."

"Sir Ronald will fire him," Peter warned. "You should caution Cobbit against drastic action."

Frank crossed his arms. "I think he and the others *should* strike, and I might go out in sympathy. Disruption is the only way to get through to Sir Ronald."

Goliath kicked Frank's ankle and indicated me with a jut of his chin.

I put up my hands. "I won't say a word to my uncle." I stood. "I have to get ready. Harmony, are you free to fix my hair before the concert?"

"I'll fix it now and again tonight."

"No need, unless it's messy." I touched my hair. Perhaps the wind had destroyed the arrangement.

She insisted on going to my room to help me prepare for afternoon tea. It wasn't until she closed the door behind us that I discovered my hairstyle was a ruse.

"Tell me all about the American in room 313," she said, taking my hand and steering me to the sofa.

"Mr. Miller?" I frowned. "Why?"

"I hear he's handsome and charming, and that you two got along *very* well at dinner last night." She couldn't have been more suggestive if she'd winked.

My frown deepened. "How do you know that? Who've you been talking to?"

"Mr. Bainbridge told me."

"Floyd?"

"Miss Bainbridge mentioned it, too."

Honestly, did they have nothing better to do? "Yes, Mr. Miller is everything you say he is. But you know my mind, Harmony. It won't go beyond friendly conversation. Now, tell me about you and Victor."

"Nicely deflected."

"Thank you. Well?"

"We're enjoying one another's company at the moment. Let's leave it at that. So what do you want to wear to afternoon tea?"

* * *

THE MURDER of Vernon Rigg-Lyon was more of a topic of conversation at afternoon tea than it had been at dinner. More details had emerged since then, although I wasn't sure how. Much of it was probably speculation. Rufus Broadman's argument with the victim before the match was analyzed in excruciating detail since there'd been so many witnesses.

"I heard they argued over a horse," said Mrs. Digby, one of Aunt Lilian's friends. Ten of us sat at the Bainbridge family table in the large sitting room. Before it became famous for its new restaurant, the Mayfair Hotel was famous for its afternoon teas. The large sitting room was often full, even during the quiet season, but in the late spring to early summer when society ladies were in town, it was impossible to get a table at short notice. Unless one was family, of course, or friends of my aunt.

One of the potted palms shielded us from the nearest

table, but even so, the group made up of Aunt Lilian's friends and two of their unwed daughters kept voices low.

"No, it was about cheating," claimed Lady Caldicott. "Mr. Broadman accused Mr. Rigg-Lyon of underhanded tactics."

"I heard it was the other way around," said Mrs. Druitt-Poore. "Mr. Rigg-Lyon accused Mr. Broadman of cheating."

Aunt Lilian dabbed at the corner of her mouth with her bone-thin fingers as she swallowed a morsel of cake. "I believe they argued about a woman."

Her friends all looked up from their plates to stare at her. "Mrs. Rigg-Lyon?" asked one with a large dose of incredulity.

Cora Druitt-Poore, a young woman around Flossy's age of nineteen, laughed. "Don't be ridiculous."

Aunt Lilian wiggled her fingers and flicked her wrist in dismissal. Her movements were jerky, and she couldn't sit still. She must have taken a dose of her tonic just before coming downstairs. "A dancer or singer, so I heard." She turned to Cora. "Why is it ridiculous for the argument to be over Mrs. Rigg-Lyon?"

Cora must have regretted her comments, because she tried to brush off the question, but with all eyes now on her, she had to clarify. "She may have been pretty once, but she hasn't aged well."

"She's only mid-thirties," said Mrs. Digby defensively.

"That's what I mean. She *looks* older. I'm sure she's lovely, though," Cora added, as if that softened her remarks.

"She's a dragon," her mother said.

"She's forthright." Lady Caldicott was always the diplomatic one. "She knows her own mind."

"She forces her opinions on others, even when not asked." Mrs. Digby leaned forward, and we all drew in closer. "I knew her when she was younger. She was very attractive then. She's a few years older than Vernon, and some say she captured him early, when he was still young enough to mold into whatever version she wanted. He was besotted, but they eventually grew apart and he strayed. I hear he kept dozens of mistresses."

Flossy gasped. "Not all at once, surely."

"I think we should change the subject," Aunt Lilian said with a glare for Mrs. Digby.

The older women quickly agreed, but the younger ones wanted to continue the discussion. "Mr. Rigg-Lyon was terribly handsome," Cora said. "It's so sad what happened to him."

"Mr. Broadman cuts quite a magnificent figure, too," her sister said. "I don't believe he killed Mr. Rigg-Lyon, no matter what anyone says. He just looks too honest and good, not at all like a murderer."

I couldn't resist and had to ask. "What does a murderer look like, Mary?"

She wrinkled her nose as she lifted the teacup. "Ugly, with a mean look about him. He probably has scars."

"Do you know what Mr. Broadman's like, aside from *looking* honest and good?"

"I hear he's charming," said Cora.

"I hear he's witty and agreeable," added Mrs. Digby. "My sister-in-law's cousin says he makes the most delightful dinner guest."

Some of the other women had heard similar stories, but none knew him personally.

"Two peas in a pod, they were." Aunt Lilian dabbed at the corners of her mouth again. "So handsome and highly regarded by everyone. So remarkably similar. It was no wonder they argued."

Her disjointed comments had us all frowning at her.

"There simply isn't room enough for two men like that," she clarified. "I do hope Mr. Broadman isn't guilty of the murder. It would be such a shame to lose him, too." Her gaze darted to mine, as if it were up to me to ensure he was innocent. Even though I'd not told her or my uncle that I was investigating, she must have realized I'd take on the case.

"What about Mr. Hardwick?" At their blank looks, I added, "The vice-captain of the Polo and Gun Club team. He was a good friend of Mr. Rigg-Lyon's, I believe. They were both going to retire from the game yesterday, but Mr. Rigg-Lyon changed his mind."

None could tell me anything about him, although the older women remembered his parents. They hadn't seen them in years.

"Mr. Broadman and Mr. Hardwick are bachelors, you see,"

Aunt Lilian explained. "If they had wives, they'd move in the same circles as us, but as bachelors, we don't associate with them. You should ask Floyd."

Cora gasped. "Are you interested in Mr. Hardwick, Cleo?"

"Or Mr. Broadman?" her sister asked with a twinkle in her eyes. "I could see you two getting along."

Flossy eyed the remaining raspberry tart on the tiered plate stand in the middle of the table. "Cleo has another gentleman in mind."

The two Druitt-Poore sisters leaned closer. "Do tell."

I spent the rest of the afternoon fending off questions about Mr. Miller.

Our little group dispersed when my aunt was ready to retire to her suite for a rest. The energizing effects of her tonic wore off after an hour these days, at which point fatigue and headaches plagued her. Sometimes she could push through it, but at other times, she either took another dose of tonic or secluded herself in her rooms with the curtains closed.

As we waited for the lift, no one saw Floyd come up behind us. "Boo," he said softly.

Aunt Lilian rounded on him and with more vitality than she'd had for the past hour, berated him. "Do you always have to be so unfeeling! You know my nerves are frayed, and yet you do something so stupid as to sneak up on me!"

"Sorry, Mother, I didn't mean to frighten you." He went to take her elbow, but she shook him off.

"Don't," she snarled.

He blinked at me then Flossy, searching for an ally, but neither of us was prepared to intervene on his behalf. We'd both borne the brunt of her ire recently, for similarly innocuous reasons. It was unsettling to be the object of her anger, given she was usually so kind, and neither of us wanted it turned on us again.

We rode the lift up to the fourth floor in silence and escorted Aunt Lilian to her rooms. Once she was settled on the sofa with a damp cloth placed on her forehead, we tiptoed out.

The moment the door closed behind us, I turned to Floyd. "Tell me everything you know about Rufus Broadman and Mr. Hardwick."

His lips tilted in amusement. "And I thought it was Miller who interested you."

"Do be serious, Floyd. A man has been murdered."

"I am being serious!"

I entered my suite and beckoned him inside. Flossy made her excuses and retired to her rooms to lie down before getting ready for an evening out.

Harmony sprang off the sofa and smoothed down the skirt of her maid's uniform. "Good afternoon, Mr. Bainbridge, Miss Fox. I was just finishing up in here." She picked up the feather duster she must have brought in with her in case she needed to pretend to be working and flicked it over the table.

Floyd took the feather duster off her and pointed it at the sofa. "You're not fooling me. I know you help Cleo with her investigations, so you may as well sit down and listen to what I have to say, too."

She sat on the sofa, feet together and hands primly in her lap. She wasn't prepared to let her guard down with a member of my family the way she did with me.

"Cleo asked about Broadman and Hardwick. I don't really know the latter. He seems like a serious chap. He doesn't carouse with the rest of us, doesn't gamble or drink much. Keeps to himself." He shrugged.

"So there are no rumors about him?" I asked.

"None. No one talks about him at all. It's a little sad."

"It sounds perfect." I gave him a pointed look. "If only no one gossiped about me."

"Don't flirt with handsome Americans and no one will."

"We weren't flirting, we were talking. It would have been a dull evening if we stayed silent. Now, about Mr. Broadman. Does he have a mistress at the moment?"

"Not that I know of. The last one decided to retire from the stage and marry a shopkeeper. Tragic loss."

"And Vernon Rigg-Lyon's mistress? Tell us about her."

"Rosa Rivera is a singer. In fact, she'll be performing at tonight's concert." He hitched up his trouser legs and sat in an armchair. "Cleo, send up for something to eat from the kitchen, will you? I'm starving."

I ordered him a bacon and egg sandwich through the brass speaking tube that connected the room to the kitchen, then joined him and Harmony in the sitting room again. "Some people are saying Broadman and Rigg-Lyon's pre-match argument was about a woman."

"That's what I heard, too. It's not surprising, since Broadman made a play for Rosa Rivera, so they say."

"He was trying to steal Rigg-Lyon's mistress?"

"Something like that. Apparently Broadman is going around today saying it was all a misunderstanding that the two of them cleared up, but I don't know when they got together to talk about it. The match was soon after the argument, and then Rigg-Lyon died shortly after the match."

"So Broadman's lying."

"That's the general consensus."

"What other gossip did you overhear today?"

"Just that the two men were fierce rivals, which we already knew."

"Ah yes. Apparently, there isn't enough room for two popular, athletic men in London society." I rolled my eyes. "There must have been more to their rift than a little sporting rivalry."

"Little?" Floyd snorted. "Clearly you don't know men very well."

"Did they often argue in public?" Harmony asked.

Floyd shook his head. "Their rivalry played out in quiet corners, with whispered accusations about each other in their own respective circles. One would tell his friends he suspected the other of cheating. The other would hear and counter-accuse his rival of doing the same. It was tit-for-tat, with each group of friends taking sides against the other. There was no crossover of group members. One could not be a chum to Broadman and also be part of Rigg-Lyon's inner circle. It just wasn't done."

"Did anyone get to the bottom of the cheating accusations?" Harmony asked. "The club manager or the bookmakers?"

"There is no gambling in polo."

Harmony and I both scoffed.

"There isn't. It's a gentleman's sport. Matches are played for the enjoyment of the game, not for money. The only point of winning yesterday was pride. It allowed Rigg-Lyon to go one-up over Broadman, something he would have enjoyed immensely if Broadman did, in fact, try to steal his mistress."

I tapped my finger on the chair arm as I thought. "I'll try to speak to Rosa Rivera tonight to find out if the rumor is true."

Floyd shook his head. "Not tonight. You need to get her alone to ask that sort of thing, and tonight she'll always be in the company of others. Trust me. I know how busy it can get backstage."

He certainly did. His last mistress had been an opera singer. They'd ended their affair on the night of the hotel's restaurant opening. I wasn't sure whether he'd taken up with another woman since then.

"Do you continue to know these things, Floyd?"

"Not lately. In fact, I find I'm free as a bird. I rather like it. It's liberating."

"Then *you* should be the one courting American guests, not me."

"Did you not hear me say I like being free?"

"I've said the same thing dozens of times, yet I was still placed next to Mr. Miller last night."

He flashed an impish grin. "And look how well that turned out."

I gave him a withering glare. "You're infuriating."

"So I've been told." He stood and chucked me under the chin. "But you adore me, nevertheless." He strode towards the front door. "Send my sandwich to my room when it arrives."

When his sandwich arrived ten minutes later, Harmony ate one half and I ate the other.

* * *

FLOSSY SPOTTED Mr. Miller several rows behind us at the Royal Albert Hall. "He's looking this way." With a fan covering her mouth, the words came out muffled. "Smile, Cleo." She lowered the fan and smiled at him.

I gave him a brief wave and turned away. I didn't want to encourage him or my cousins. They were insufferable enough when it came to my love life, or lack of it.

The music was lovely, but I found I couldn't enjoy it as much as I usually would. A single thought tapped constantly throughout the entire first session until I could ignore it no longer.

I simply *had* to sneak into Rosa Rivera's dressing room. If I couldn't talk to her tonight, looking through her belongings was the next best way to learn about her. There was no better opportunity to do so than when she was on stage.

The singer was part of an ensemble of vocalists who were scheduled to perform immediately after the interval. Flossy and I stretched our legs during the break, joining the throng taking refreshments and chatting to friends in the foyer. I almost got caught by Mr. Miller, but spotted him before crossing his path. I told Flossy I was returning to our seats, then slipped away, disappearing into the crowd.

Finally, the gong sounded and the audience left to enjoy the second half. I waited until no one was looking before heading through the door that led backstage.

The corridor smelled musty with an undercurrent of sweat. Electric lights were placed too far apart to illuminate the whole way brightly, but it was enough to see by. The floor was covered with carpet to muffle the sound of footsteps as backstage hands traveled to and fro.

Only two men asked who I was and what I was doing there. I informed them I'd been sent backstage by the manager. I'd always found that speaking with confidence went a long way towards convincing people. Referencing a higher authority did the rest.

I found Rosa Rivera's dressing room just as the muted sounds of the orchestra resumed. Her name was on the door along with another woman's from her vocal ensemble. Both would currently be on stage. Hopefully no one would have the same idea as me and try to rifle through the dressing room in their absence.

I entered and closed the door. At least it smelled better than the corridor. Jasmine and lily of the valley with a hint of rose. The room was small. Between the two dressing tables, two trunks, and racks of ball gowns and costumes, the space was tight. I read the names on the cards accompanying the bouquets of flowers to determine which dressing table belonged to Rosa. The two women were popular with gentle-men, although Rosa had two more bouquets than her co-star. Word had probably spread that she was available after the death of her lover.

There wasn't a single photograph of Vernon Rigg-Lyon in the room, but that didn't strike me as unusual. This was her place of work, after all. The dressing table was cluttered with hairpieces, combs and pins, costume jewelry, face creams and makeup. I lightly stroked the feathers attached to a headband. They'd been dyed a coral color. There was also a scarf hanging from the edge of the mirror in a similar shade.

I opened the top drawer and my breath hitched. Several lengths of ribbon were laid out in strips.

They were all exactly the same shade as the one I'd pulled from Vernon Rigg-Lyon's pocket.

CHAPTER 5

Finding the ribbons that matched the one I'd discovered in Vernon Rigg-Lyon's pocket was a breakthrough that had my mind whirling with more questions. Had Rosa Rivera given it to him before she murdered him? Or did he snatch it off her during an argument that had been the catalyst for his murder?

Most intriguing of all—why had the major removed it from the scene of the crime?

My preoccupation with the dressing room discovery meant I didn't see the gentleman striding across the foyer towards me until it was too late.

"Miss Fox? Why are you coming from there?" Mr. Miller must have been outside for some fresh air and was returning late to the performance.

"I was lost," I said.

His gaze rose to the sign above the door with STAFF ONLY written in block letters. "May I escort you back to your seat?"

"It might be best if we go in separately. We wouldn't want any misunderstandings if anyone sees us arrive together."

"Yes, of course. After you." He gave me a polite bow and waited in the foyer while I headed off.

I slipped back into my seat, earning a glare from Flossy.

"Where were you?" she hissed.

"Investigating."

"Father noticed you weren't here. He looked cross that you weren't seated when the curtain went up."

I kept my gaze forward rather than risk glancing at my uncle. "Do you know which one is Rosa Rivera?"

"The one with black hair, on the left. Isn't she elegant?"

She was indeed. She had a confidence about her, more so than the other woman in the ensemble. Rosa moved about the stage as she sang, acting out the emotional music through her facial expressions and body language, whereas the other woman stood still and let her beautiful voice do all the work. I wondered if the passion Rosa poured into her performance was due to sorrow over her lover's death.

When the concert was over, the audience filed into the foyer again and made for the door like a tide. One moment Floyd stood beside me, and the next I found Mr. Miller in his place.

He smiled at me. "Did you enjoy the performance, Miss Fox?"

"Very much. You?"

"Superb singing, but I prefer comedic operas."

"So do I."

"We should see one together while I'm town."

My heart sank. I shouldn't have been so agreeable. "I'll have to check my diary, and that of my aunt."

"Of course, but it's my understanding Lady Bainbridge is unwell. Do you have no other chaperone?"

My hesitation allowed Flossy to chime in. "We'll find one." She looped her arm around mine. "We wouldn't want a little thing like a lack of a chaperone to keep you two apart."

"Excellent. I'm so pleased."

Flossy looked pleased, too.

Once we emerged from the building, Mr. Miller touched the brim of his hat and set off, trotting down the stairs.

"Is it just me or does he have an extra spring in his step?" Flossy asked, grinning.

"I am not going anywhere with him, so you can wipe that smile off your face."

I might as well not have spoken. "He's very keen on you," she said. "And he's handsome, tall, charming, clever and has gainful employment. Just your type." She squeezed my arm.

"He's every woman's type, I suppose, but I know you're very particular when it comes to men."

I extracted my arm from her grip. "Flossy, I am not going to encourage Mr. Miller."

She sighed. "Just get to know him better before you dismiss him."

Trying to convince her I didn't want to marry wasn't working. She would never believe me, as she couldn't believe any woman would want to be a spinster. I needed a new tactic.

"Do you truly not love me as much as I love you?" I asked.

She grabbed my hand. "Cleo! How could you say such a thing? I know we've only known one another six months, but I adore you. You're like a sister to me."

"Then why do you want me to go to America?"

She stared at Mr. Miller as he trotted down the steps ahead of us. "He might want to move to England to be with you."

"He can't. His uncle's company is in New York, and Mr. Miller is on a path to becoming senior manager by the time he's thirty." That part at least was true. I had no idea if the company planned to expand to England and would require someone to oversee operations here. It could be the reason behind Mr. Miller's visit, for all I knew. And the reason for his interest in courting an Englishwoman.

"Oh. No." Flossy gave a decisive shake of her head. "I'm not losing you now that I've found you." Her grip tightened on my hand. "You are staying here in London with me. You're right not to encourage him. Now all we have to do is convince my father and Floyd."

"I knew Floyd wanted to push us together, but your father, too?"

"It was his idea."

I was up against a more formidable foe than I realized. Convincing Uncle Ronald that Mr. Miller wasn't the man for me wouldn't be easy. The problem was, he didn't factor in emotions when it came to marriage, so telling him I wasn't romantically interested in Mr. Miller wouldn't work. I needed another angle.

But I couldn't think of one.

* * *

I'D EXPECTED to flop into bed the moment I arrived back at my suite, but I had a surprise visitor. Two, in fact. Victor and Harmony were waiting for me. Going by Harmony's mussed hair and Victor's askew tie, they hadn't been bored while they waited.

"I hope my rooms haven't become your secret meeting place," I said as I removed the combs from my hair.

"It wasn't appropriate for Victor to wait for you alone," Harmony said. "So I joined him for the sake of your reputation."

"How very selfless of you." I sat on the chair and kicked off my shoes. "Did you learn something from your friend, Victor?"

"I did. He said there's been gossip about Rigg-Lyon circulating among the staff at the Polo and Gun Club ever since my friend started working there two years ago. Rigg-Lyon couldn't keep his hands off the female staff."

I liked him less and less.

"There were also rumors he seduced more than one young lady."

"Did these seductions occur while he was with Rosa Rivera or before they were together?"

"Concurrently."

"If she learned about them, she might have killed him in a fit of jealous rage." I told them about discovering the coral ribbons in her dressing room at the Royal Albert Hall. "The same could be said about his wife, although I can't imagine her losing her temper. She was unemotional today when Harry and I met her."

"Nothing says murderess like an unemotional widow," Harmony pointed out.

"I also asked my friend about Hardwick," Victor went on. "He said Hardwick and Rigg-Lyon were best of friends. They did everything together."

"So when Rigg-Lyon changed his mind about retiring, his good friend would have been upset," I said. "They were supposed to retire from the sport together."

Harmony shook her head. "That's not a strong enough motive to kill him."

"Are you going to question Hardwick?" Victor asked me.

"Tomorrow." I glanced at the clock on the desk. "Today."

Even if he wasn't guilty of murder, as the good friend of the victim, Mr. Hardwick might have some insights. Like who did Vernon Rigg-Lyon upset with his roving eye and wandering hands?

* * *

INSTEAD OF TAKING coffees up to Harry's office the following morning, I joined him in the Roma Café when I spotted him seated beside the two elderly men perched on stools at the counter. All of them, including the owner, Luigi, looked up as the door swung closed behind me.

"Good morning, Miss Fox," Luigi said brightly. His looks might be classically Italian, but his accent was decidedly Cockney. "You look real nice today."

"Thank you, Luigi, that's very kind. May I have a coffee, please? Something strong. It was a late night."

"Another one? You should rise later in the mornings to catch up on your sleep."

"I would if I didn't have an investigation to conduct. There's far too much to do." I smiled at the two elderly men, greeting them in Italian. My father had taught me before he died when I was aged ten, while my mother had taught me French. I was fluent in neither, but I had enough to get by if I ever traveled to France or Italy.

Both men nodded a greeting then turned as one to Harry.

Harry rose from the stool. "*Buongiorno, Cleo. Come stai?*"

"You've been learning Italian?"

"They've been teaching me a few words every morning."

"Marvelous. *Sto bene.*"

"*Voglio baciarti.*"

The leathery creases on the faces of the old men folded like an accordion with their laughter. Luigi pressed his lips together but failed to hide his snicker.

Harry rounded on them. "I see I fell for an old trick. Very mature, gentlemen."

Luigi shrugged an apology, but the two glued to their stools continued to grin like naughty boys. One of them clapped Harry on the arm and said something I couldn't quite catch, although the Italian word for "true" was in there.

Harry pulled out a chair for me at one of the tables. "Sorry about that. I hope I didn't say something too rude."

"I don't know the translation, but perhaps refrain from saying it to anyone else."

Luigi brought over two cups of freshly brewed coffees. "These are free. If you really want to learn Italian, I can ask my cousin to teach you in the evenings. She teaches Italian and Spanish to young toff ladies during the day."

Harry told him he'd think about it. "It's not as though I'll ever travel to Italy," he told me after Luigi was out of earshot.

"You might. Perhaps you'll fall in love with your Italian tutor and want to meet her family." The moment I said it, I wished I could take it back. The thought of Harry with an Italian beauty made me as queasy as seeing him with Miss Morris had. "I have much to report on our case, but first, did you find out anything from Scotland Yard?"

"Only that the detective assigned to this investigation is worse than I thought. He has not made arrangements to question the rest of the witnesses. He's decided that Liddicoat was telling the truth about seeing a man in a brown coat leave the vicinity, and he thinks seeking out the cab driver who collected him from the front gate is the way forward. He refused to listen to me when I offered other suggestions. Forrester did warn me he'd be stubborn, but I didn't believe him. I do now." He sipped his coffee. "So what did you learn?"

I told him about the gossip I'd overheard yesterday afternoon and my discovery of the coral ribbons in Rosa Rivera's dressing room. Instead of congratulating me, he frowned at me over the rim of his coffee cup.

"You broke into her dressing room?"

"Yes."

"Did you have your cousin stationed as lookout?"

"I went alone."

"Did anyone see you?"

"Only Mr. Miller, the American guest. I told him I was lost, but I don't think he believed me."

Harry's eyes narrowed at the mention of Mr. Miller. "Why was he there? Was he spying on you?"

"No! If he had been, he would have confronted me when I went in, not when I came out. Don't worry about Mr. Miller. He won't cause problems."

He didn't look convinced as he continued to sip his coffee.

"I think we should call on Mr. Hardwick before we speak to Miss Rivera about the ribbon." I told him what Victor had learned from the cook at the Polo and Gun Club. "It'll be best to go armed with as much information about Rigg-Lyon's attachments as possible when we confront her. Who better to ask than his closest friend?"

Harry checked his pocket watch. "It'll be too early for Miss Rivera, anyway. We'll speak to her at the theater later this afternoon. If you have an afternoon tea to attend, I can call on her alone."

"I have a luncheon today, and a ball tonight, so I can come with you in between."

"You should be careful not to overdo it."

"If I give anything up, it'll be tonight's ball. I won't miss the fun of the investigation."

He chuckled. "You are the most unique woman I've ever met."

"Thank you. Now, our next problem is, where will we find Mr. Hardwick on a Monday morning?"

Harry had been given Hardwick's address by Detective Forrester, who'd taken a peek in the official file, so we began there. The landlady at the lodging house where he kept rooms said we'd find him at the bank, where he worked as an assistant to the deputy governor.

We traveled into the city and, after a long wait staring at the wooden wall paneling in an antechamber, were shown into a reception room with more seating, floor-to-ceiling bookshelves, and a desk. I recognized Mr. Hardwick. A woman hovered at his side, a stack of papers in her arms. Her foot tapped impatiently as she waited for him to finish speaking into the telephone. When he looked up and saw us, he raised a finger to invite us to wait.

When he finally hung up the receiver, he accepted the stack of papers from the woman, spoke to her about the contents, and rose. He knocked on the door beside his desk and entered when a voice on the other side gave permission. A few minutes later he returned without the papers, closed the door softly, and resumed his seat.

"You wish to see me, not Sir Ian?" He jerked a thumb at the door.

Harry handed him a business card and introduced us. "We're investigating the murder of Vernon Rigg-Lyon."

Mr. Hardwick scrubbed a hand over his mouth and jaw. "At least someone is. I have no faith in the police." He wasn't as handsome as either Rigg-Lyon or Broadman, with his receding hair and sunken chin, nor did he exude their level of confidence. "Who hired you?"

"That's confidential," Harry said.

Mr. Hardwick indicated we should sit. "I'm very busy, but I can spare you a few minutes, although if you have any follow-up questions, you should call on me at home in the evening, when I'll have more time."

He shuffled some papers then set them aside on top of a catalog from Tattersalls, the nation's biggest auction house for horses. There was also a photograph of a horse on his desk and a painting on the wall behind him of a majestic chestnut with a polo player seated in the saddle. The plaque below the painting stated the rider's name as Walter Hardwick, not Barnaby.

"Your father?" I asked.

He nodded. "He and my mother live on the family estate. I return home every now and again to see them and discuss strategy."

"Polo strategy?"

"Horses. They breed stock for polo, and I act as agent here in London. It's just a part-time occupation at the moment, something I squeeze in when I'm not here, but we hope to scale up and make it a thriving concern one day. You look familiar. What did you say your name was?"

"Cleopatra Fox. I was second on the scene in the stables after Mr. Broadman."

His lips pinched. "That cur. If you want to find the killer, I'd look there first. He hated Vernon."

"The feeling was mutual, apparently," Harry said.

"Vernon wasn't nearly so vehement in his dislike. Broadman was persistent in his accusations of cheating against Vernon. Almost maniacal, you could say."

"Is that what they argued about before the match on the steps of the clubhouse?"

Mr. Hardwick shifted his weight in the chair. "I don't know. We didn't have an opportunity to discuss it."

It seemed unlikely he didn't discuss it with his friend before the match, but I didn't press the point. "Did Mr. Broadman ever present any evidence of Mr. Rigg-Lyon's cheating?"

"No, because he didn't have any evidence."

Harry took over the questioning. We'd agreed that he should be the one to ask about Rigg-Lyon's affairs. "There has also been a suggestion that they argued over a woman."

"As I said, I don't know what their disagreement was about."

"Mr. Rigg-Lyon was something of a ladies' man."

Mr. Hardwick's lips twitched. "Women were attracted to him."

"Did his wife know he kept mistresses?"

"You'd have to ask her."

"How serious was his relationship with Rosa Rivera?"

Mr. Hardwick hesitated. "No more serious than any of his other affairs. He wouldn't leave his wife for her, if that's what you're asking."

"Did Miss Rivera know that?"

"Again, you'd have to ask her." After a brief pause, he added, "A woman like Rosa must have known."

"A woman like her?" I echoed.

He separated his hands before clasping them again. "Vernon wasn't her first lover. She was...experienced with how these things worked. Only a naive fool would expect him to leave his wife for a mistress, and I can assure you, Rosa is neither naive nor a fool."

"There is also a rumor that Mr. Rigg-Lyon ruined the reputations of young ladies."

"Certainly not! That's an outrageous lie." As if he suddenly realized how loud his voice had risen, he leaned forward and lowered it. "Vernon may have had a reputation with women, but he paddled in the entertainment pool only. Singers, dancers, that sort. Not ladies of good breeding." He sat back again. "Did Broadman say otherwise? You shouldn't listen to him, or his cousin, Liddicoat."

"You know him, too?" Harry asked.

"Not well, but he's naturally going to take Broadman's side, isn't he? I mean, ask yourselves, why did Liddicoat lie about seeing a man with a brown coat if not to make the police look elsewhere instead of at the culprit standing over the body holding the murder weapon dripping with blood?"

"It wasn't dripping," I pointed out. "The blood had dried. Also, he wasn't discovered standing over the body. He was outside the stables, calling for help. If he were guilty, he'd have left the scene quietly."

"Or he's cleverer than the police think because he predicted that's what they'd assume. Don't let him fool you, Miss Fox. He may not be the brightest star in the sky, but his cousin is intelligent. Liddicoat knew that seeing a brown-coated man would distract the police away from Broadman."

"What makes you think it's a lie?"

Mr. Hardwick made a scoffing noise. "No one else saw the fellow in the brown coat. You were second on the scene so must have been in the vicinity. Did *you* see him?"

It was a good point, one that unsettled me. Was I biased in favor of Mr. Liddicoat because I wanted him to be telling the truth for Miss Hessing's sake?

Mr. Hardwick expelled a deep breath, as if expelling his anger, too. "Is that all? I have work to do." He put up his finger to indicate to the woman hovering in the doorway with another armful of papers that he wouldn't be long.

"We're nearly finished." Harry indicated me. "Miss Fox noticed your surprise when Mr. Rigg-Lyon announced he'd changed his mind and no longer planned to retire."

"It's true. I was surprised, even a little annoyed, that he hadn't informed me. We planned on announcing it that day together, win or lose."

"Why wouldn't he tell you something like that? You're good friends."

"I suppose it was a spur-of-the-moment decision. The thrill of winning the cup would have got his blood up. Being on the podium, accepting the accolades...it's a heady feeling, one that can overrule all other thoughts and emotions."

"Why did you both decide to retire?" I asked. "You're not old."

"I'm thirty-five, Vernon was thirty-six. Our bodies need to be in peak physical condition to play at the elite level, and we're not as young as we used to be. Besides, we both had other interests to pursue." He indicated the photograph of the horse.

"One more question," Harry said. "Where were you between three-fifty and four-ten on Saturday afternoon?"

Mr. Hardwick started to laugh then stopped abruptly. "You can't seriously think I killed him?"

We stayed silent.

He shifted his weight in the chair. "I was in the privy, if you must know."

"Did anyone see you leave?"

"No. There was no one about. It wasn't until I went outside that one of the staff told me Vernon was dead."

The woman strode up to the desk and pointedly cleared her throat. It was our signal to leave.

Mr. Hardwick rose, too, and shook our hands. "Find my friend's murderer, Armitage. Vernon didn't deserve that ending. He was a giant among men." He swallowed heavily. "There'll never be the likes of him again."

He turned away, but not before I saw his eyes fill with tears.

The woman placed the documents on Mr. Hardwick's desk then escorted us through the warren of corridors and staircases to the ground level where the public queued to see one of the bank tellers stationed behind the long counter.

We waited until we were in a cab before discussing Mr. Hardwick's comments.

"Did you believe him?" I asked.

"I believe he's upset over his friend's death, but that

doesn't mean he didn't do it himself. As to the rest, I'm not sure. What do you think?"

"I think he lied about the retirement issue. I think he was more upset than he let on. He looked angry when he stormed off after Rigg-Lyon announced his change of heart, not merely annoyed. The thing is, I can't work out why he'd be furious about something like that. Upset, yes, and annoyed that his friend didn't confide in him, but angry? It seems excessive."

We agreed that I should put in an appearance at the hotel before heading out to luncheon with Aunt Lilian and Flossy. We would interview Rosa Rivera later when we could be sure she'd be at the opera house preparing for her evening performance.

I arrived at the Mayfair to see Uncle Ronald stopped at the front door by Frank. Although he kept his features schooled, it was clear my uncle was cross from the slicing motion of his hand cutting off Frank's words. He strode inside, leaving Frank to glare after him.

"What was that about?" I asked.

"I tried to talk to him about Cobbit's concerns. He wouldn't listen."

"Perhaps now isn't the right time."

"It never is."

"Frank, are you sure this is the hill you want to die on?"

"You know I'm a Bainbridge man, Miss Fox. Always have been, always will be. But a man's got to stand up for what's right, and this is right." He stabbed his finger into the palm of his hand. "First it'll be automobiles taking over the stables and putting good men like Cobbit out of work, next it'll be me."

"All is not lost. Cobbit can retrain as a mechanic."

"Cobbit's an old dog like me. He ain't got what it takes to learn a new trick." He tapped his temple in case there was a misunderstanding.

A guest approached and Frank opened the door for him. I entered the hotel and smiled at Goliath, arranging luggage on a trolley for the couple standing at the check-in desk. My uncle chatted to two ladies, Mr. Hobart at his side. They laughed at something one of the women said, then Uncle Ronald made his excuses.

He joined me on the stairs and greeted me jovially. "I'll walk up with you, Cleopatra." I'd never seen him take the stairs all the way to the fourth floor. Given he was a thick-set man, whose enjoyment of food and wine was evident from the strain of his waistcoat, it was no surprise he preferred the elevator. "How are you today, my dear?"

"Very well, thank you, Uncle. And you?"

"Couldn't be better. Are you going out to lunch with Florence and Lilian?"

"I am. Do you have plans?"

"I'm lunching at my club with a couple of hotel guests. I believe you know one of them rather well. Miller? American, uncle and nephew, in London for business."

Now I understood why he was taking the stairs instead of the elevator. I picked up my pace. "The nephew and I sat together at dinner the other night."

"Ah, yes, I thought so. Good man, young Miller. Good prospects. The uncle's in construction in New York, and doing well, I hear."

I suspected this was my uncle's attempt at a subtle approach. Speak highly of a young gentleman, drop hints about his connections, but don't push me in his direction. Going by the inept way he went about it, I suspected the approach was a new method for him. Subtle wasn't a word I'd usually associate with my uncle.

I didn't have to do anything more than smile and nod because we'd reached the second floor landing and Uncle Ronald was puffing like a steam engine. "I think I'll take the lift the rest of the way," he said between breaths.

* * *

Luncheon was mercifully short, but even so, it was three-thirty by the time I telephoned Harry from Mr. Hobart's office and suggested we meet outside the Royal Albert Hall. The doorman let us in without question when Harry showed him his business card and explained our reason for needing to speak to Rosa Rivera.

We found her alone in her dressing room, practicing her

vocal scales while she arranged a wig on a stand into an elaborate style.

"Put them with the others," she said without turning around. Her accent was underpinned by a hint of Spanish, but it wasn't strong. She pointed the comb she was holding at the two bouquets of flowers on the dressing table.

Harry cleared his throat and she spun around. "Our apologies for the interruption."

Her gaze unashamedly took Harry in, ignoring me altogether. Being overlooked by women when in his presence was somewhat familiar to me now, but it was still not something I liked. She put out her hand, not for him to shake, but to kiss.

He lightly grasped it and performed a perfunctory bow. He was more accustomed to these uninvited flirtations than me. He'd been the object of them for years. "Good afternoon, Miss Rivera. My name is Harry Armitage, and this is my associate, Miss Fox. We're private detectives."

"You want to speak to me about Vernon's death? I expected to be questioned, although I thought it would be by the police." She was even more beautiful up close, with glossy black hair cascading to her waist in waves, chocolate-brown eyes, and smooth skin. She wore a dressing gown which slipped off one shoulder, revealing the slender strap of an undergarment. Her fingers skimmed over her bare skin before slowly drawing the dressing gown back up to cover herself.

Being ignored wasn't necessarily the worst thing to happen to a detective. While her attention was on Harry, I sidled closer to the dressing table. The top drawer was open. Inside were cards that must have accompanied the flowers, as well as stationary items, ink and writing implements. But no ribbons.

She'd got rid of them. Why?

Had she merely cleaned out her top drawer? Or had someone warned her that her coral ribbon had been found on the body of her deceased lover, and if duplicates were discovered in her dressing room, it would make her the prime suspect in his murder?

CHAPTER 6

I kept my mouth shut as Harry asked Rosa questions. We hadn't discussed beforehand who would take the lead in questioning her, but it was obvious she would respond better to him than to me. Harry must have thought so, too. Our silent agreement to the tactic was one of the ways we worked well together.

"I'm sorry I have to ask this, but it's a standard question," Harry began. "Where were you between three-fifty and four-ten on Saturday afternoon?"

"Here, being measured by the dressmaker." She waved a hand at the rack of beautiful gowns. "It may have been a little before that. I didn't look at the time when we finished, but Mrs. Warden will know. She's very punctual."

"You didn't wish to see Rigg-Lyon play in the final?"

"No. His wife was going to be there. We had an agreement that I stay away if she was going." She leveled her gaze with his. "I did not kill Vernon, Mr. Armitage. I was fond of him. He was good to me." She reached for a handkerchief on the desk and pressed it to her nose. It was swollen from crying and her eyes were red.

"Do you know he pursued other women while he was with you?"

"Of course." She tilted her head coquettishly. "Although I like to think I was his favorite."

"You didn't mind?"

"At first, yes, but I came to realize I wasn't in love with him, and when one is not in love, one cares a little less. As I said, I was fond of him, he was fond of me, but it wasn't love. There was affection and respect between us, that's all." She adjusted her dressing gown at her shoulder again as she turned to me, acknowledging me for the first time. "May I offer you some advice, Miss Fox? Life is easier if you do not fall in love."

Harry cleared his throat. "Do you know Rufus Broadman?"

"A little."

"There is a rumor that he and Rigg-Lyon argued over you."

She placed a hand to her chest. "Me?"

"Rigg-Lyon thought Broadman attempted to steal you away, so the rumors say."

She wagged a finger. "Ah, I know what that is about. We talked one night at a party. It was nothing, just idle chatter, a little flirting. Vernon did not say anything at the time, and he did not seem angry. I think the rumors are making a mountain out of a molehill."

"Did you ever see them argue?"

Her gaze shifted away.

"Miss Rivera? Did you ever witness an argument between them?"

"I once saw Rufus accuse Vernon of cheating at polo. Vernon denied it. How does one cheat at polo?" She shrugged in answer to her own question.

"A ribbon was found in Rigg-Lyon's pocket after he was murdered. Do you know anything about that?"

She blinked rapidly at him before reaching under the desk to retrieve an embroidered bag. She opened it and pulled out a coral ribbon. "Was it this color?"

Harry's gaze met mine.

"Yes," I said. "Why did he have it?"

She smiled sadly and clutched the ribbon to her chest. "He once told me he carried my ribbon during his matches for luck, but I thought he was just being sweet. You know how men are." She withdrew a fistful of ribbons from the bag. "I have so many, I didn't miss one."

"You say you were never at the same polo matches as Mrs. Rigg-Lyon," Harry went on. "But did you ever see her with her husband?"

"No, never."

"Did he ever mention her to you?"

She looked offended. "A gentleman does not mention his mistress to his wife, or his wife to his mistress. The only time he spoke of her was to tell me she had no right to be upset about me. He says she had affairs, too."

I couldn't imagine the frail, standoffish woman taking a lover. "Are you sure?"

She shrugged. "He believed it. He saw regular entries in her appointment diary for someone named John C. Or John S? I can't recall now."

"When did he tell you this?"

"Two or three weeks ago."

"Did he confront her?"

"I don't know, but I doubt it. He didn't care enough about her for it to matter to him. Besides, if he forbade her from taking a lover, she might do the same to him, and he wouldn't want to give me up."

Harry handed her a business card. "Thank you for your help, Miss Rivera. If you think of anything, let me know."

She tucked the card and ribbons into her bag. "I hope you catch the person who did this. Vernon wasn't a perfect man, but he was wonderful to me. I will miss him."

Harry and I didn't leave the Royal Albert Hall immediately. We went in search of the dressmaker to verify Rosa's alibi. We found Mrs. Warden in a large dressing room that must be used by several women. The dressmaker was alone, kneeling on the floor with a large red cape spread out before her and a measuring tape in hand. The cape was smudged with dirt, which I supposed was the required effect for the costume.

Harry put out his hand to assist her. The gray-haired woman accepted it gratefully and pushed to her feet with a grunt.

"Thank you. My knees aren't what they used to be." She lowered the spectacles hanging on a leather strip around her neck and peered at him. "Are you the new tenor? I'm Mrs.

Warden, but you'll be wanting my husband. He's around here somewhere."

Harry handed her a business card. "We're private detectives investigating the murder of Vernon Rigg-Lyon."

She returned the spectacles to her face and inspected the card. "You must be here to see Rosa Rivera. I believe those two were…acquainted."

"We've just come from her dressing room. She claims she was with you on Saturday afternoon."

"That's right. I was making adjustments to some of her outfits." She frowned. "Do you think she did it? Lord, I hope not. I like her."

"We're just establishing where everyone was at the time of the murder. Do you remember what time you last saw her?"

"I left her dressing room at three thirty-five."

"You seem very certain."

"I'm particular about appointments, and she made me five minutes late to my next one."

Rosa wouldn't have reached the Elms Polo Club before ten past four—the latest time the murder could have occurred—if she left the Royal Albert Hall by three thirty-five.

Harry wasn't convinced, however. "We need to test it," he said as we descended the steps to the pavement. "A single horse and carriage wouldn't make it at a regular pace, which rules out cabs. I think a private vehicle could do it with two horses if the coachman was willing to push them to their limit. I'll ask Cobbit if it can be done."

"What about an automobile? That would make it on time." Automobiles were uncommon enough that we could probably identify all of them currently in the city. "Floyd will know who owns one."

I resolved to speak to my cousin, while Harry's task was to check with Cobbit.

We decided to walk to the hotel, taking Rotten Row through Hyde Park. The clouds had settled in, providing a light coverage from the sun and keeping the heat at bay. The fine weather brought out the riders, showing off their high-stepping horses and fashionable outfits. Sumptuous open landaus and barouches drove past slowly so that the ladies' hats didn't blow off, while smaller, lighter curricles and private hansoms tried to pass. Each vehicle was polished to a sheen, every buckle and button gleaming. The horses, liveried coachmen and footmen were presented as superbly as their passengers. It wouldn't do for a society household to send out an equipage with a smudge or old nag.

We pedestrians kept to a sedate pace on the pavement to avoid being sprayed by dust flicked up by wheels and hooves on the gravel or stepping in horse deposits. Harry bought a newspaper from a boy at Hyde Park Corner before we crossed to Piccadilly. He told me there used to be a man with an ice cream cart stationed there on warm days with the most varied flavors of ice cream for sale, but he'd not returned since the banning of penny licks last year.

"You were taking your life in your hands eating ice cream from one of those cups," I told him. "My parents used to tell me they carried disease years ago, before the general public became aware of the dangers."

"Carlo's chocolate ice cream was worth the risk."

"You should try Mrs. Poole's."

"The hotel's restaurant is a little out of my budget right now."

I winced. "Sorry. That was unfeeling of me."

"Not at all. It's something to aim for. When the agency is successful, I plan on eating there until Sir Ronald admits he made a mistake dismissing me."

"You'll be dining there every week, in that case. Uncle Ronald believes he's always right. And, to be fair, he doesn't want your agency to fail."

"True. He's not vindictive, just stubborn."

I thought we'd part ways at the front of the hotel, with me going inside while he continued to the mews, but he stopped at the front entrance to speak to Frank.

"Do you know if Victor's working today?"

Frank folded his arms over his chest and thrust his chin forward. He was still reluctant to give Harry any quarter. He would always believe Uncle Ronald did the right thing in dismissing him. "Why do you need to know?"

"I need his expertise."

"Why?"

"Frank," I snapped. "It's for the investigation. If you don't help Harry, it means you're being a hindrance. Do you really want to be the reason the murderer isn't caught?"

Frank lowered his arms to his sides. "I suppose not," he muttered. "Victor's shift finishes at eleven."

Harry thanked him and moved off. Instead of going inside, I hurried after him. "What do you need Victor for?"

"It's best if you don't know."

"That will work with others, but not me. We're partners, Harry, as well as friends. I want to know if I need to worry about you."

He quickened his pace before slowing again. "Very well. I'm going to take a look at Mrs. Rigg-Lyon's diary. We need to know for certain if she is having a liaison with a man before we confront her about it."

"What a good idea! If we can find letters from him, even better."

He stopped and rounded on me. "Not 'we', Cleo. You're not coming."

"There's no reason I shouldn't come."

"You have a ball tonight."

There was that. "It's not far from Mrs. Rigg-Lyon's house. I could sneak away for a few minutes. No one will notice."

"You underestimate how popular you are as a dance partner. They'll notice."

"You have no idea how popular I am."

He smirked. "I'm an investigator. Of course I know."

I rolled my eyes. "This is my investigation, too. I should be there."

"You only want to come because it's more interesting than a ball."

"Well, yes."

"Go to the ball. Dance and do whatever it is people do at balls when they're not dancing. Enjoy yourself. I'll let you know tomorrow what we discovered."

It turned out that he didn't wait for the morning. He required my assistance, after all.

* * *

WHEN A BALL IS HELD once a week, they cease to be special. More often than not, I found them exhausting. There were all the dress fittings in the weeks beforehand, the hours of preparation on the day, the last-minute adjustments to hairstyles, not to mention the sore feet on the night, the pressure to fill silences with witty conversation, and the late finish. It was enough to make even the most exuberant girl groan when she received yet another invitation. The smart hostess held her event earlier in the social season, when guests were fresh and before couples had been paired.

Sometimes, however, I still found them worth attending. As information-gathering sessions, they could prove valuable to an investigation. The one held around the corner from Mrs. Rigg-Lyon's house promised to be one such event with both Mr. Broadman and his cousin, Mr. Liddicoat, in attendance.

The house wasn't grand so the guest list was small enough that the evening felt more intimate. I'd met everyone at least once at other events, which would usually make for an enjoyably full evening. But tonight, I would have preferred to blend into the walls and observe one of our main suspects.

On the few occasions I was able to surreptitiously watch Mr. Broadman, he appeared unaffected by the death of his polo rival. He was amiable and flirtatious. Occasionally, he turned grave, but only when others mentioned the demise of Vernon Rigg-Lyon.

Mr. Liddicoat stayed glued to his cousin's side. This fact wasn't lost on me or Miss Hessing, who lamented that she couldn't speak to him alone when we met at the refreshment table.

"I would very much like to know if he is all right," she said as we studied the array of sliced ham, cold tongue, sandwiches and fowl that had been cut into bite-sized portions. "But I can't get him away from Mr. Broadman."

I selected a sandwich from the silver platter. "Mr. Liddicoat seems kind-hearted."

"Oh, he is." She sighed dreamily as her gaze searched out her paramour.

He didn't notice, however. He was at Mr. Broadman's side, listening intently to something he said to another gentleman.

"Should I go to him?" she asked. "Perhaps I should. It would look odd if I don't. Everyone has seen us dance together on numerous occasions, so they would wonder why we haven't danced tonight. They'll think we've had a falling out when that is quite untrue. My mother won't mind."

I placed a hand on her arm to show my support. "I'm sure she won't. She hasn't forbidden you to see him, after all, so you can speak to whomever you want. I think it's a good idea to speak to Mr. Liddicoat. The other fellow is moving off and he and Mr. Broadman are alone by the tea table."

She smiled in relief at my suggestion and was about to join them when she paused. She bent down to my level. "Don't look now, Miss Fox, but Mr. Miller is watching you from the other side of the room."

I took her advice and kept my gaze on the refreshments table. I didn't want to encourage Mr. Miller. Although we'd had one dance together, I'd made sure not to find myself trapped with him since. It was a shame that my family was trying to match us, as I would like to have a conversation with him without it implying something more.

"Now Sir Ronald is with him," Miss Hessing whispered. "They're both looking this way. You should go to them. I think Mr. Miller would be very pleased if you did."

"I'd rather speak to your Mr. Liddicoat."

"You don't like Mr. Miller? He seems nice and is very handsome. My mother knows his family and she claims they're hardworking to the point of being a little dull, which is not the negative she makes it out to be." She gave me a cheeky smirk. "If my mother finds someone interesting, you should run the other way."

"He is nice, but he's not for me. It's better to let other girls know he's available if I have no intentions towards him myself. Speaking of other girls, there are two making a beeline for Mr. Liddicoat. We have to hurry if we want to get there first."

We took our supper plates and joined Mr. Broadman and Mr. Liddicoat before the two other ladies who'd spotted them alone reached them. The prettier one pursed her lips at seeing her quarry caught, but the other girl merely shrugged and moved towards the refreshment table. I turned my back to Uncle Ronald and Mr. Miller but still felt their gazes on me.

Mr. Liddicoat and Mr. Broadman greeted us with gentlemanly bows. Mr. Liddicoat immediately sidled closer to Miss Hessing, asking her in a quiet voice if she was well and enjoying the night. His tone was intimate, even if his questions were not.

Mr. Broadman was therefore stuck with me. "It's a pleasure to see you again, Miss Fox, albeit under pleasanter circumstances."

"Indeed. Nasty business on Saturday. Have you recovered from the shock?"

"Not entirely, but I'm keeping busy and trying not to think about it. My cousin was just telling me you're related to the Bainbridges. Lady Bainbridge is your aunt, I believe."

"She is. I moved into the Mayfair Hotel just before Christmas. I lived in Cambridge before that."

"That's quite a move for a young lady on her own. It mustn't have been easy for you."

I blinked in surprise. Not many people acknowledged how difficult it had been for me to move to a new city, leaving behind everything and everyone I knew. I'd not expected him to be so empathetic.

"I'm about to move myself." He nodded at Mr. Liddicoat, still talking quietly to Miss Hessing. "My cousin suggested we lease some rooms together. We move in this week. It'll be quite a change for us both, having to share."

There was only one reason two gentlemen bachelors shared lodgings—it lowered the cost for each. Well, there was another reason, but I didn't think either Mr. Broadman or Mr. Liddicoat was the sort of man who preferred each other over women.

I wondered if Harry knew about Mr. Liddicoat's financial predicament and had noted it in his report to Mrs. Hessing. I didn't want to ask in case he hadn't. He'd feel obliged to add it, and I didn't want Mrs. Hessing to use it as a reason to keep Mr. Liddicoat away from her daughter.

But what if Mr. Liddicoat's situation was precisely the reason why he was pursuing an heiress in the first place?

My thoughts and the conversation were in danger of being

diverted down a path that wouldn't help me solve the murder, so I steered it back. "What will happen to the Polo and Gun Club's main team now that Mr. Rigg-Lyon is gone and Mr. Hardwick is retiring? Do you think he'll come out of retirement to honor his fallen captain?"

"I doubt it. Hardwick has other plans."

"Oh?"

"Expanding his father's horse-breeding business or something like that. Do you ride, Miss Fox?" Once again, he was shifting the conversation back to me. He was rather an expert at diversion. Either that or he was just a very good flirt and knew the way to get into someone's good graces was to ask them about themselves.

Unlike in the hectic moments after the murder, I was able to see Mr. Broadman in his element. He cut a fine figure in a black tailcoat and waistcoat over a crisp white shirt, with his hair parted down the middle. He towered over me, but I never felt dominated by him. I could see why Flossy and the other girls were enamored.

"I don't know the first thing about horses," I said.

"You should learn. I could teach you. May I call on you at the Mayfair Hotel?"

Oh Lord, this wasn't going at all to plan. "Are the rumors untrue?" I asked innocently.

"What rumors?"

"That you are courting someone and she is the reason you and Mr. Rigg-Lyon argued on the steps of the Elms clubhouse?"

Mr. Broadman's reaction was slight, but I was on the lookout for any change to his pleasing features, so the flare of his nostrils wasn't lost on me. "You shouldn't listen to gossip, Miss Fox. It's almost always untrue when it comes to men like me. That argument was nothing more than a little release of pre-match nerves."

"You don't strike me as the nervous type, Mr. Broadman."

"Outward appearances can be deceptive. For instance, you seem like a charming woman of good breeding, but it turns out you are a meddlesome gossip like all the rest." He spun on his heel and strode off.

I was left staring at his back, wondering how I could have handled that better.

Beside me, Mr. Liddicoat hurriedly made his excuses to Miss Hessing and went to follow his cousin.

I stepped into his path, blocking him. I'd lost one source of information; I didn't want to lose another. "I'm afraid I may have upset your cousin by asking him how he's coping after Saturday's tragedy." My sympathetic look wasn't false. The murder was tragic and my questions were intrusive. If Mr. Broadman was innocent, then I was sorry for him. He may not have been close to Vernon Rigg-Lyon, but they'd been long-time acquaintances, and Mr. Broadman had been accused of his murder. Both were upsetting situations. "He wanted some time alone to reflect." I took hold of his arm to secure him at my side.

"Yes, of course," he murmured. "It's been a very trying few days for Rufus."

"Have the police continued to hound him?"

He shook his head, his gaze still on Mr. Broadman who'd been waylaid by a group of young ladies that included Flossy. "Thankfully they believed my account about the man wearing the brown coat."

It seemed like an odd choice of words. "Why wouldn't they believe you?"

He blinked as he finally focused on me. "It's a figure of speech. Being the cousin of the man who found the body, they might assume I have a vested interest in providing an alternative suspect."

"You must have been nearby when you heard Mr. Broadman's shout. You came quickly."

"I was taking a walk through the wooded area near the clubhouse while I waited for him. We planned to return to the city together."

"Were you there for some time?"

"I headed there after the presentation of the winner's cup. The crowd had become a little overwhelming and I wanted to be alone."

If he was amongst the trees, how could he have seen the suspect in the brown coat in the vicinity of the stables? The woods were on the opposite side of the clubhouse.

I kept my features smooth. I didn't want him suspecting that I now doubted his story. I wasn't finished with my questions. Unfortunately, I didn't get the opportunity to revisit the argument between his cousin and Mr. Rigg-Lyon, as Mr. Miller joined us.

A somewhat awkward conversation followed before the music resumed. Mr. Liddicoat asked Miss Hessing to dance, and Mr. Miller asked me. I couldn't get out of it and graciously accepted.

As we parted from the others, he bent to my level. "That fellow was rude to you earlier, the one who walked off. I could tell something he said troubled you."

"Mr. Broadman? Not at all. I think I said something to upset him, not the other way around."

"Are you sure you don't want me to call him out? I can challenge him to a duel."

I laughed. "Do you have dueling pistols?"

"Alas, no." He sighed theatrically. "The fellow should count himself lucky."

I continued to smile as we chatted throughout the waltz. Mr. Miller was a good dancer and a better conversationalist, a combination that meant the time passed quickly.

I enjoyed myself until I spotted my aunt and uncle watching us. Aunt Lilian's foot tapped on the floor in time to the music and one swaying hand conducted the string quartet. She must be in the throes of her tonic. She'd taken a dose just before we left the hotel, but that would have worn off some time ago. She must have it with her and taken more to get her through the evening.

It was worrying, but what worried me more was the small smile both she and my uncle sported. It was the sort of smile I gave Miss Hessing and Mr. Liddicoat when I saw them together.

"Your cousin is trying to get your attention."

I followed Mr. Miller's gaze to see Floyd standing at the edge of the circle of dancers. He mouthed "After the dance" and jerked his head towards the exit. Considering Floyd wanted to pair me with Mr. Miller, it must be important for him to call me away.

"It's probably something to do with the investigation," I murmured.

"What investigation?"

I bit the inside of my lower lip. I'd been so distracted by Floyd, and so comfortable with Mr. Miller, that I'd forgotten to be careful. While I didn't care who knew that I worked as a private investigator, Uncle Ronald would be furious to know I'd let it slip to a guest.

I was debating whether to brush him off, deny it, or admit the truth when Mr. Miller gave me no option.

"Miss Fox?" he pressed. "Are you and your cousins detectives?"

"Just me, although they're both sources of information on occasion."

"I see. And on this occasion? What are you investigating?"

"The murder of the polo player."

He mistimed a step, causing me to stumble. He caught me around the waist, then resumed his smooth rhythm. "I thought you were going to tell me that you find lost dogs or misplaced items. Murder is…well, it's dangerous."

"I'm very careful."

We continued dancing in silence for a few moments, but I could tell his thoughts were brewing. Finally, he told me what was on his mind. "I think having a hobby that engages the mind is admirable in an unmarried lady."

"But not in a married one?"

"She'd be too busy for investigating. Married women have a great deal on their plates. They raise children, manage a household, organize charity functions. It's not a light load. We men have an easier time of it. We just go to the office each day." This he said with a soft laugh, so I assumed it was meant as a joke. "I do know one married lady who writes articles for a women's journal. She does it in the evenings when she has no social engagements."

"Perhaps that's not enough for some women." I gave him a perfunctory smile. "Excuse me, Mr. Miller, this must be important or Floyd wouldn't interrupt."

I moved away as the dance ended, but not before I saw Mr. Miller's look of confusion. I wasn't sure what confused him. The fact that I investigated murders or that my family knew about it and even helped occasionally? Probably all of it.

I joined Floyd, but instead of telling me why he wanted to speak to me, he led the way out of the ballroom.

"Floyd? What is it? What do you want to tell me?"

"It's not me who wants to talk to you." He trotted down the stairs so quickly that I couldn't keep up.

I picked up my skirts and raced after him. "Floyd, slow down. Who wants to speak to me?"

"Armitage, another fellow who looks vaguely familiar, and Miss Cotton."

If Harmony, Harry and Victor were here, then it could only mean one thing. They'd discovered something unexpected at Mrs. Rigg-Lyon's house. Something that urgently required my attention.

CHAPTER 7

I followed Floyd down the stairs to the entrance foyer where a footman stood guard, determined not to let Harry, Harmony and Victor go any further. Dressed in black overalls, caps and gloves, they clearly weren't guests. Even Harmony wore an outfit more suited to a burglar than a maid. She clutched a small book in one hand; their evening had been fruitful.

"Why do they need to speak to me?" I asked Floyd.

"It's not just you. They need to speak to me, too. Something about my French being better than yours. Come on. Let's find out, then you can go back to the ballroom and dance with Miller." This last part was said loud enough for the trio to hear.

Harry suddenly looked up as we approached. He drew in a sharp breath as his gaze fell on me. "Cleo. You look...well."

"Yes, she does," Floyd said pointedly. "It's all that dancing with a gentleman named Marshall Miller. You don't know him, but he's a fine fellow. All the girls want to dance with him, but he only has eyes for my cousin."

My withering glare was lost on him as he smiled triumphantly at Harry.

Harry's lips thinned and he looked away.

It was left to Harmony to finally answer my question as to why they were there at all. "Victor and Harry found this diary, but we think it's in French." She showed us the small leather-bound book that fit neatly into her palm. "We hoped you could decipher it, Cleo. But when we saw Mr. Bainbridge on the landing, we thought we'd ask him too, since he's fluent."

Floyd accepted the diary from her. "Where did you find it?"

"Uh..." She appealed to Harry then Victor. Neither answered.

Floyd had opened the diary to the first page but quickly closed it again upon seeing the inscription. "This belongs to Mrs. Rigg-Lyon," he hissed. "We shouldn't be looking through it. It's private, not to mention it was probably obtained under dubious circumstances."

Harmony and Victor exchanged worried glances. Harry's expression was unreadable.

I took the diary from Floyd. "Don't pretend you've suddenly acquired some morals. Besides, you owe Harry and me for getting you out of a particularly sticky situation. Would you like me to tell your father what that was, or would you prefer to help us catch a murderer?"

Floyd held my gaze for a moment, then gave in with a sigh. "Don't tell me how you came across it."

"We didn't plan to," Harry told him.

Floyd re-opened the book and flipped through the pages. Together, we inspected the entries. It was an appointment diary with three lines dedicated to each day of the week. Mrs. Rigg-Lyon's handwriting was contained and neat, a no-nonsense style for a no-nonsense woman.

"Why is it in French?" Floyd asked.

"She's French," I said. "You've never spoken to her? She has an accent."

He shook his head as he turned the pages.

"It's mostly names," Harry said. "I suspect they're friends she's meeting socially. It's easy enough to guess the translation of a few other words—café, reunion."

"Meeting, not reunion." Floyd pointed to some words that confirmed Harry's theory. "Lunch, afternoon tea... They must have been redecorating in January and February. These are the words for drapes and carpet." He flipped to last week's page and pointed to Saturday's entry. "Polo is the same in French and English."

"Go back through the last month's entries. There's a John S at least once a week, usually Thursdays, but sometimes on a Monday."

Floyd found the entries. Each time John S was noted down, a time for their meeting was beside it, along with the letters R M before the word Mont. "*Mont* is mount or mountain in French. Perhaps she's referring to a mountain with a name that begins with R and M."

"That's what we thought," Harry said. "But there are no mountains in London."

"It could be a hill on the outskirts." My suggestion was met with shrugs and shakes of the head from the native Londoners.

Floyd continued to flip through the pages, but aside from the mention of John S, the last month was quite empty. Given it was the social season, that was odd.

Floyd handed the diary back to Harry. "Any idea who John S is?"

"Rigg-Lyon believed it was his wife's lover," Harry said.

"How do you know what Rigg-Lyon thought?"

Harry met Floyd's gaze levelly. "I'm not at liberty to divulge that information."

Floyd rolled his eyes. "Suit yourself. So, if Mrs. Rigg-Lyon did have a lover, he must be considered a suspect for her husband's murder. Jealousy is a curse, as they say. Fortunately for me, I've never experienced the emotion firsthand. I'm far too cool-headed to fall in love."

"Cold-hearted, more like," I bit back, only partially teasing.

He didn't seem upset by my judgement. "I'm not convinced she has a lover."

"Why not?"

"If I'm cold-hearted then she's made of ice, so my friends say."

"There is one way to find out for certain."

"How?" Harmony asked.

"We follow her." I pointed to an entry for Wednesday, two

days hence. "She is due to meet John S at R M Mont at 11 AM."

Floyd pulled out his watch by its gold chain. "Come on, Cleo, it's growing late. Your dance partner will want another dance before the evening ends."

We left the others and returned upstairs to the ballroom. With the investigation on my mind, I wasn't quite ready to resume dancing, however. Before we entered the ballroom, I caught Floyd's arm.

"I've been meaning to ask you about automobiles."

That got his attention. Balls and dinners were rather dull affairs for most young gentlemen. They found automobiles far more interesting. "What about them?"

"How many people own one?"

He scoffed. "I don't know everyone, Cleo. There must be hundreds in England."

"I mean how many people have them stabled in London right now? Particularly ones that can travel faster than fifteen to twenty miles per hour."

He folded his arms as he thought. "Most don't bring them to the city. Too difficult to drive in traffic and find stabling for them, so they leave them at their country estates. I can think of only three who brought them to London for the season, one of which was Lord Dunmere. There are a few more who keep them permanently stabled here." He frowned. "I think one of those is currently not working. Do you want me to make inquiries?"

"A list would be a big help. Thank you. And Floyd? Do stop pushing me towards Mr. Miller. I have no interest in him."

He lifted a shoulder in a shrug. "All right by me. I don't really want you to move to America. I've grown used to you. But *you're* breaking the news to Father. Anyway, I only mentioned him to put off Armitage. I didn't like the way he looked at you."

"Leave Harry out of this."

He put up his hands in surrender then offered me his arm to escort me back into the ballroom. "Is Armitage's girl pretty?"

"Miss Morris is a beauty, and very charming and sweet

natured. She's perfect, in fact." It wasn't a lie. She *was* perfect...just not perfect for Harry, something he'd said himself after he ended their relationship.

I wasn't going to tell Floyd that part. Not yet. Not until both he and my uncle had given up trying to turn me into a proper lady who didn't undertake detective work. Until then, Miss Morris would remain a part of our lives, in name only.

Aunt Lilian managed to last another hour before she was ready to leave. It was Uncle Ronald who informed Flossy and me when we came off the dance floor with our partners. The two gentlemen bowed to us before departing, then Flossy went in search of her next partner to inform him she couldn't oblige him with their scheduled dance. My own card was quite free so I followed Uncle Ronald downstairs to the entrance hall where Aunt Lilian sat on a chair. With her eyes closed, she appeared to be asleep, but I suspected she was merely attempting to block out the light from the overhead chandelier.

Mr. Miller emerged from the shadows at the base of the stairs as we reached the bottom step. It was as if he'd been waiting for us.

My uncle didn't seem surprised to see him there. "Ah, Miller. Just the man. Would you mind keeping Cleopatra company while I fetch the ladies' stoles?" The hovering footman was perfectly capable of fetching our stoles from the cloakroom. It was his job, after all.

Mr. Miller smiled at me as Uncle Ronald walked off. "Did you enjoy your evening, Miss Fox?"

We exchanged a few minutes of pleasant if inane chatter before Floyd and Flossy arrived. My uncle took a few minutes more. He handed my velvet stole to Mr. Miller, who placed it around my shoulders. His thumb stroked the bare skin of my shoulder before he withdrew his hand.

It was an intimate gesture; one I would welcome from a gentleman I liked romantically. In Mr. Miller's case, the gesture was not welcome.

A prickle of panic swept down my spine as I realized he could fit in our carriage if we all squeezed together, but Floyd suggested they go on to a private club next for a quiet drink with his friends. Mr. Miller politely agreed and warmly said goodbye to me.

As he escorted me out of the house and down the front steps to the pavement, Floyd bent to whisper in my ear. "You're welcome. By the way, I discovered who currently has their automobile in London, and which ones of those can travel at fifteen or more miles per hour. I'll slip a list under your door when I get home."

"Thank you, Floyd."

He was about to assist me up to the seat of our waiting carriage when Uncle Ronald loudly cleared his throat. When he got our attention, he jerked his head in Mr. Miller's direction.

Floyd dutifully offered my hand to Mr. Miller. He seemed a little embarrassed to have been summoned so crudely, but he smiled through the awkwardness, nevertheless. He assisted me into the carriage, then helped Flossy, while Uncle Ronald offered his hand to Aunt Lilian.

"What an amiable fellow," Uncle Ronald declared once we were seated and the carriage lurched forward. "He's a great admirer of yours, Cleopatra. How many times did you dance together?"

"I lost count," I said.

Uncle Ronald beamed. "What good fortune that he came tonight. I'm glad he asked me."

I frowned. "Asked you what?"

"Whether you were going to attend. He received an invitation but wasn't sure if he would go. Yesterday he asked me if you'd be there with your cousins, and I assured him you would." He took Aunt Lilian's hand in his big paw and patted it. "You made a good impression on him at dinner the other night, Cleopatra. Going by the way he attended to you tonight, I'd say he's smitten. What do you think, Lilian?"

Aunt Lilian pressed her fingers to her temple. "My head is pounding. If you wouldn't mind keeping your voice down."

"Of course, dear, of course." He patted her hand and beamed at me the rest of the way back to the hotel.

* * *

AT BREAKFAST, Harmony and I pored over the list Floyd had slipped under my door during the night. There were only six motor vehicles listed. A manageable number.

Harmony folded the paper and tucked it into her apron pocket. "I'll send the others out to speak to the drivers."

"Have them ask where the vehicle was on Saturday afternoon. I want to know if one of them collected Rosa Rivera from the Royal Albert Hall and drove her to the Elms." I placed a piece of toast on my plate and picked up a knife and the pot of strawberry jam. "You took a risk going with Victor and Harry last night."

"A minor risk and one I was willing to take. I merely kept watch outside the house and would whistle if Mrs. Rigg-Lyon or a servant came home. All was well and I wasn't needed. Still, I felt better for being there."

I understood the sentiment. I worried about Harry being caught, too. If he were discovered, it could be disastrous given his conviction for theft as a child. A judge wouldn't give a light sentence for a second offence, even if they occurred years apart.

Harmony inspected the hard-boiled egg in the cup before scooping the middle out with a spoon. "Sorry for interrupting your evening. I was against it, but Harry insisted."

I paused with the toast halfway to my mouth. "He did?"

"I thought we could work out the diary entries on our own, but he said we required someone who spoke French. I suggested we wait until morning, then return the diary tonight, but he insisted we do it all at once."

"I suppose he wanted to get it over with." I bit into the toast.

"That's not why. He wanted to see you in your ball gown."

I choked on the piece of toast.

"He also wanted to see Mr. Miller," she went on. "It's a pity they didn't get to meet."

"Harry couldn't possibly know Mr. Miller would be there. I didn't until I saw him."

"He knew." She sported a wicked smile as she poured herself more coffee from the pot. "I told him."

"How did *you* know?"

"Lady Bainbridge's maid told me when we walked back to the residence hall together after you'd all left the hotel. She overheard Sir Ronald tell Lady Bainbridge that Mr. Miller had asked him if you'd be attending the ball."

"Are there no secrets in this hotel?"

"There are some benefits to being invisible."

Treating servants as if they weren't there was a mistake many people like my uncle made. It was a benefit in an investigation, but not so much for keeping family matters private.

"Harry is a little jealous of Mr. Miller," she went on, that smile still in place. "Even more so after we left the ball, thanks to Mr. Bainbridge pointing out that the American chose to dance with you above all others."

"Floyd still thinks Harry and I are interested in one another."

"I wonder why," she murmured into her coffee cup.

We went our separate ways after tidying up my suite. Harmony pushed her cart along the corridor while I headed downstairs. The senior staff of Mr. Chapman, Mrs. Short, Mrs. Poole and Peter emerged from Mr. Hobart's office, followed by Mr. Hobart himself. They must have just finished their morning meeting. I greeted them individually and received greetings in return, some of them warmer than others. Mrs. Short's was the curtest of all, but that was simply her nature rather than anything personal.

"You're in a good mood this morning, Miss Fox," Mr. Hobart said, smiling.

"Am I? Yes, I suppose I am."

"The ball must have been enjoyable."

"It was as expected."

Frank opened the front door for Goliath, who was pushing a trolley full of luggage. The doorman scowled at the porter then at us before returning to his post outside.

Peter nodded in Frank's direction. "Don't linger to talk to him or your good mood will be extinguished faster than a candle in a storm."

"Wise words," I said as I waved goodbye.

I couldn't resist giving Frank the cheeriest of greetings but wasn't surprised when I received a grunt in return. His mood was grimmer than usual.

Harry wasn't himself either. He was cool rather than grim, however, when I met him at his office. We exchanged the briefest of pleasantries then he got straight to business.

"Even if we can't locate John S, Mrs. Rigg-Lyon's diary proves that Rosa Rivera wasn't lying. He exists. If he is her lover, he's a suspect."

"We'll know more after following her tomorrow morning," I said.

"There's another polo match tomorrow afternoon at the Elms Club. It'll be worth attending and observing some of our suspects."

"I'll see if Floyd can acquire some vouchers. Speaking of Floyd, he gave me names of automobile owners who currently have their vehicles stabled in London. Harmony will find out if any of their mechanics collected Rosa Rivera from the Royal Albert Hall. What did Cobbit say? Does he think it's possible for a horse and carriage to get from the hall to the club in under thirty minutes?"

"He offered to run a little experiment this morning." He checked his watch. "We'd better go downstairs to meet him."

I stood and waited while he put on his jacket. "Doesn't he have work to do?"

He plucked his hat off the stand. "Either he doesn't or he's on strike already."

The thought left me unsettled. Uncle Ronald would be furious if Cobbit went on strike. Perhaps furious enough to dismiss him. If Frank and other staff joined Cobbit, it would severely impact the smooth running of the hotel.

The coachman was in no mood for talking, however. He greeted us with nods and ordered us into the cabin. Harry gave him final instructions before joining me.

He closed the door and we both checked our watches for the time then tucked them away. Harry peered out of the window as we lurched forward. His profile gave nothing away, but his silence was unlike him.

"Harry, is something the matter?"

He turned to me with a smile. "Not at all."

I didn't believe him. That smile was too benign, and his eyes lacked their usual spark. An investigation always ignited something within him, but this morning he seemed distant, distracted.

"I was just thinking about the case," he went on. "I telephoned Detective Forrester before you arrived this morning. He says the investigating detective has been searching for more witnesses who saw the brown-coated man leaving the Elms. They've found none."

"They couldn't possibly have questioned every cab driver in London."

"True, but they've made it known they're looking for someone. This morning's newspapers have published Scotland Yard's request for anyone who saw a man dressed in a brown coat at the polo to come forward. They've also questioned ground staff at the Elms. Nothing. We have to consider the possibility that Liddicoat is lying to protect his cousin."

Perhaps Harry's gloomy demeanor was because he wanted Mr. Liddicoat to be innocent for Miss Hessing's sake. What I was about to tell him wouldn't improve his mood, but it had to be said.

"I think Mr. Liddicoat did lie. I spoke to him at the ball last night and he claimed he was walking among the trees near the clubhouse at the time of the murder. But from what I remember of the estate's layout, the stables aren't visible from the woods."

"So he couldn't have seen anyone in the vicinity of the murder." He frowned. "You didn't confront him, did you?"

"No. I think that should be left to the police. When you speak to Detective Forrester again, you should mention it. I also spoke to Mr. Broadman and learned something interesting."

"Go on," he prompted when I hesitated.

"He and Mr. Liddicoat are moving into new lodgings together."

"To save costs?"

"I assume so. Did you know Mr. Liddicoat was having financial problems?"

He shook his head. "I couldn't find any significant debts

or signs of money troubles. He's not wealthy, but he comes from a good family, none of whom are in debt either, that I could see. Of course, private arrangements can be made with money lenders."

"Do you think Mr. Liddicoat is in debt to any of them?"

"It's impossible to say."

I watched the shops slip past as we traveled as quickly as the traffic would allow. "Harry...don't put it into your report to Mrs. Hessing."

"I won't speculate on his financial situation, but I will mention he's moving in with his cousin and provide an address. She can draw her own conclusions."

"What if she concludes that he's a fortune hunter?"

"Then so be it. She's paying me and has a right to know. Besides, it's best if she does know. Don't you want to protect Miss Hessing from fortune hunters?"

"Yes, of course, but..." I sighed.

"Just because you don't want him to be a fortune hunter doesn't mean he isn't one." He sat back and rested his elbow on the windowsill. "Marriage is as much a financial arrangement as a personal one and should be treated with the same precaution taken when going into business with a new partner."

"I didn't know you held such a cynical view."

"I haven't given it much thought until recently." He folded his arms over his chest. "Not from the view of wealthy people, like the Hessings. When you have nothing, then entering into marriage with someone else who has nothing isn't problematic. But a wealthy woman should go into it knowing everything about the gentleman."

"Very wise. Fortunately, my family are aware of the dangers. Any gentleman who shows an interest will find himself interrogated more thoroughly than any suspect in a murder inquiry." I laughed.

Harry did not. "I thought you had no plans to marry. Has that changed?"

"I was referring to Flossy."

His gaze shifted to the view out of the window. "Does Miller know you have no plans to marry?"

"I've not encouraged him, so the issue is irrelevant."

"Is it?" he said dully.

Once we left the traffic behind, the two horses picked up speed. They couldn't maintain it the entire distance to the club, however. Both Harry and I checked our watches again as we pulled to a stop at the gates.

"Too slow," I said. "Rosa couldn't have arrived here in time to murder Rigg-Lyon, even if she departed the moment the dressmaker left her dressing room."

Cobbit confirmed it. "The horses are spent. I want to rest them awhile."

"Take your time," Harry said.

There were no journalists present today and the gates were unlocked. A few grounds staff tended to the garden, and some players practiced on the field. Two little boys played with toy sailboats at the edge of the lake while their mothers or nannies watched on, wide hat brims angled towards the sun. The glassy surface of the water was broken by a pair of ducks gliding effortlessly across the center but was otherwise still. The butterflies and bees dancing from flower to flower were a little more energetic, but their nectar-gathering efforts only enhanced the peaceful scene. It was hard to imagine a murder had taken place here mere days before.

We headed first for the copse of beech trees to the side of the clubhouse where Mr. Liddicoat claimed to have been walking after the post-match presentation, right up until he heard Mr. Broadman's shout. We walked through it, but there wasn't a single spot where we could see the stables.

We asked a gardener tending to the rose bushes growing near the clubhouse if he'd been here on Saturday. He had, and we asked if he'd seen a man wearing a brown coat.

"No. I didn't see anyone wearing a coat, brown or otherwise, but I wasn't really looking at the people. My attention was on the roses." He cut off a pink one and handed it to me. "This suits your outfit, Miss, if you don't mind me saying."

"I don't mind at all. Thank you." I smelled the rose and tucked the stem into my brooch pin.

He indicated another gardener sitting atop a steam-powered lawn mower. "The police have already asked us about the brown coat man. No one saw him, but that doesn't mean he wasn't here. There's a lot of people around on match day."

We thanked him and were about to return to Cobbit and the waiting carriage when Major Leavey's assistant, Watkins, hailed us from the front steps of the clubhouse.

He trotted down the stairs to meet us. "I thought I saw you both. I wanted to tell you something that might help your investigation. It's about Vernon Rigg-Lyon. I saw him arguing with one of the grooms a few weeks ago. I only just remembered it late yesterday when I saw the same groom. I rarely go into the stables, but I was looking for the major."

"Do you know which groom?" Harry asked.

"I think his name was Bert."

"Do you know what they were arguing about?"

"Rigg-Lyon was threatening Bert. He said he'd tell the major Bert's secret if he didn't do as he was told."

"Do you know what Rigg-Lyon wanted him to do?"

Watkins shook his head.

"What about the secret? Do you have any idea what that could be?"

"No, sorry. I don't know the grooms at all."

We thanked him and headed to the stables. Robbie and Bert were standing out the front, tending to a horse that had just been brought in. It was still saddled, the rider already several feet away as he strode past us, mallet in hand.

Robbie saw us first. "You two again. Got more questions, have you?"

"Our questions are for Bert," Harry told him.

Bert's face blanched. His grip tightened on the reins.

"A few weeks ago, you argued with Vernon Rigg-Lyon."

Bert shook his head, but I didn't need to be a psychic to know he was lying. Guilt was written all over his face.

"A witness told us he threatened you," Harry went on. "He was going to tell the major your secret if you didn't do as he asked. What was that about?"

"Nothing!" Bert cried. "I didn't kill him!"

"We're not accusing you of killing him, we're just trying to understand the victim. Come now, Bert. A witness heard you being threatened by Rigg-Lyon. Tell us what it was about so we can—"

"No!" Bert jumped into the saddle with athletic grace and urged the horse with a swift kick. The startled animal leapt forward, nostrils flared.

It headed straight for me.

CHAPTER 8

*H*arry grabbed my arm and yanked with such force that I slammed into him. We both toppled to the ground, my fall cushioned by him. We lay there, face to face, breathing heavily, but not from exertion. Being so close to a man, feeling his muscular contours beneath me, was a new experience. One made all the more intoxicating because I desired him.

Our gazes connected for a brief, hot moment. It was all the time I needed to see that he desired me, too.

Robbie cleared his throat, a polite reminder that we weren't alone.

Nothing dampens desire more than embarrassment. The realization that I'd almost been trampled by a horse probably had something to do with it, too.

Robbie assisted me to my feet. "You all right, miss?"

"Fine, thank you. Harry?"

Harry stood and glared daggers in the direction Bert had ridden. "When I catch him…"

I brushed off the back of his jacket. "We'll have words."

He seemed too angry to think clearly, so it was left to me to question Robbie. "Do you know why he fled?"

Robbie picked up Harry's hat from where it had fallen and dusted it off. "No. Took me by surprise. He's a nice bloke, quiet, never causes trouble."

"Did you know Mr. Rigg-Lyon threatened him?"

"No."

"Do you know what he wanted Bert to do for him? Or the secret he threatened to expose?"

He shook his head and handed the hat to Harry. "Are you going to report this incident to the major?"

"Do you think we should?" I asked.

"The major'll dismiss him on the spot." He scratched his head again. "Bert's a hard worker. He's good with horses, but not with people. I don't think he meant to hurt you, miss. He just didn't want to answer your questions."

"That's no excuse," Harry snarled.

Robbie edged away, then scuttled sideways into the stables, keeping a wary eye on Harry until he was inside.

"We won't report Bert," I said. "If the major dismisses him, we'll lose access to one of our suspects."

"Our prime suspect," Harry said, striding off.

I picked up my skirts and hurried after him. "We need to keep a level head about this, Harry. Just because he fled, doesn't mean he's guilty of murder. Although I do think he has something to hide."

He stopped and rounded on me. "You could have been killed, Cleo!"

"Yes, but probably not on purpose. I think Bert simply couldn't control the horse. It seemed frightened when he jumped into the saddle. I happened to be standing in their path, that's all."

He sucked in a deep breath and released it slowly. Some of his anger seemed to release along with it. "I'm still going to throttle him when I see him."

"I know you mean that figuratively."

"Do I?" He went to walk off, but I caught his hand.

"Thank you, Harry. You saved my life." I stood on my toes and kissed his cheek.

When I released his hand, he crossed his arms high over his chest and looked everywhere except at me. "Yes. Well. Try not to make a habit of almost dying."

* * *

COBBIT DROVE TO THE MEWS, not the front of the hotel. My uncle stood in the middle of the cobbled lane, hands on hips. For one panicky moment I thought he was there to scold me, but his glare wasn't directed at me.

"Where have you been?" he shouted at Cobbit as we pulled to a stop.

"Miss Fox had errands to run," Cobbit shouted back. "Sir."

I sighed. It seemed I was going to be caught in their dispute after all. I turned to Harry. "It's probably best if you stay in here until he leaves." I opened the door and climbed out. "Good morning, Uncle. Cobbit drove me to the Elms Polo Club and back. He had no other duties this morning—"

"He did! He was supposed to drive me to a meeting." His gaze moved past me to Harry as he alighted from the carriage.

I should have known hiding wasn't Harry's style.

My uncle lowered his arms to his sides and grunted, as if he expected Harry to be involved in Cobbit's disobedience.

"Cobbit?" I said. "You told us you had nothing else to do this morning."

He shrugged. "It wasn't on my running sheet. If it ain't on the sheet, it ain't scheduled."

"I told you yesterday," Uncle Ronald growled. "You always put these things on the sheet yourself."

Cobbit merely shrugged again, but his grip on the reins was tight. The coachman wasn't the sort to play games. He was usually candid to the point of bluntness, rather like my uncle. With their ideologies so far apart, their characters would make it difficult to build a bridge between them.

Yet I had to try. "He can take you now," I said to Uncle Ronald.

"It's too late. I caught a cab there and back."

One of the grooms emerged from the stables and Cobbit climbed down from his perch. "We'd better settle the horses before that vile machine gets back and upsets them," he said, his gaze firmly on my uncle.

"That's another thing," Uncle Ronald said. "Lord Dunmere claims you argued with his mechanic."

Cobbit's jaw firmed. "His contraption was in the way, and he refused to move it."

"I gave him my permission to stable it here. You know that."

"I never agreed."

"You don't have to agree, Cobbit! You have to do as you're ordered!" He pointed a finger at the coachman. "Make room for the automobile and leave the mechanic alone."

"This ain't fair, *sir*. I know my rights."

"Do you also know I can dismiss you? And him?" He jabbed his finger in the direction of the groom.

The poor lad paled.

"And you…" He pointed at Harry. "Why are you here? You've been forbidden from stepping foot on my premises."

Harry put up his hands in surrender. "We were merely investigating the murder."

Uncle Ronald's gaze narrowed. "You've been advising Cobbit, haven't you? You saw your chance to get revenge on me and have been stoking the flames."

"I have not," Harry said, evenly.

"I know your type, Armitage."

"Stop it!" I snapped. "Harry has done no such thing. In fact, he deserves your gratitude for what he did today, not these baseless accusations."

"Cleo," Harry said sternly. "There's no need to tell him how I made a breakthrough in the case."

I blew out an exasperated breath, but he was right to stop me. If my uncle knew the danger I'd been in, he would forbid me from continuing with the investigation.

Fortunately for us, Uncle Ronald turned his attention back to Cobbit. "I don't want any more complaints from Lord Dunmere, is that clear?"

"Crystal. Sir."

Uncle Ronald glared at him a moment longer then stormed off down the lane. He stopped halfway and turned around. "Cleopatra! Are you coming?"

It was not a good time to refuse. "See you tomorrow morning," I whispered to Harry before hurrying after my uncle.

We didn't speak a word on the short walk to the hotel.

Frank opened the door for us but signaled with a jerk of his head that he wanted me to linger. I waited for the door to close behind my uncle before I asked Frank what he wanted to talk about.

"Is Sir Ronald upset with you?"

"He's angry with Cobbit. Apparently, he refused to let Lord Dunmere's mechanic stable his vehicle with the coach, then he was driving Harry and me to the Elms when he should have taken my uncle to his meeting."

"A strike without going on strike. Gets the point across but he still gets paid. Good move, Cobbit, good move." He eyed the door, as if considering how he could do the same.

"I support fair wages and conditions, Frank, but I'd be careful playing games with my uncle, particularly over a point like this. He has to accommodate guests' needs or risk the hotel falling behind the times."

If he jutted his chin any further, he'd topple forward. "I'll do as my conscience dictates, Miss Fox."

I left him with his conscience and entered the hotel. Peter had been conversing with guests but made his excuses and approached me. "Harmony was just here. She wants to see you in the staff parlor before you go shopping with Miss Bainbridge."

"That's today? Drat. Have you seen Floyd?"

"He left an hour ago."

"Is Mr. Hobart here?"

"In his office."

"I need a quick word with him. If Harmony can meet me in a few minutes, I'll go to the parlor after I talk to him."

He went to find Harmony while I headed to Mr. Hobart's office.

One end of the entrance foyer used to lead to the offices for the senior staff, as well as their private accommodation and sitting room. When the new restaurant was installed on the ground floor of the neighboring building, the wall had been knocked through to create an entrance so that hotel guests didn't have to walk outside. The renovation resulted in the loss of some of the offices. To recreate an office for each senior staff member, their private quarters were converted. Since Peter and Mr. Hobart both lived off site, the change only affected the housekeeper, Mrs. Short, and steward, Mr. Chapman. They had been temporarily housed in the residence hall along with most of the other staff, but I wasn't sure if they still lived there.

Mr. Hobart's kindly face creased with his welcoming smile. "Miss Fox, what a pleasure. I hear you and Harry have been investigating together this morning."

"News travels fast."

"Goliath informed me a few minutes ago. It's his day off today, so when I saw him here, I became curious. Apparently, Miss Cotton has him working for you."

"Just a little sleuthing task. Speaking of which, Harry and I need to go to the polo tomorrow."

"You can't get in without vouchers." He pulled the telephone closer. "Is it just the two?"

"Flossy will probably be upset if she's not included. And since Harry and I need to poke around, she'll need a companion or she'll be on her own. I'll ask Miss Hessing to join us."

"Four vouchers." He rested his hand on the receiver before lifting it off the hook. "I'll make it five. Mrs. Hessing doesn't let her daughter out of her sight, lately."

"You can get them without Floyd's help on such short notice?"

He gave me a look to say I ought to know better.

I left him to perform the miracle of acquiring five vouchers to the Elms Polo Club for the following afternoon's event, and headed for the staff parlor. Harmony, Victor and Goliath were already there. Harmony wore her maid's uniform, but Victor and Goliath were dressed in ordinary clothes.

"This won't take long," she said as she glanced at the clock. "Which is fortunate, because you have to change before you meet Miss Bainbridge."

I looked down at my day dress of steel-blue cotton offset with a V-shaped panel on the bodice to show the white blouse beneath. "There's nothing wrong with this outfit."

"It's too plain."

"For shopping?"

"For going out with Miss Bainbridge. You don't want to

look dowdy next to her. I've laid out the gold dress with the turquoise embroidery on the collar and hem, and matching hat."

"Turquoise?" Goliath asked.

"A fancy word for green," Victor clarified.

Harmony rolled her eyes. "It's between blue and green, like the shallows of a pristine sandy bay in the tropics."

We all stared at her.

"So I'm told," she added. "Victor, give Miss Fox your report."

He straightened, but still managed to look like he didn't care what anyone thought of him. "Harmony gave me the addresses of three motor vehicle owners currently in London. I questioned the drivers this morning. One of the vehicles needs repairs and hasn't been working for a week. The other two went nowhere near the Elms on Saturday."

Harmony indicated Goliath should give his report next.

He puffed out his chest. "I also checked on three vehicles. Their mechanics confirmed they didn't collect anyone from the Royal Albert Hall on Saturday and didn't go anywhere near the polo club, either."

"Thank you," I said. "So Rosa Rivera does have an alibi for the time of the murder. She was with her dressmaker until three thirty-five and couldn't have reached the polo club before four-ten, the latest time when the murder could have occurred."

"Unless there's an automobile we don't know about," Victor pointed out.

"Yes. There is that."

He checked the clock then rose. "I have to change for my shift."

We parted company outside the staff parlor. They headed towards the service corridor while I went in the opposite direction to take the stairs up to the fourth floor. As I passed the lift, John opened the door and Mr. Miller stepped out.

"Miss Fox! What luck. Do you have a moment?"

I attempted a friendly-but-not-too-friendly expression but it felt stiff, unnatural. "A very brief one. I have to meet my cousin."

His face fell. "I was going to ask you to have lunch with me."

"Perhaps another time. Excuse me, I really must dash or I'll be late." I picked up my skirts and raced up the stairs before he could stop me.

* * *

AFTER SHOPPING, Flossy and I had afternoon tea with friends at the hotel, then the entire family attended a dinner party, so I didn't have time to think about the investigation. My energy lagged in the late evening, but not as much as Aunt Lilian's. She looked worn out by the time we returned to the hotel at around midnight. She leaned heavily on Uncle Ronald, her eyes mere slits as he steered her towards the lift.

I slept well and felt refreshed the following morning. Mr. Hobart had procured vouchers for the polo, so I slipped invitations under the doors of Flossy and the Hessings, with another to notify my aunt of our plans for the afternoon. I took Harry's voucher with me and handed it to him, along with his coffee, when I arrived at his office.

He pocketed it and indicated I should leave ahead of him. "Did Sir Ronald say anything to you after you left the mews with him yesterday?" he asked as he locked the door.

"Not a word."

"I'm worried about Cobbit. Even if he realizes he can't win, he's too stubborn and proud to back down. He'll fight a losing cause all the way to the end."

I lifted my skirts clear of my feet and headed down the stairs. "It is a losing cause, I fear. Floyd and his friends talk about automobiles the way Flossy and her friends talk about jewelry. They all desperately want one. The hotel's stables and coach house will have to accommodate them permanently, soon. Lord Dunmere is merely the first guest to bring his, but there will be others, I'm sure of it."

Harry agreed, but his only solution to solving the standoff between my uncle and Cobbit was for Cobbit to capitulate, and we both knew he'd never do that.

We took a cab to Marylebone and waited in it for Mrs. Rigg-Lyon to make an appearance. We weren't sure if she would walk to meet John S at their appointed time, or if she'd need to drive, so we decided to keep the cab for the time being. We'd arrived thirty minutes before the time noted in her diary for the meeting in case she required that long to get there. But fifteen minutes later, I was concerned we hadn't arrived early enough and she'd already departed.

I was about to suggest that I knock on the door and ask if Mrs. Rigg-Lyon was home, when a carriage pulled up. She exited the house, dressed in mourning black, her face as stark as the moon beneath her hat.

We directed our driver to follow her conveyance. Ten minutes later, I pointed out the street sign to Harry as we turned a corner. Marchmont Street.

"M Mont," he said with a wry smile. "It's short for Marchmont—a street, not a mountain or hill. But she wrote R M Mont in her diary. Why the R?"

"*Rue.* It's French for street. Marchmont Street is *Rue de Marchmont* in French."

The buildings were a mix of row houses and shops, located in a good area away from the busier parts of the city. Mrs. Rigg-Lyon's carriage pulled to a stop, but Harry asked our driver to continue and park a few doors down.

We watched through the rear window of the cabin as she alighted and climbed the front steps. She didn't knock but went straight in. She must be very familiar with the occupant if she didn't need to be invited.

We followed, not sure how we would proceed. Knock and ask for John S, or make inquiries at the service entrance?

Neither approach was required in the end. A brass plaque beside the front door answered one of our questions: Dr. Johns, Physician.

"She's not having a relationship with a man named John S," I said. "She's seeing Dr. Johns because she's ill."

"Or with child," Harry suggested.

"I'd wager she's ill. She looks sickly."

We agreed that questioning the doctor would get us nowhere, but we disagreed on whether it was worth asking Mrs. Rigg-Lyon about her ailment. I didn't think she'd tell us anything, but Harry thought she might if he informed her that her husband thought she'd been having an affair. We were discussing whether the regular visits to the doctor were relevant to the murder at all when Mrs. Rigg-Lyon emerged, tucking an envelope into her bag.

She stopped at the top of the steps when she spotted us. "Did you follow me here?"

"Mrs. Rigg-Lyon, may we have a word?" I asked.

"Why did you follow me? What does my medical appointment have to do with my husband's death?"

"That's what we're trying to find out." Now that we'd been caught, we might as well see if we could gather any useful information. I had an inkling how the visits could be linked to the murder, but I didn't want to reveal it to her.

She advanced down the steps towards us. "This is an outrageous breach of my privacy."

"We apologize for following you," I went on. "But we're trying to solve a murder, and sometimes that requires us to use unorthodox methods."

"I understand that, Miss Fox. But you're wasting your time with me. I did not kill my husband. Why would I? I'm dying."

What does one say to that? "I'm sorry," I muttered, although it felt woefully inadequate. Her admission took me by surprise, although the dire prognosis didn't. She looked so thin and drawn, a walking skeleton dressed in the color of death.

Harry offered to assist her into the carriage. "Thank you for your honesty. We're very sorry to have troubled you."

She took his hand, but the effort required to get up the step to the hansom's seat was still too much. He almost had to lift her and when she eased onto the seat, her breathing was heavy and uneven. Once she was settled, Harry closed the panel that protected her skirts from dirt flicked up by the horses.

"I know you think I was jealous and angry over my husband's affairs, and you're right. I was. But when I learned that the cancer was going to kill me, everything changed. I *wanted* him to find happiness with another."

Harry moved away from the hansom as it drove off, then we returned to our waiting cab. "Do you believe her?" he asked.

"I believe that she's dying. But I don't believe she wanted Vernon to be happy with another woman after she's gone, particularly with the woman he was already keeping as his mistress. Besides, her dying makes it easier for her to murder him. If she's caught and sentenced to hang, it matters little to her since she's going to die anyway. By telling us her prognosis, I don't think she's exonerated herself. I think she gave us a better motive."

* * *

We parted ways at Harry's office and agreed to meet inside the grounds of the polo club. I returned to the hotel to change into an outfit suitable for a high-society picnic then met Flossy in her suite before heading downstairs.

"Why do we have to go with Mrs. Hessing?" she whined as we waited for the lift. "I like Clare, but her mother is awful."

The lift door opened and John the operator greeted us.

"She'll find some friends to chat to," I said as we descended. "We can do as we please. Oh, and Flossy. Will you keep Miss Hessing busy when I'm not there?"

She frowned. "Where will you be?"

"Investigating."

She didn't have a chance to protest because the lift stopped on the ground floor, and the Hessings were waiting for us when John opened the door.

Miss Hessing took our hands and squeezed. Her face glowed, making her look very well indeed. "I'm so pleased we're going together. It'll be such fun." She held us back and let her mother walk ahead across the foyer. "Mr. Liddicoat will be there. I'm going to try to get away to meet him. If I do, will you make sure my mother is occupied so she doesn't worry?"

"Of course," I said, squeezing back. "Flossy and I will both be on mother-minding duty. Won't we, Flossy?"

My cousin looked like she wanted to throttle me. I wasn't surprised. If I was investigating, and Miss Hessing was having a rendezvous with Mr. Liddicoat, Flossy would be left alone with Mrs. Hessing.

* * *

BEING A WEDNESDAY, the crowd wasn't as large as the one that gathered for the previous Saturday's cup final. Even so, I couldn't immediately find Harry. I did, however, run into Floyd, who had seen my sleuthing partner a few minutes earlier, so he told me through lips pursed so tightly they hardly moved.

"You got him a voucher, didn't you?"

"Mr. Hobart did, if you must know."

"Using your name, no doubt."

"He probably used yours, since the Bainbridge name holds more weight than the Fox one." I tried to step around him, but he blocked my path. "Don't make a scene, Floyd."

"He shouldn't be here, Cleo. Guest vouchers should be reserved for guests of members."

"Your snobbery is unbecoming and not worthy of you. Harry has helped you. You should be grateful."

"I am. And I'm not a snob."

I barked a laugh.

"I'm not! It's the rules. If the club manager found out someone obtained a voucher through dubious means, he'd issue less of them next time. If he found out you were behind it, then he might banish me, or Flossy. She'd be humiliated."

I wouldn't put it past Major Leavey to banish me, but more to stop me uncovering a secret than because I broke the rules. A secret that explained why he'd removed Rosa Rivera's ribbon from the victim's body.

The players from the Elms team walked past us, leading their horses. Mr. Broadman saw me and slowed his pace. He looked like he was about to say something, but his teammate urged him forward and Mr. Broadman continued on.

The gathered crowd cheered, the loudest applause of all coming from Mr. Liddicoat as he watched his cousin with pride. I searched for Miss Hessing and saw her watching her paramour from where she sat on the picnic blanket beside Flossy. Her mother was in deep conversation with a friend who'd joined them, and didn't applaud at all. She gave no indication that she'd seen the polo players, or even intended to watch the match.

Floyd followed my gaze. "Why didn't you invite Mother to chaperone you, instead of Horrid Hessing?"

"Mrs. Hessing is here because I thought Miss Hessing would make a good companion for Flossy while I'm investigating. Besides, Aunt Lilian looked dreadful last night. She should rest today so she's feeling refreshed for dinner."

We both knew no amount of rest would refresh her, however. Despite being fatigued, sleep was difficult to find. She was restless after the effects of her tonic wore off, and increasingly anxious. It was difficult to know if the anxiety was a result of her lack of sleep or a symptom of the melancholy the doctor was supposed to be treating her for. Either way, the tonic he'd prescribed had become less and less effective.

Anxiety. Restlessness. Fatigue. Listed together like that, her symptoms sounded very familiar to another list I'd heard at this very club. When cataloged alongside her other symptoms, like loss of appetite and an increasingly short fuse, a hollow feeling in the pit of my stomach opened up.

All were experienced when the effects of her tonic wore off. Alone, they made me curious, but not suspicious. But when added to the symptoms she experienced *immediately after* she took the tonic—energetic, alert and hungry—the similarities between the two cases were too many to ignore.

Aunt Lilian wasn't the only one affected by whatever ingredients were in the tonic.

Vernon Rigg-Lyon's horse was, too.

CHAPTER 9

J went to walk off but stopped when I realized I had no idea where I was going. "Where did you see Harry?" I asked Floyd.

"Skulking near the tack room."

"Harry isn't the sort to skulk."

I headed to the tack room near the stables, angling my parasol so that my face couldn't be seen by anyone passing by. I found Harry around the side. Or, rather, he found me. He stepped out from the shadows and signaled for me to join him.

"Harry, I've thought of something." I peered around the corner to the stables. "On the day of the murder, Mr. Rigg-Lyon's horse, Panther, was in one of the stalls. He was restless, unsettled, and we put it down to sensing his master's death. Then the following day, when you and I returned here and questioned Bert and Robbie, Robbie mentioned Panther was a very fast horse, but afterward, he lost his appetite, was tired, twitchy. He showed signs of aggression, too, kicking Bert and not letting the grooms near."

"Are you suggesting those aren't merely Panther's character traits?"

"They could be. But they're also symptoms I witness every day in Aunt Lilian."

He rubbed a hand over his jaw as he took that in.

"When she takes her tonic, she's very energetic immediately afterward. She can't be still or quiet, and she has an enormous appetite. But once it starts to wear off, she becomes tired very quickly. She gets headaches, her muscles twitch, and she loses her appetite altogether. She hardly eats a thing."

"That explains why she's so thin."

"She is also anxious and easily annoyed lately. The other day, Floyd came up behind us and she jumped when he greeted us, even though he wasn't loud. Her scolding was excessive."

"Are you saying Panther has been fed the same tonic as Lady Bainbridge?"

"In a larger dose, but yes. Someone has given him the tonic right before the match to make him faster. That someone is most likely his owner, Vernon Rigg-Lyon, but he might have had help from one of the grooms. Bert was assigned to Panther that day."

"And he ran off when we asked about their argument." Harry gazed at the stables. "What if their argument was about administering the tonic? Rigg-Lyon needed Bert to give Panther the tonic before the matches, but Bert refused. He only capitulated when Rigg-Lyon threatened to reveal his secret to the major."

"Bert does care about the horses. Robbie says so."

"The question is, was Bert upset enough over his involvement in doping Panther that he killed Rigg-Lyon? Or did someone else kill him after finding out Rigg-Lyon was cheating at polo?"

I wished we could prove Panther was being doped, but he wasn't here today. None of the horses from the Polo and Gun Club were. Their teams weren't in the day's competition. "Why bother, though?" I asked. "Floyd says there are no wagers placed on the outcome of polo matches."

Harry scoffed. "Even if they're so-called gentlemanly arrangements, I'd bet my fee that gambling exists. Not only that, but there's also a lot of pride involved. Winning is everything to some."

For men like Broadman and Rigg-Lyon, whose identities were so closely linked with their athleticism, losing would be soul-crushing. Perhaps enough that they'd kill if they learned they'd lost because the opposition cheated.

We couldn't see the polo field from where we stood, but my gaze wandered in that direction anyway. "Perhaps that's what Rufus Broadman and Vernon Rigg-Lyon argued about on the day of the murder. Perhaps Broadman found out about the doping and confronted Rigg-Lyon."

"Do you know what's in your aunt's tonic?"

"The label doesn't say."

"It sounds like cocaine. The stimulating effects, the withdrawal symptoms..." Harry leaned a shoulder against the wall. "I've seen addicts before. Something should be done to limit its sale."

Cocaine could be found in a number of tonics, lozenges, and gargles available from pharmacies to cure everything from toothache to lethargy. Although Aunt Lilian was the first person I'd met who was addicted, I'd read about its dangers before, in journals and even in fiction where characters used it. Harry was right. Now that the negative effects of addiction were better understood, the sale of cocaine should be controlled.

Any controls would come too late for Aunt Lilian. We had to wean her off the tonic somehow. It wouldn't be easy, given she didn't want to stop. She'd been prescribed the tonic for melancholia, a disease that had afflicted her for years, apparently. She believed herself to be dull without it. She'd once told me that my mother was known for her wit and intelligence, and she felt inferior to her in their youth. It saddened me to hear it. Aunt Lilian had so many wonderful qualities, yet she couldn't see them. Until she realized how wonderful she was, she would not give up the cocaine tonic.

This was the first I'd heard about it being administered to horses, however. "I can see how doping a thoroughbred with cocaine would help it win races. It's not against the rules?"

"It's not illegal—yet—but it is unethical. It's not just cocaine. Racehorses are doped with caffeine, too. The substances are often mixed together, and the concoction is injected into the horse before a race. It seems polo isn't immune to doping. So much for it being a gentleman's sport.

If horses are being doped, then wagers must be made on the outcome of matches, after all."

"Poor Panther."

Harry's jaw hardened. "He was Rigg-Lyon's horse, and yet he was actively doping him. Rigg-Lyon blackmailed Bert into injecting Panther before the match, but Bert didn't want to."

"It seems so. It was Robbie who mentioned Panther's symptoms, not Bert, and it was Robbie who said Bert was assigned to Panther. Bert kept that detail to himself. He was afraid he'd be a suspect if we knew."

"So Rigg-Lyon threatened to expose Bert's secret if he didn't administer the cocaine to Panther, something that went against his horse-loving nature. If Bert was angry about that, he might have killed Rigg-Lyon in retaliation."

"Or he killed Rigg-Lyon because Rigg-Lyon revealed that he knew Bert's secret. A secret Bert apparently couldn't risk getting out."

Harry indicated the stables. "He's here today."

"He'll run off again the moment he sees us."

"We'll avoid him. I want to look around the stables, see if I can find any clues, but I'll have to wait for the grooms to leave."

That would be some time away, and I had to leave with the others at the end of the match. Mrs. Hessing would never allow me to stay behind. "You'll have to do it alone. But there is something we can do now. Look, Robbie is leaving the stables. We should speak to him again."

Harry pushed off from the wall and strode towards the groom. I picked up my skirt with one hand, and clutched my parasol in the other, and followed. Robbie was heading to the outbuildings, his head down so he didn't see us until we were directly in front of him.

"You two again! Does the major know you're here?"

"Panther was being doped with cocaine," Harry began.

"Bloody hell." Robbie frowned. "Are you sure?"

"Rigg-Lyon forced Bert to inject the horse."

Robbie shook his head vigorously. "Bert wouldn't. He loves horses." He removed his cap and scratched his head. "Are you sure Panther had cocaine in his system? I've heard of racehorses being injected, but polo? Seems a bit excessive."

"You described Panther's symptoms to us yourself," I said. "They all point to signs of an addiction to a stimulant like cocaine."

"And you reckon Bert injected him?"

"Not willingly," Harry said. "Can you recall any times Bert seemed distressed after being in Panther's stall?"

Robbie shrugged. "I don't know…" His gaze slipped past us. "I've got to get back to work." Instead of continuing on his way to the clubhouse, he turned and hurried back to the stables.

"You two!" came a shout from behind us. "What are you doing here?"

I glanced over my shoulder to see Major Leavey striding towards us, pointing a stick in our direction. With bushy brows and stern features, all that was missing to complete the military cliché was the uniform.

"You can still escape," I told Harry. "I'll stop him going after you."

"I'm not leaving you to face him alone. Besides, what can he do to me? Forbid me from obtaining another guest voucher? I'm hardly going to be sad about being barred from match days."

"He could throw you out now." Going by the way the major's eyebrows had drawn together to form one thick line, he was angry enough to do it.

Harry merely smiled. "Good afternoon, Major. A pleasant day for the polo."

The major tucked his stick under his arm, conforming even more to the stereotype. I pressed my lips together to stop my smile. "I see that smirk, Miss Fox. And you, Armitage. Don't move."

Harry put his hands in the air. "As you wish."

"Don't play games with me. How did you get in?"

"I gave my guest voucher at the gate, like everyone else."

"How did you obtain one in the first place? Well?" When we didn't answer, he shook his finger at us. "I've asked around about you two. I know Miss Fox is related to the Bain-bridges, and that's how she obtained her voucher, but you,

Armitage…you're merely an employee of the Mayfair Hotel. You shouldn't be here."

"Former employee," Harry countered.

He seemed quite unconcerned to be the object of Major Leavey's ire. Perhaps, like me, he suddenly found the major a little ridiculous with his military pomposity and the wiggling of his eyebrows as if they were attached to puppet strings. I couldn't see how anyone under his command would take him seriously.

The major set his feet apart and jutted his chin at me. "Do Sir Ronald and Lady Bainbridge know you sneak about with their former staff?"

"They do," I said coolly. "And we were simply taking a walk, not sneaking."

The major grunted. "Kindly return to your chaperone, Miss Fox. And you, Armitage, get going."

"Where to?" I asked.

"The gate. He's leaving."

"But he had a guest voucher!"

He looked up at Harry. "Don't make a scene or I'll have you thrown out."

Harry put up his hands again. "It's all right, Cleo. I've realized the polo doesn't interest me, after all."

He walked off. The major looked torn between following him and making sure he left, or following me and making sure I didn't do any more sleuthing. I took advantage of his hesitation.

"Why did you remove the ribbon from Vernon Rigg-Lyon's pocket? And why did you lie about it?"

Harry wouldn't have liked me asking questions now. If the major was the murderer, it might place me in danger if he felt threatened by my knowledge. But I couldn't help it. Sometimes when I was angry, emotions spilled out of me and I said things I later regretted. And I was *furious*. The way he spoke to Harry was rude and condescending. At least Floyd was polite to Harry's face.

I didn't regret letting my emotions rule me this time. I was glad I accused the major of stealing the ribbon. For one thing, some of my anger was released when I voiced my question, and for another, it got a result. Instead of trying to deny it as an innocent man would, the major flushed scarlet and stormed off.

* * *

HARRY and I hadn't made an arrangement to meet, but I assumed we would. I stood in the hotel foyer as I considered whether to telephone him first or just show up with coffee at his office when Mr. Miller greeted me. I shouldn't have stalled in such a visible space without checking my surroundings first. He'd been standing near one of the large vases of flowers with his uncle and mine. He broke away from them when he saw me, much to the delight of the two uncles who exchanged knowing smiles.

"Miss Fox, I'm so glad to see you this morning." Mr. Miller reached inside his jacket and removed a small leather-bound book from his pocket. "I've been carrying this with me since yesterday. I saw it in a bookshop and thought of you." He handed it to me with an air of expectation.

I read the title. "*Poems and Essays* by Walt Whitman. A dead man made you think of me? How flattering."

He chuckled. "He's my favorite writer, and I thought you might like to read some of his work. Or have you read him already?"

"I haven't. This is very kind, but I can't accept it."

"Of course you can." He lowered his voice. "It'll give me an excuse to write to you. I leave in a few days, but naturally I'll want to know what you thought about my favorite writer, so I'll send a letter when I reach home soil. You'll respond, all very formally, of course. Then I'll write again and before you know it, we'll be regular correspondents." He said it with such effortless charm it didn't feel unduly forward. Coming from another man, it would have been oily.

There was a commotion at the front door as a guest stormed inside and demanded to see the manager. Mr. Hobart appeared from goodness knows where to see why he was required, and Uncle Ronald joined them.

I was too distracted to give Mr. Miller his gift back before he bowed politely and walked off with his uncle.

I sighed and tucked the book into my bag. I was about to

head outside, past the guest venting his frustration in hushed tones to Mr. Hobart and Uncle Ronald, when I spotted Miss Hessing emerging from the lift, alone. She smiled when she saw me.

"Good morning, Miss Fox. What a lovely day."

"Is it? I haven't been outside yet. You look cheerful in that shade of yellow, Miss Hessing. And, may I say, that hat is fetching. Is it new?"

"I bought it just the other day to go with this outfit. I'm so pleased you like it. I'm trying out some new designs. There's a dressmaker we found in Bond Street who understands my tastes so well."

It gladdened me to see her shed her dowdy outfits for something pretty and modern. With her mother's style tending to the garish end of the scale, Miss Hessing often compensated by going to the other extreme. She hid herself in ill-fitting dresses in plain colors. Where her mother wanted to be noticed, Miss Hessing wanted to blend in. She blended in so well that she almost disappeared, if one didn't look hard. It was wonderful to see her come out of her shell. I was quite sure Mr. Liddicoat's attentions were to thank for that.

If he were to suddenly disappear from her life, she'd be devastated. And yet if he was after her for her fortune, she needed to know.

Miss Hessing glanced around then leaned closer to me. "My mother has gone out, so I'm going to meet Mr. Liddicoat now. Would you like to walk with us?"

The question may have been asked out of politeness, but I wasn't going to say no to the opportunity. "Thank you, that will be a very pleasant way to spend ten minutes or so."

Her smile didn't waver, proving she hadn't simply asked out of politeness, after all.

We slipped through the front door just as Uncle Ronald ordered Goliath to go to the mews to see why Cobbit was late collecting the guest and his luggage. I nodded a greeting to Mr. Hobart, but he was too busy reassuring the guest that he would reach the station on time to make his train.

We joined Mr. Liddicoat, waiting some feet away. He greeted us both amiably while reserving most of the warmth for Miss Hessing. Perhaps my constant questions about his cousin cooled his opinion of me. If that were the case, I was about to turn down the temperature even more.

I waited for the pleasantries to be over, and we reached the edge of Green Park. "I saw you at the Elms Polo Club yesterday, Mr. Liddicoat, cheering on your cousin. You're a great admirer of his."

His eyes brightened at the mention of Mr. Broadman. "Rufus has a lot of admirable qualities."

"Is that why you're moving in together? Because you like one another's company?"

He blinked at me. "We're moving in together because it makes sense for us to share the cost of lodgings." His gaze shifted to Miss Hessing then back to me. They sported twin frowns as they regarded me. "Clare knows our plans, and why. As do you, I see."

"Mr. Broadman told me."

"It's not a secret."

Miss Hessing looped her arm through his. "It is where my mother is concerned. She doesn't know, so please don't tell her, Miss Fox. She'll jump to the wrong conclusion."

"Mrs. Hessing is a resourceful and clever woman. She might find out."

"We'll cross that bridge when we come to it."

"Wouldn't it be best just to tell her yourself?"

Mr. Liddicoat raised his brows at Miss Hessing. Clearly they'd had this discussion, with her urging him not to say anything to her mother.

"She'll think I'm a fortune hunter if I keep it a secret," he said, as if picking up a conversation they'd just left off.

"She'll think that anyway if she finds out," Miss Hessing countered. "Perhaps she won't find out." She sighed, not believing her own words.

Mr. Liddicoat was right. It would be better coming from them rather than hearing it from Harry. And Harry *would* tell Mrs. Hessing. He felt obliged to.

I caught Miss Hessing's arm, stopping them both. "Tell her. It's for the best. Tell her today. Don't delay it a moment longer."

She drew in a deep breath and let it out slowly. "All right. If you think we should."

"I do." I released her and we continued on, ambling along the path with no particular destination in mind. An awkward silence descended, and I knew they wanted to be alone. But I had one more issue to broach first. "While I was at the polo club, I went for a walk in the woods. You know the one, Mr. Liddicoat. It's where you said you were the other day when Mr. Rigg-Lyon died."

"I recall. It's a nice spot, good for a walk to clear the mind. My peace and quiet was shattered when my cousin shouted, though."

"You could certainly hear a shout coming from the stables from there. But you couldn't have seen anyone in the vicinity of the stables."

Mr. Liddicoat abruptly stopped. He spluttered a nervous laugh. "Of course you can. You must have been in the wrong area."

"I wasn't. You said the trees near the clubhouse, and there is only one wooded area there. Mr. Liddicoat, why did you lie about seeing a man in a brown coat and hat leave the stables?"

He laughed again, only to cut himself off with a scoffing sound.

Miss Hessing tightened her grip on his arm. "This is silly. He wouldn't lie, Miss Fox. You must have made a mistake. You must have thought he meant a different wooded area."

I tilted my head to the side. "Mr. Liddicoat?"

He closed his eyes and expelled a long breath. "All right. I didn't see a man dressed in a brown coat and hat near the stables that day."

Miss Hessing removed her arm from his and stared at him.

"I did see someone dressed like that, just not there," he quickly added. "He was also in the woods. He didn't see me, I'm quite sure. He had his head down, with his collar up and hat pulled low. Why would he dress for a cold, windy day when it was sunny and warm, unless he's trying to hide his appearance?"

"Why did you lie?" I asked.

"To protect my cousin. The man in the brown coat *must* be the killer. I simply said he was in the vicinity of the stables so the police would look for him. I wanted them to take the sighting seriously."

"By lying."

"Rufus isn't the murderer. That man in the brown coat is."

Miss Hessing took his arm again. "He's right, Miss Fox. The man in the brown coat sounds suspicious."

"Please, you must believe me," he went on, his voice rising. "Rufus is innocent."

Miss Hessing bit her lip. "My mother will forbid us from seeing one another if Mr. Broadman is found guilty of murder." She rubbed her paramour's arm and gave him a worried smile. "We want to be together. We're in love. But if Mr. Broadman is found guilty...well, you know what she's like."

Mr. Liddicoat stepped towards me, his eyes flashing. He wasn't a large man, but he was intimidating in that moment. Desperation can change a person. "Find my cousin innocent, Miss Fox. Please. Prove he's not a killer. I beg you."

I nodded. What else could I do in the company of my friend?

But I wouldn't strike Mr. Broadman off our list based on a plea. I needed evidence, and Mr. Liddicoat's lie hadn't helped his cousin's cause. He was still very much a suspect until proven otherwise.

Miss Hessing didn't want to be out of the hotel too long in case her mother returned, so we parted ways with Mr. Liddicoat and walked back together.

All was calm at the front door. The guest must have been collected, whether by Cobbit or a cab. I didn't dare ask Frank. I didn't want to open a can of worms and be forced to listen to his litany of complaints.

I said goodbye to Miss Hessing and continued along Piccadilly. As I passed one of my favorite teashops near the Circus, I looked through the window. I stopped when I spotted Harry seated with a woman, a pot of tea between them. I couldn't see her face. It was obscured by an enormous hat covered with orange dahlias. She wore colorfully jeweled rings over her gloved fingers and a walking stick had been hooked to the table's edge. I didn't need to see her face to know it was Mrs. Hessing.

It would seem my warning to Miss Hessing had come too late—Harry had decided to report Mr. Liddicoat's tight financial situation to his client, after all.

I hurried back to the hotel to warn her. It was the least I could do since it was my fault Harry had found out.

CHAPTER 10

After warning Miss Hessing, I passed the teashop a second time. Harry and Mrs. Hessing were no longer inside. I continued to his office where I found him seated at the desk, writing a letter.

He looked up as I placed my parasol into the umbrella stand. "You didn't bring coffee."

"I didn't think you'd want it since you just had tea."

He slotted his pen back into the holder and flipped the lid of the ink pot closed. "Good detective work."

"I saw you through the window, then I returned to the hotel to warn Miss Hessing. She's going to tell her mother about Mr. Liddicoat's change of address the moment she enters their suite, before she has a chance to get a word out. It's the only way to salvage the situation. If it is salvageable."

"Don't look at me like that, Cleo. I'm not the villain. I didn't tell her about Liddicoat's financial situation."

I sat heavily on the chair. "You didn't?"

"No. But I do think Miss Hessing ought to tell her." He showed me the letter he was writing. It was addressed to Miss Hessing and suggested she inform her mother about Mr. Liddicoat's change of address and the reason for it. It wasn't finished.

"Were you going to breach your client's confidentiality and tell Miss Hessing her mother hired you?"

"No. I was going to leave it vaguely worded. If she

worked it out based on this, then so be it."

I smiled warmly. "That's kind of you, Harry. Your letter won't be needed now. And don't worry, Miss Hessing still doesn't know her mother hired you. I simply warned her she was about to learn the truth without saying how. If you weren't telling Mrs. Hessing about Mr. Liddicoat, what were you two discussing?"

He screwed up the letter and tossed it into the waste basket. "That's confidential."

I narrowed my gaze. "What have you learned?"

He stood and buttoned up his jacket. "I thought we'd call on the Rigg-Lyon household and speak to the servants. It's the only way to find out if Mrs. Rigg-Lyon came home immediately after the presentation of the winner's cup on Saturday."

I swiveled in the chair as he passed me. "Stop avoiding the question."

"I'm not avoiding it. I gave you my answer." He picked up my parasol and held it out to me. I stood and accepted it, but he did not let go. "I don't want to argue with you, Cleo."

There was a simple way he could assure there was no argument—he could answer my question. But since he was as stubborn as me, I knew he wouldn't. I'd simply have to employ my detective skills to find out on my own.

It suddenly occurred to me. There was something else he'd learned in the last few days about Mr. Liddicoat. "Did you tell her he lied to the police about seeing the brown-coated man?"

"No! If the lie leads to us proving Broadman committed the murder, *then* I'll inform her. But only then."

"Good, because I asked him about it this morning and he admitted he lied."

Harry had been about to open the door but stopped. "You confronted him?"

"He claims he *did* see a man wearing a brown coat and hat, but he wasn't in the vicinity of the stables. He was in amongst the trees, too."

"Nowhere near the stables." He opened the door and followed me out. "He could have lied about that, too. Perhaps the brown-coated man is completely made up."

It was entirely possible. His lie had been convincing. We'd all fallen for it, and we could no longer believe anything Mr. Liddicoat said.

* * *

LOYAL SERVANTS ARE a problem for detectives. They can't be bought or charmed. Mrs. Rigg-Lyon's housekeeper proved to be one such employee, refusing to be drawn into answering our questions when we spoke to her. The young maid who'd greeted us at the staff entrance seemed terrified of disobeying the housekeeper's instruction to speak to no one about the death of Mr. Rigg-Lyon and had immediately fetched her superior.

With a squaring of her shoulders, the doughty housekeeper indicated the open door and the steps beyond leading up to the pavement. "If you don't mind, I have work to do."

"As do we." I spoke tartly out of sheer frustration. Our investigation was in danger of stalling if we didn't find a way to push forward. "Don't you want to find out who murdered Mr. Rigg-Lyon?"

"Of course. But any questions you have about Mrs. Rigg-Lyon's movements can be answered by Mrs. Rigg-Lyon. I suggest you ask her directly instead of coming down here and engaging in gossip."

"Your refusal to answer makes your mistress look guilty."

She went very still.

It was a small sign that I might be able to convince her to talk. It was enough to encourage me to press on. "We know she's dying. She informed us herself."

The housekeeper swallowed heavily.

"Who will defend her when she's gone? If she's innocent—"

"She is!"

"The killer might seize upon her death and use it to his or her advantage. They might point the finger at her. With Mrs. Rigg-Lyon gone, who's to stop the police from recording her as the murderer? The killer will walk free, and her memory will be tarnished."

The housekeeper's eyes filled with tears. "The police won't believe such a blatantly false accusation."

Harry shook his head sadly. "I know the detective assigned to this investigation. He's lazy. He'll look for the easy route, and what could be easier than blaming a dead woman with no connections in this country? No one to defend her honor?"

The housekeeper pressed a hand to her chest. "All right. You've made your point. She returned home at around four o'clock. I don't know if that exonerates her or not, but I can assure you, she's not a murderess."

It exonerated her, if it was the truth. For Mrs. Rigg-Lyon to be back at home in Marylebone by four, she had to have left the polo club before the murder occurred.

"Now stop bothering her. She's got enough on her plate, and she didn't do it. They had their problems, like all married couples, but I never heard a harsh word exchanged between them. You should be looking at those who argued with him, like *that woman*." She all but spat the words.

"Rosa Rivera?" I asked.

"She was here a few days before he died. She must have waited for Mrs. Rigg-Lyon to leave, because she arrived a few minutes later. Mr. Rigg-Lyon was furious and told her to stay away for the time being, that they'd have more freedom soon. I suspect he was talking about after his wife's death."

It seemed so, but Rosa Rivera claimed Rigg-Lyon thought the appointments with John S were liaisons with her lover. Either Rosa lied to us about him knowing or he'd lied to her.

"What did Miss Rivera say to that?" Harry asked.

"She never got a chance to ask; not while I was there, anyway. He saw me, so I had to move away to where I couldn't hear them." For someone who refused to answer us moments ago, the housekeeper was very free with her words now. It was as if she'd removed a stopper to release one answer but couldn't put it back and now more poured out. "I peeked through the gap in the door and watched. That woman was angry at first, but he calmed her down and they made up." She pulled a face. "Obscene, it was, all that kissing."

"Did Miss Rivera often show up in Mrs. Rigg-Lyon's absence?" I asked.

"No. Never."

"So why did she come that day?"

The housekeeper shrugged.

Harry and I thanked her and climbed the stairs to return to street level. We were both lost in our own thoughts, neither speaking until we reached the main road where he hailed a cab. I directed the driver to the bank where Mr. Hardwick worked. We'd planned to call on him after speaking to the Rigg-Lyon servants, and I saw no reason to change our plan. While Rosa Rivera's arrival at the house was interesting, it was irrelevant. She had an alibi for the time of the murder.

Harry's thoughts did not follow mine, however. "She could have hired someone," he said when I voiced my opinion on her innocence. "Or she might have another lover prepared to murder at her bidding."

"You think a lover would kill a rival for her? That's rather extreme."

"Some men will do anything for love."

It didn't ring true to me, however. Rosa didn't appear to have other lovers, and her only recent disagreement with Rigg-Lyon was over her showing up at his house. They were otherwise content with their arrangement.

"I can spare a few minutes between meetings," Mr. Hardwick said when we finally got to see him. "How can I help this time?"

His cheery manner felt odd coming less than a week after the death of his close friend. His sorrow had been evident the last time we called on him, but there was no sign of it now.

Before we asked about doping horses, there was something I wanted to check. "How well do you know Rosa Rivera?"

"Didn't we already discuss her? Are you accusing me of something?"

"Was she seeing another man at the same time as Mr. Rigg-Lyon?"

"Why would I know a thing like that?"

"You were very good friends with Mr. Rigg-Lyon. Did you never talk about her with him?"

"No." He scoffed.

"But she was flirtatious."

"Aren't all those girls?"

Everything within me recoiled. I wanted to rebuke him for painting every woman in the entertainment industry with the same brush, but I needed him to talk. I stayed silent in the hope he'd fill the void. Harry remained still, too.

Mr. Hardwick fell into the trap. "I don't think Rosa had other lovers, but it's true that she was a flirt. That's why Broadman believed he was in with a chance. She teased him, led him like a puppy on a leash, and made him fall in love with her." He sniffed. "But when it came to it, she rejected him."

"I didn't think you and Mr. Broadman were close," I said. "How do you know this?"

He picked up a letter he'd been writing when we came in and pretended to read it. "Common knowledge."

"Hardly."

He lowered the letter. "And how would either of you know what's common knowledge amongst gentlemen of a certain caliber?"

My coiled insides tightened further.

Harry was as collected as always, however. "You once told us Rigg-Lyon kept other lovers and that Rosa would have known about them. Can you tell us their names?" An excellent question, and one we should have asked last time.

"There was no one he was serious about. Rosa was his favorite, but she knew where she stood in the scheme of things. I'm sure he explained that to the other women who benefited from his attention."

A woman holding a piece of paper hovered in the doorway. She signaled to the door behind Mr. Hardwick, which led to the deputy governor's office.

"One moment," Harry told her before Mr. Hardwick could respond. He gave her a smile and she smiled back, dipped her head, then disappeared from sight. Harry turned to Mr. Hardwick. "Panther was being doped with cocaine."

Mr. Hardwick's jaw dropped. He stared at Harry. "No! That's an outrageous lie! Who's spreading that despicable rumor?"

"So you didn't know?"

The square jaw suddenly hardened. "How could I, when it's not true?" He stabbed a finger into the desk. "Is it Broadman? Is that who concocted such a ridiculous story?" *Stab, stab, stab.* "It was him, wasn't it? He can't face the fact we beat him. He's a poor loser." *Stab, stab, stab.* "Panther is naturally quick. They come from good stock."

"They?"

"My horse, Leopard, is Panther's brother. They were bred at my father's stables. Their sire was a champion polo pony. There's no need to dope animals with that pedigree. They're born superior. By claiming Panther was being doped, you're tarnishing my family's reputation as breeders of quality. It's not on." He signaled to the woman at the door who'd returned and seemed anxious to come in. "If there's nothing else, I have work to do."

We waited until we were outside to discuss Hardwick's claims. "He seemed adamant that Panther wasn't doped," I said.

"He can deny it all he wants, but if the evidence states otherwise…" He hailed a cab and we waited for it to pull over. "We need to speak to Bert and get to the bottom of it."

"What did you think about his claim that Rosa's flirting led Broadman on, like a puppy on a leash?"

"Hardwick seemed angry towards her about it. A little too much, if you ask me, considering it's Broadman he doesn't like. Why not place the blame on him?"

"Because he was referring to himself, not Broadman. Everything he accused Broadman of doing with Rosa actually happened to him."

Harry agreed with my theory. "But that doesn't help build a case against him. If anything, it exonerates him. His anger was directed at Rosa, not Rigg-Lyon. He didn't seem jealous of his friend, just annoyed that his mistress rejected him. He has no motive for the murder."

"Perhaps. But we need to remember that he has no alibi for the time of the murder. He claims he was in the privy but admits no one saw him leave because the foyer was empty. The major's assistant said he wasn't manning his desk in the foyer at the time because he was in the restaurant helping tidy up, so that detail of Hardwick's is feasible, at least."

The hansom stopped and Harry assisted me up the step then settled beside me on the seat. "Where to now?"

"I have to return to the hotel. I've got yet another luncheon to attend."

He opened the panel in the roof and gave the driver instructions before closing it again. "Who are you having lunch with?" It was an innocent question, but the hint of intrigue with which he voiced it made it sound like my answer mattered.

I turned to face him squarely. "Friends of my aunt's. Why?"

"No reason."

I stared at him. He pretended not to notice. "Harry, why are you being so mysterious today? First you won't tell me what information you passed on to Mrs. Hessing this morning, and now you want to know who I'm having lunch with. What's going on?"

"Nothing."

I arched my brows.

"Nothing, Cleo."

I settled my skirts around me and didn't speak to him the rest of the way. It wasn't until we reached the hotel that he realized he didn't have enough money to pay the driver.

"I'll pay," I said, opening my bag. I removed the book of poems by Walt Whitman and fished out my purse. I paid the driver through the roof slot and went to climb out.

Harry blocked the way. He indicated the book. "I didn't know you read Whitman."

"I don't. At least, I haven't yet. It looks like I have no excuse not to, now."

His gaze narrowed. "Where did you get the book?"

"Mr. Miller, the American guest, gave it to me." I made a shooing motion. "Even if you're continuing on, you have to move so I can get out."

He stepped down to the pavement and offered me his hand. Once I was alongside him, he told the driver he had no further need of him. The driver urged the horse forward and the hansom rolled away.

All the while, Harry continued to hold my hand. And we were right outside the hotel.

I squeezed his fingers. "Is something the matter?"

As if he suddenly realized he still clutched my hand, he let go. "Cleo…I need to tell you something. I didn't pass on information to Mrs. Hessing this morning; I wanted information *from* her."

"What kind of information?" I asked carefully. There couldn't be many reasons why he'd be so hesitant to mention that he'd gone to Mrs. Hessing for help, not the other way around. Indeed, I could think of only one.

"I asked her what she knew about Miller."

"I see. Why mention it to me now and not earlier?"

"Because I wasn't sure what his intentions were towards you. Now I know." He indicated my bag, containing the book. "He gave you a gift. Not just any gift, but something you would appreciate."

"I appreciate jewelry, too." My joke fell flat. The spiked tone saw to that, as well as Harry's obvious discomfort. "What do his intentions have to do with you telling me this now? What precisely did you learn from Mrs. Hessing?"

"He abandoned his betrothed at the altar on their wedding day. Rumor has it that he found out her father lost his fortune mere days earlier in the economic depression of '93."

"I don't believe all the gossip I hear, Harry, you know that. Anyway, that was seven years ago. He would have been young."

"Mrs. Hessing also told me he has no money. He works for his uncle, but he won't inherit anything. His uncle has young sons who'll one day take over the company."

"Oh dear, he has gainful employment. What a dreadful fellow."

My sarcasm fell on deaf ears. "Apparently Marshall Miller's wages are not enough to support his lifestyle. He's in deep debt." Harry dipped his head to meet my gaze. "It gives me no joy to tell you this. I want you to be happy, Cleo. But with someone who deserves you, not someone who wants you for your connections."

The fact that I wasn't an heiress was moot. The first night

I'd met Mr. Miller, I had suspected he assumed I was as wealthy as my Bainbridge cousins. No doubt he thought I'd inherited my grandparents' fortune through my mother, not knowing she'd been disinherited. I'd not said anything to disabuse him of the opinion. I should have. I could have saved myself this uncomfortable discussion.

Even so, Harry had overstepped. He'd gone to Mrs. Hessing not knowing if Mr. Miller had done anything wrong. He'd extended his fishing net out to sea without knowing if there were fish swimming there. I wasn't sure if I was angry with him or not. What he'd done he'd done because he cared about me, and if I were being perfectly honest, it made me feel warm all over. But he shouldn't have done it in secret.

"Say something, Cleo. If you want to tell me that I shouldn't have asked Mrs. Hessing then go ahead. Get it off your chest." At least he understood that he'd overstepped. That was something.

"Doesn't Mr. Miller deserve the chance to explain?"

He blinked in surprise. "Of course. That's why I'm presenting you with the information, so you can do what you want with it." He cleared his throat. "So…what are you going to do with it?"

"Nothing."

"Will you return the book?"

"I have to go."

He expelled a measured breath. "Right. It's none of my business. But Cleo—"

"I'll see you in the morning." I turned away, aware of the terseness of my response. It would seem I was upset with him, after all.

I went to walk off, but he caught my hand.

"Cleo. I am sorry for the subterfuge. I didn't ask your permission to investigate him, because I thought you'd forbid me."

I withdrew my hand from his. "You're right. I would have." I headed towards Frank, standing ready to open the door, my skirts whipping around my ankles with my brisk strides.

* * *

I GAVE the book to Terence at the post desk to pass on to Mr. Miller when he collected his mail. After exchanging pleasantries for a few minutes, I returned to my suite to change into something pretty for luncheon. I was pinning my hat in place in front of the dressing table mirror when there was a knock on my door. It was Harmony.

"Just the person I need to see," I said, pulling her inside. "I have so much to tell you."

"It'll have to wait. Sir Ronald wants to see you."

"Now? I have to meet Flossy and Aunt Lilian."

"I wouldn't keep him waiting if I were you. He seemed angry."

"Why?"

"I'm just the messenger."

Perhaps he'd learned that I'd rejected Mr. Miller and was upset that his matchmaking efforts had come to nothing. But that seemed unlikely. I'd only just returned the book, and I didn't think my rejecting him would make Uncle Ronald angry, just a little deflated.

What would anger him was me telling Mr. Miller at the ball that I was a detective. Uncle Ronald had made it clear that I could continue investigating as long as it didn't interfere with my social engagements or tarnish the Bainbridge name. It had just slipped out at the time, because I'd felt comfortable with Mr. Miller and didn't think it mattered. Yet it clearly had mattered to him. He couldn't understand how important it was to me to continue. If he'd mentioned it to my uncle in the meantime, Uncle Ronald would be furious that someone outside the family knew.

I steeled myself and prepared my responses.

"Why did he send you?" I asked Harmony as she escorted me to my uncle's office further along the corridor.

"I asked him if there was anything I could do for him. He said there was and he sent me here to fetch you." She sighed.

I clasped her arm. "Keep trying. I'm sure a task more worthy of your skills will crop up soon."

She knocked on Uncle Ronald's office door, then opened it and announced me before leaving me to face the music alone.

Uncle Ronald wore his emotions on his sleeve, so it was obvious that he was indeed angry, although from the tone he used to invite me to sit, I suspected the anger wasn't directed at me.

"Is something the matter?" I asked.

He leaned back in the chair and rested his clasped hands on the mound of his stomach. "I've just had a very difficult discussion with Miller and his nephew, and now I'm afraid I need to have a difficult discussion with you."

I held my breath. "Oh."

His thumbs dueled with each other over his clasped fingers. "I'm furious with them. Livid, in fact."

"With *them*?"

"I'm sorry, Cleopatra. This ought to come from your aunt, but she's unwell and I didn't want to trouble her." He leaned forward and moved his clasped hands to the desk. He fixed me with a sympathetic gaze, which was somewhat unsettling, since Uncle Ronald rarely felt sympathy for anyone. "It came to my attention that the nephew is no gentleman. He broke off an engagement with a young lady when her father's fortune disappeared." He shook his head. "Apparently, Miller is quite poor and is reliant on his uncle's goodwill. Now, I was prepared to give him the benefit of the doubt. Perhaps he wasn't in love with the girl, and that's why he abandoned her. However, it crossed my mind that if he was a fortune hunter, he might only want to marry you because he assumed you were an heiress. Naturally, as your guardian and protector, I wanted to test him to find out for certain if he does love you and would accept you as you are." He cleared his throat. "So I told Miller your situation and gave my blessing to your union."

"You had no right to do that without discussing it with me first." It was probably not the moment to point it out, but it needed to be said. "And who informed you of Mr. Miller's situation?"

He barreled on as if I'd not spoken. "I'm sorry, Cleopatra, but he bowed out. Not only that, he had the gall to claim that you'd made your feelings clear and weren't interested in him." He suddenly threw his hands in the air. "The nerve of him, after everyone who saw the two of you together could see how much you enjoyed his company. You danced at least three dances with him at the ball. You smile whenever he's near, and the look on your face this morning when he handed you that book…he'd become dear to you, I could tell."

He was even less adept at reading signs than I thought him to be. But it wasn't his misunderstanding that interested me. There was something more pressing at stake.

"It's kind of you to worry on my behalf, but it's not necessary. I had no feelings for Mr. Miller." I watched him carefully so that *I* didn't misread any signs. "Uncle, who told you about Mr. Miller's broken engagement and financial situation?"

"That's confidential."

That was a convenient response. It was also a familiar one, that I'd heard a few times just that morning.

He cleared his throat and reached for a folder that had Cobbit's name on it. It must be his employee file. "This automobile business needs to be addressed with the coaching staff. You have a good grasp of the situation, Cleopatra. Do you have any suggestions?"

I rose, stiffly. My entire body ached with tension. "I have a luncheon engagement."

"Of course, of course." He offered me a sympathetic smile. "Enjoy yourself. Talk to Florence about…" He waved his hand in the air. "I'm sure she'll offer a sympathetic ear."

"Yes," I said flatly.

"I know you feel as though you'll never recover, but I assure you, someone better suited will come along and you'll forget all about Miller. You're a wonderful girl. It's a shame he couldn't see that."

I thought about telling him again that I felt nothing for Mr. Miller, but he probably wouldn't believe me. I was indeed feeling both sad and angry over a betrayal, but not the one he assumed. Harry must have come straight in to see Uncle Ronald after he'd informed me, while I was at the post desk.

It was one thing to investigate Mr. Miller without my knowledge, but it was quite another to speak to my uncle. He had no right to intervene, and no right to assume I couldn't handle the situation in my own way and in my own time.

I would tell him as much when I saw him again.

CHAPTER 11

Luncheon would have been more pleasant if Aunt Lilian had been up to it, and I'd been in a more cheerful mood. But she was suffering from a headache, and I remained cross with Harry.

I hoped a vigorous walk with Flossy on Rotten Row in Hyde Park would help release some of my frustration, but unfortunately the walk was a slow one. We stopped frequently to talk to friends who'd gone with the same aim as my cousin—to be seen. Some of the men certainly saw her. With her pretty looks and curvaceous figure, she was openly admired by several gentlemen, many of whom I recognized from the balls we'd attended over the previous weeks. She showed no particular interest in any of them, however.

The sudden arrival of Floyd put an end to their interest. It wasn't anything he said or did, it was simply the fact he was there. None of them were interested enough in Flossy to go through her older brother first.

Floyd didn't seem to notice. In fact, aside from a cursory lift of his chin, he barely acknowledged his sister at all. He wanted to talk to me.

"I've been asking around about Rosa," he said.

"Who's Rosa?" Flossy asked.

He hushed her. "Keep your voice down. This doesn't concern you. It's information about one of Cleo's suspects."

Flossy stormed off ahead, twirling her parasol so fast it was in danger of creating its own weather pattern.

"What did you learn?" I asked Floyd.

"It's very unlikely she had other lovers. Despite being an outrageous flirt, she was faithful to Rigg-Lyon."

"It's hypocritical that a mistress is admired for being faithful to her *married* lover."

"That's a debate I'm not having with you today."

"Because you know you can't win."

He dismissed the issue with a flick of his wrist. "Rigg-Lyon was also a flirt, but he tended to follow through, if you understand my meaning." He winked, just in case I was unsure.

"You mean he was unfaithful to both his wife and mistress?"

"Precisely."

"He gets worse and worse," I muttered.

Floyd shrugged. "In for a penny, in for a pound." He cleared his throat when he noticed my glare. "Anyway, the point is, Rigg-Lyon was a lock-up-your-sister type. I didn't know him well before, but my inquiries have revealed that he made a play for almost anything in a dress aged under twenty-five."

"Even girls of good families?"

He nodded.

Mr. Hardwick claimed his friend only took performers as mistresses, not genteel ladies. Perhaps he'd lied about other things, too, such as knowing the reason for Rigg-Lyon and Broadman's argument before the match.

"Does Broadman have a sister who may have fallen victim to Rigg-Lyon's, er, charms?" I asked.

"Not that I know of. I still think the rumor that Broadman attempted to steal Rosa from Rigg-Lyon is the reason for their argument that day. More than one person claimed Broadman tried to poach her at a party one evening."

That didn't mean they hadn't got their information from the same source who was trying to spread that rumor —Hardwick.

Floyd suddenly frowned at his sister, several steps ahead, and quickened his pace. "The devil."

A gentleman walked alongside Flossy, his fingers lightly skimming her elbow. He smiled at something she said, and she giggled behind her hand in response.

I hurried after Floyd and reached them in time to see the glare he fired in the gentleman's direction. He gave Floyd a condescending bow and a smirk to go with it, before ambling away.

Flossy turned on her brother. "That was rude of you. Why did you glare at him like that?"

"He's a cad, Floss. Stay away from him."

"We were just having a conversation," she said hotly. "I had to talk to somebody."

"Flossy is capable of deciding for herself if a gentleman is a cad or not." My defense was just as terse as Flossy's, earning me curious looks from both of my cousins. "She doesn't need you to make those sorts of decisions for her, Floyd."

"And how is she to make a decision when she doesn't have all the information?" He turned back to his sister. "If it were still legal for a gentleman to challenge another to a duel for trying to seduce his wife, then that fellow would be dead five times over. You may not be someone's wife, Flossy, but you're my sister. I don't want you falling in love with a lecherous, amoral turd."

Flossy looped her arm through her brother's. "Thank you, Floyd. But I don't think I would have fallen for him. His eyes are too close together."

They walked on arm in arm with me alongside them. They chatted for a while about some gentleman or other, but I wasn't listening. I couldn't stop thinking about Harry. He'd intervened in my life just as Floyd had done for Flossy. The difference being, Floyd hadn't gone behind his sister's back to find information, nor had he gone to Uncle Ronald.

But Floyd would have told Uncle Ronald if Flossy had expressed an interest in the cad.

Perhaps I should have done what Flossy did and made sure Harry knew I had no feelings for Mr. Miller. Perhaps he would have acted differently.

The thought cooled my temper a little, but it didn't disappear altogether.

* * *

THE HOST for the evening's party was a prominent cricketer who played for the national team as well as the Middlesex Cricket Club. With the only international matches for the year being played at the Olympic Games, he and many of his teammates were in London for an upcoming county game. Naturally, the players of one gentlemen's sport knew several members of the other great gentlemen's sport, and there were several polo players from the two London clubs in attendance.

Considering their fierce rivalry and the mystery surrounding the death of Mr. Rigg-Lyon, the air crackled with tension. The arrival of Mr. Broadman caused a series of whispers to ripple through the gathering. Heads turned. Players from the Polo and Gun Club stiffened, while those from Mr. Broadman's Elms team closed protectively around him. It made for a welcome distraction from my thoughts, something which the conversations about ducks, Ashes, maidens, and silly points failed to do.

Although the host and hostess hadn't called their event a ball, it had all the hallmarks of one, with dancing, music and refreshments. For once, there were more gentlemen than ladies, so Flossy and I were never short of partners. She enjoyed the attention immensely, but after several dances in a row, I wished I could disappear into the wallpaper and simply observe.

The only gentleman I wanted to dance with was Mr. Broadman, so I could get his measure a little more, but he danced only twice, both times with the prettiest girl in the room. Instead, I made do with his cousin.

Mr. Liddicoat hadn't asked a single girl to dance all evening. If Miss Hessing had been here, he probably would have danced several times with her already, but Mrs. and Miss Hessing hadn't been invited. Not moving in the cricketing circles probably meant they'd never met our host and hostess, whereas both Uncle Ronald and Floyd were keen on the sport.

"It's good of you to ask me," I said politely as Mr. Liddicoat led me to the middle of the floor.

"You don't appear in need of rescuing, Miss Fox." He settled his hand on my waist as the music began. "Indeed, I've wanted to dance with you since I arrived, but had to wait until now."

"You're in the habit of rescuing young ladies without partners." It wasn't a question. I'd had several opportunities to observe him over the past few weeks, and I'd noticed he only asked the friendless girls, the ones who were ignored, at best, or outwardly ridiculed by other men at worst. Early in our acquaintance, Miss Hessing had been the victim of some cruel taunts, and often found herself on her own while all the other girls danced. That was until Mr. Liddicoat came along. Ever since their meeting, she'd enjoyed not only his company at parties, but that of other men who thought she might be worthy of a closer look.

"You've asked around about me," he said.

I remained silent.

"It's true that I tend to choose my partners from among the wallflowers, but there's no reason for that except self-preservation. I'm not like my cousin, Miss Fox." He nodded at Mr. Broadman, surrounded by his chums and a cluster of girls hanging on his every word. "Most ladies don't throw their dance cards at me as I pass. I'm not handsome, athletic, rich or interesting. I don't like to see a girl wrinkle her nose when I ask her to dance, so yes, I choose my partners from those who welcome my attention. It so happens that I found a lady with many fine qualities that way. A lady whose company I enjoy above all others, and one who likes me in return. To be honest, I cannot believe my good fortune. You're Clare's friend. I don't think I need to list all the wonderful things about her. You already know them."

It was a fine speech, and I found myself feeling somewhat better about him courting Miss Hessing.

"Her fortune makes her vulnerable," I said.

"No, Miss Fox. Her low self-esteem does. Her wealth makes her desirable, if that's what a man is looking for in a wife."

"Many are."

"True enough. But not me. I don't think there's anything more I can say to convince you otherwise."

"You don't have to convince me, Mr. Liddicoat. It's Mrs. Hessing who needs the reassurance."

"I'm not so sure about that. Mrs. Hessing may control the purse strings, but it's not Clare's purse I want. If her mother cuts her off, then so be it. We'll manage. It's *you* I need to reassure that my intentions are honorable. It's you who have influence over Clare. If you tell her I'm not worthy, then she'll listen."

It was a rather stunning thing to hear, and unnerving, too. A weight of responsibility descended upon me. So much so that we finished the dance in silence, and once the music ended, I avoided dancing for a long time by claiming my feet were sore.

Refreshments couldn't come soon enough. Flossy and I made a beeline for the tea table and were soon joined by two gentlemen we'd danced with earlier. We fell into a conversation about the best cricketers of the last decade. Or, rather, they discussed their favorites while Flossy pretended to listen and I nodded from time to time.

My gaze wandered, however, seeking out my suspects. I was just in time to see Mr. Hardwick take a swig from a silver flask when he thought no one was looking. It wasn't the first time he'd sipped from it. Earlier in the evening, he'd been more discreet, leaving the room to partake. But as the night wore on, he'd become more and more careless.

I thought him unaffected by the flask's contents until a player from the Elms Polo Club team bumped into him. The bump was light, but Mr. Hardwick stumbled into the woman next to him, causing her food to slide off her plate.

Mr. Hardwick recovered his balance, but instead of seeing if the lady was all right, he rounded on the fellow who'd bumped him. "Watch where you're going!"

The man apologized to the lady and offered to refill her plate. She graciously accepted and handed it to him as the staff cleared away the mess.

Mr. Hardwick wasn't satisfied with that. "No wonder the Elms lost." He snorted. "You have as much coordination as a giraffe on skates. And your horse is as slow as an elephant."

The other man pulled himself up to his full height and

puffed out his chest. "You can slander me, sir, but my mount is off-limits. He's a king among horses."

"Oh ho!" Mr. Hardwick rocked back on his heels. "So you can slander *my* horse, and that of my teammates, but I cannot point out an obvious truth about yours?"

Mr. Broadman and his Elms Club teammates gathered around their besieged friend. "No one is slandering your horse, Hardwick. If only your playing was as imaginative as your mind."

The Elms Club team chuckled at their captain's joke.

Mr. Hardwick stabbed a finger in Mr. Broadman's direction. "You, sir, are a slanderer and a liar, and quite possibly more."

Mr. Broadman's fists closed at his sides. "I beg your pardon?" he growled.

Mr. Hardwick continued, undaunted by the reddening face of the man towering above him. He must be even drunker than I thought to be so unconcerned. Mr. Broadman was positively rigid with anger. "You think nothing of damaging my reputation and that of my family, so it's time you received a dose of your own medicine."

Oh no. This was all our fault, mine and Harry's. Mr. Hardwick thought Mr. Broadman told us about Panther being doped with cocaine, and we'd not denied it.

Mr. Broadman, however, wasn't helping the situation. He stood toe to toe with Mr. Hardwick, glowering down at the smaller man. "I'm not the one taking medicine, Hardwick. Nor am I injecting it into anyone…or *anything*."

Mr. Hardwick may have been drunk, but not drunk enough to slow him down. He punched Mr. Broadman in the stomach before the latter could react and dodge out of the way.

Mr. Broadman doubled over from the blow, giving Mr. Hardwick a more advantageous angle with which to punch him in the jaw. It was a nice move from a shorter man to bring a bigger man down. It sent Mr. Broadman reeling back.

A shocked Mr. Liddicoat and a friend caught him, while two others retaliated. One caught Mr. Hardwick's right arm and the second returned the punch to the stomach.

Several ladies screamed. One fainted, and because all eyes

were on the fight and not her, nobody caught her. She crumpled to the floor in a puff of skirts.

Flossy and I stood on our toes to get a better look, but were ushered out of the way by Floyd and Uncle Ronald, who'd swooped in from goodness knows where.

Flossy clicked her tongue in frustration. "Spoilsports," she muttered.

The rest of her words were drowned out by shouts, as the host and his friends ordered the fighters to desist and leave. Mr. Hardwick was muscled out of the room between two cricketers, his teammates following in his wake, and Mr. Broadman was shown to another room to tend to his bloodied lip. A half dozen girls volunteered their handkerchiefs to clean it, while others offered to fetch him tea, punch, sandwiches, and just about everything else available from the refreshment table.

The hostess shooed them away, earning another click of the tongue from Flossy, who must have been considering how she could be of service too.

I distanced myself from her and the other disappointed young ladies and circulated amongst the men. I caught whispered explanations about the doping accusations, and comments to the effect that it was a slur on the Hardwick family's breeding business. While all condemned Mr. Hardwick's violent outburst, I got the feeling some secretly thought it justified, particularly if Mr. Broadman were guilty of Mr. Rigg-Lyon's murder. It seemed not everyone was convinced of his innocence.

My information-gathering session was cut short by Uncle Ronald, who decided Flossy and I shouldn't be exposed to any more overtly masculine behavior. The hostess apologized profusely for the way the evening had turned out, and asked us to pass on her regards to Aunt Lilian, who hadn't attended due to her ill-health. Flossy and I both assured the hostess the evening had been a triumph, overall, and that one incident wouldn't color our memories.

Going by Flossy's bright eyes and the way she couldn't stop talking about the fight in the cab on the way home, I suspected it would be the only thing she remembered in a week's time.

"Cobbit couldn't collect us tonight?" I asked my uncle as we passed the fountain in the center of Piccadilly Circus.

"He said the horses are unwell."

"You don't believe him?"

His only answer was a grunt.

Flossy put a gloved finger under her wrinkled nose. "I hope they get better soon. This taxi smells."

* * *

I SLEPT POORLY THAT NIGHT. My nerves felt frayed, and not because of the fight. I couldn't stop thinking about my upcoming meeting with Harry, replaying several scenarios until they blurred together in the small hours.

"You look terrible," Harmony said with a frown as she settled the breakfast tray on the table in my sitting room the next morning. "You'll need a very big hat to distract from the shadows under your eyes."

I grasped the coffee cup between both hands and held it out to her. "Your honesty is always refreshing and sometimes bruising. But I agree with you today. I look how I feel...tired."

She poured coffee into my cup. "Is it the investigation? Is something about it bothering you?"

If I admitted it was something else, she'd pester me until I told her, and I didn't feel like talking about Harry and what he'd revealed to Uncle Ronald about Mr. Miller. I didn't want her to think poorly of him.

So instead, I nodded. "There was a fight at the party last night between two of our suspects." I told her what had happened and why.

"You should discuss it with Harry today," she said.

"I will."

"Good." She peered at me over her coffee cup. "You need to talk to him."

From the earnest way she said it, I wondered if she was referring to something other than the case. But she couldn't possibly know what really bothered me. She was insightful and empathetic, but she wasn't a psychic.

* * *

My ARRIVAL at Harry's office was met with a relieved smile. It quickly vanished, however, when I didn't return it. "You're still cross with me," he said flatly.

I sat down and considered how best to broach the topic. None of the scenarios that had kept me awake all night felt right. In the end, I went with a direct approach. "Yes, I am."

He shifted in the chair, leaning forward a little, a sign he wanted to get his point across. "Cleo, I did what I did because I don't want anyone taking advantage of you."

"You never gave him a chance, Harry. You'd never even met Mr. Miller when you decided to investigate him. Nor did you wait to find out my opinion of him."

He sat back. "If I waited for you to form an opinion, it may have been too late. I thought it best to get in early, before you grew too attached."

"I can decide for myself what's best for me."

He lowered his gaze. "You're right. I'm sorry." He put up his hands, warding me away or creating a barrier between us, I wasn't sure which. "Your life is nothing to do with me."

"Harry," I chided, "that's not what I'm saying, although I do appreciate the apology."

His gaze lifted, his brows arched. "If I promise not to over-step again, can we return to being friends?"

It was hard not to forgive him when he looked at me with the shadow of vulnerability darkening his velvet-brown eyes, but I hadn't finished. "It's not just the fact you went behind my back, it's that you did it again, *after* our discussion."

He frowned. "I don't understand."

"Yesterday, when you told Uncle Ronald what you'd learned about Mr. Miller. You must have gone to see him after we parted outside the hotel. Or did you ask Mr. Hobart to pass it on?"

His jaw dropped lower and lower with every sentence I uttered. "I didn't inform Sir Ronald, Cleo. I would never discuss anything about you with him."

My stomach plummeted. "Oh." It came out more of a breath than a word. "It must have been Mrs. Hessing who told him."

He placed both palms flat on the desk and studied them a

moment before pushing himself to his feet. "We should speak to Bert about doping Panther."

I watched as he put on his jacket. He wouldn't even look at me. "I'm sorry, Harry. I jumped to the wrong conclusion." I stood and followed him to the door. "At least we're balanced now. I'm cross with you about investigating Mr. Miller, and you're cross with me for assuming it was you who told my uncle."

"I'm not cross with you. I'm just…" He heaved a sigh and shook his head. "I hoped you knew me well enough to know I wouldn't go to Sir Ronald with my concerns."

"The timing pointed to you being the culprit."

"Did it?"

"Yes! Mrs. Hessing has known about Mr. Miller's past all along, so why wait until yesterday?"

"Perhaps she didn't want to spread gossip unnecessarily. Perhaps she only decided to bring it up when she thought you two were serious."

"A conclusion she came to because you asked about him."

"Or because she saw the two of you together."

I narrowed my gaze. "Just because I enjoy a gentleman's company, it doesn't mean I want to be more than friends."

His lips pressed together as he indicated I should walk down the stairs first. His reaction was baffling. His original inquiry about Mr. Miller even more so.

Was he jealous?

If so, it was both flattering and unnerving. I wasn't sure what to do about it. Enjoy it or discourage him? Remind him that my future plans didn't involve marriage?

Or kiss him?

It was entirely possible I was misreading his reactions and he wasn't jealous. When it came to Harry, I seemed to make a habit of misunderstanding. My confusion led to my silence. It was safest to say nothing to avoid increasing the tension between us further.

The tension and the silence remained all the way to the Elms Polo Club where we alighted from the cab. Focusing on something else was a relief, and I dove into the investigation with renewed enthusiasm.

The gate was unlocked, but we couldn't just roam around

at leisure this time. The major had thrown us out on Wednesday and would do so again if he spotted us. We needed a way to enter unobserved, and not just by Major Leavey.

"Bert will probably run away again when he sees us," I said.

"Then we won't let him see us until it's too late for him to run."

My parasol gave me the perfect way to hide my face, but Harry was more conspicuous. Even if he lowered his hat brim, his height and broad shoulders gave him away. Fortunately, the grounds staff were too busy to take any notice of us. It was Friday, which meant they were preparing the playing field and spectator areas for another day of matches tomorrow. Weeds were removed, rose bushes dead-headed, and pavilion seating cleaned. We avoided the clubhouse and headed to the outbuildings.

We had a clear view of the stables and tack room as we rounded the corner, but no one was outside working this time. If Bert was inside, he was trapped.

Bert was not inside the stables. It was devoid of humans, so Harry said when he re-emerged. I'd remained at the entrance to keep watch and alert Harry if the major approached.

We made our way to the tack room next, our gazes continually scanning the area for the major or Bert. We were only a few feet away when we heard a deep, angry voice coming from inside. Although we couldn't make out the words, the tone was clearly threatening.

We quickened our pace. Instead of keeping watch, I entered the tack room behind Harry.

It took my eyes a moment to adjust to the dimmer light after the bright sunshine, but when they did, I spotted Mr. Broadman towering over Robbie, his fist buried in the groom's shirt front. Robbie was forced onto his toes, the veins at his throat bulging over his collar, pulled tight by Mr. Broadman.

"Liar!" Mr. Broadman snarled. "You must know!"

Robbie's denial came out as a squeak.

"Let him go!" Harry ordered.

Mr. Broadman whipped around, then suddenly released Robbie. The groom staggered as he lost his balance, falling back into the wall, just missing the bridles hanging from a row of hooks. He rubbed his throat, his wide gaze on Mr. Broadman.

Mr. Broadman scrubbed the back of his hand over his mouth. "I, uh, was just questioning him."

Harry stepped between the two men. "Your methods leave something to be desired."

"You do it, then. You ask him about doping Panther, Leopard, and God knows how many other horses from the Polo and Gun Club team." He turned a cold glare on Robbie.

"I didn't do it!" Robbie cried.

"You must have known. Confess!" He tried to lunge past Harry, but Harry blocked him and managed to keep him back.

Even so, Robbie sank into the wall. "I didn't know anything about it. I swear to you."

Mr. Broadman shoved Harry away. "You must know. You're all in it together, all of you grooms." Again, he advanced, and again, Harry blocked him. This time he grabbed him, forcing him further back.

"Calm down," Harry growled. "If you want answers, this isn't the way to get them."

"This is because of last night, isn't it?" I asked Mr. Broadman. "I was there. I saw Mr. Hardwick accuse you of spreading rumors that Mr. Rigg-Lyon's horse had been doped. But you didn't know before that, did you?"

The muscles in his jaw bunched. "I suspected but wasn't sure. Hardwick's accusation confirmed it, in my mind. The way he reacted…he wouldn't have behaved so abominably if he and Rigg-Lyon were innocent."

"Is that what you argued about on the clubhouse steps before last Saturday's match?"

He nodded. "Rumors had been swirling among polo circles for weeks, but that was my first opportunity to discuss it with Rigg-Lyon."

"Discuss? You almost came to blows."

Mr. Broadman blinked rapidly, and his fiery stare was extinguished.

"Do you have any new evidence that Mr. Hardwick was involved, aside from his reaction last night?" I asked.

"That's enough evidence for me." He jerked his head at Robbie. "I came here to question the groom who took care of Panther that day. If Panther had been doped before the match, the cocaine would have to be injected beforehand. The groom assigned to him either did it himself or knows who did."

"His name's Bert." Harry indicated Robbie. "This isn't him."

"I know, but Bert ran off when he saw me."

I frowned. We hadn't seen anyone as we made our way to the tack room, and I'd been outside the stables while Harry checked inside. I didn't get the chance to ask about it, however, as Mr. Broadman continued to growl his way through an explanation.

"Robbie must know about the doping, too. They all do, all the grooms. How much did Rigg-Lyon pay you?" he snapped.

Robbie shook his head. He looked terrified as he sidled closer to Harry.

Harry put his hand up to ward Mr. Broadman off. "I grant you that Bert is probably guilty. He has run away twice now to avoid questioning. But what evidence do you have that Robbie is involved?"

"They present a united front, this lot. They protect one another."

"The grooms each have minds of their own."

Mr. Broadman's response was a tightening of his lips into a thin line.

"I don't understand why," I said. "Why dope your horse to win a match that no one bets on? Why go to such lengths to cheat?"

"Because Rigg-Lyon's the sort that has to win at everything," Mr. Broadman growled. "He hated to lose. He was like a child, always needing the adulation, the accolades, and prizes. The women." He snorted. "If there was a contest for the longest dive off a cliff, he'd plummet to his death just to win."

It was in poor taste, considering, but Mr. Broadman seemed beyond caring. I'd never seen him so riled up. He was always so polished in company, so polite and charming. It was as if his mask had been ripped off, revealing the ugliness underneath.

Harry sometimes wore a mask to get what he wanted, but when his mask slipped, it didn't reveal a lesser man. There was honesty and goodness under his mask. I wasn't so sure Mr. Broadman could claim the same.

"You can't come here and tar all the grooms with the same brush without evidence," Harry said.

Mr. Broadman scoffed. "I was trying to get evidence out of Bert, but he ran off. I told you that."

"Which direction did he go?" I asked.

Mr. Broadman looked to Robbie.

Robbie pointed at the large double doors that stood open. "Bert spotted Mr. Broadman coming here and knew he was done for. So he legged it in the other direction. Left his kit behind and all, he was that scared." He indicated a battered and stained burlap sack hanging from a hook near the door.

I took it down and opened the drawstring closure. Inside were a few meager belongings—a wooden comb missing some teeth, a spoon, tin bowl and cup, and a dirty waistcoat that smelled like horse and sweat.

"Do you think Bert was complicit?" Harry asked Robbie. "Do you think he injected all the horses, not just Panther?"

He shrugged. "He loved horses. He wouldn't hurt them willingly."

There was something in the waistcoat pocket. A letter, going by the shape of it. I fished it out.

"What about *unwillingly*?" Harry pressed.

"I s'pose, if he thought he had no choice."

"We know Rigg-Lyon threatened to reveal Bert's secret if he didn't do as he ordered. We can now safely assume he was attempting to blackmail Bert into doping Panther, and possibly Leopard and the rest of the team's mounts, but what secret did Bert have that would be bad enough to force him to go against his horse-loving nature?"

It wasn't a letter in the pocket, it was a series of photographs. Three of them, to be precise, and they were all of the same person, taken from different angles. I took a moment to study them thoroughly.

"I don't know," Robbie answered Harry. "Bert's secretive. Keeps to himself. The rest of the lads think he's strange, but I reckon he just doesn't like people. He was mostly a good worker, although…"

"Although?" Harry prompted.

"Sometimes he couldn't be found immediately after a match. It's when he's needed most, so it was noticeable."

"Where did he go?"

"He wouldn't say, but I saw him coming from the direction of the courtyard."

"The other outbuildings?"

If Robbie nodded, I didn't see. I was too focused on the photographs to look up.

"Cleo?" Harry asked as he approached. "What have you found?"

I handed the photographs to him. "I know Bert's secret."

CHAPTER 12

$\mathcal{H}$arry returned the photographs to the waistcoat pocket. He cleared his throat and wouldn't meet my gaze. "Well, those are…"

"Educational?" They were for me, at least. I'd seen photographs of a naked man before, as part of another investigation, but these were more explicit. They were probably meant to arouse the viewer, but I couldn't help the giggle that bubbled out of me.

Harry arched his brows but said nothing. Even so, I detected a hint of amusement dancing in his eyes.

I bit the inside of my cheek in an attempt to regain composure and focus on the task at hand. The photographs. I didn't know the identity of the man in them. He was probably a model, paid by the photographer for his time. My guess was that he was a laborer, used to physical work. His muscles bulged as much as his—

"What is it?" Mr. Broadman barked. "What did you find?"

Harry stuffed the waistcoat containing the photographs back into the sack. "Evidence."

"For the police?"

"For the major. I think he should deal with this."

As if Harry conjured him by speaking his name, Major Leavey suddenly appeared inside the door. He squinted in our direction. "You two again! I told you not to come here."

He strode in our direction, pointing his finger aggressively. "Remove yourself from these premises at once!"

Mr. Broadman put out a hand to keep him back. "Let them stay. They've found a clue. One of the grooms has been doping the horses."

"What!"

"Not ours. The Polo and Gun mounts. Rigg-Lyon's, at least, and probably Hardwick's and the others."

The major stared at him. Then his eyes narrowed. He turned to Robbie.

Robbie put his hands in the air. "Not me, sir!"

"Bert," Mr. Broadman explained.

If Harry or I had accused one of the grooms, the major wouldn't have believed us. But he was willing to listen to Mr. Broadman. "I assume you have evidence."

"Watkins told us about an argument he witnessed between Bert and Rigg-Lyon," Harry explained. "Rigg-Lyon threatened to expose Bert's secret if he didn't do what Rigg-Lyon wanted, but we weren't sure what that secret was—until now." Harry showed him the photographs.

The major merely glimpsed them before pulling a face and shoving them back at Harry. "Disgusting." He waggled his finger as Harry returned them to the waistcoat pocket. "Don't let Miss Fox see those."

No one mentioned that it was too late.

"So Rigg-Lyon found those in Bert's possession?" he asked.

"He may have," I said. "Or he may have discovered Bert's...interests lay in that direction another way."

The major slapped his hands together behind his back and rocked on his heels. "I think you should stop there, young lady. This is not a conversation you should be privy to."

I continued as if he hadn't spoken. Sometimes the only way to respond to a man who is pushing you in one direction is to push back. "Do you recall us mentioning the small peep-holes drilled into the changing room shower cubicles?"

The major folded his arms and said nothing.

"What?" Mr. Broadman turned on his heel and marched out of the stables.

We all followed, leaving the burlap sack with the

photographs behind. Instead of going inside the changing room, he turned the corner and found the wall with the small holes drilled through the brickwork. He bent and peered through one.

"Bloody pervert." He didn't seem upset at the notion of being spied upon, but perhaps he would later, after the violation had time to sink in.

The major and Robbie peered through the other holes in silence. Neither commented.

"Of course, we can't be certain that Bert was the one who made those holes," I pointed out. "But given what we just found in his belongings, it's a safe assumption. Those photographs tell us that he has a predilection for the male nude."

The major stiffened. "Don't say that word. It's not becoming for a young lady to even utter it."

I bit down on my tongue to stop myself repeating it. As much as the wicked side of me wanted to ruffle his feathers a little more, it wouldn't be helpful.

Harry must have been worried that my self-control would waver, because he rushed to fill the silence. "It's not just the photographs. Apparently Bert's often late getting to the stables after a match and can be seen coming from this direction. The showers are occupied immediately after a match by the players, are they not?"

Mr. Broadman nodded. "From both teams." He traced a finger over the hole. "I had no idea. No idea whatsoever."

"Rigg-Lyon must have noticed," Harry went on. "He probably caught Bert in the act and decided to use the information to blackmail him."

Mr. Broadman's face darkened. "The bloody nerve." I thought he was referring to Bert's peeping until he added, "He's not worthy of being called a gentleman." Apparently Mr. Rigg-Lyon's crime was the worse of the two in his view.

"Did you know?" I asked Robbie.

He'd been silent ever since leaving the stables, and now he looked dazed. "No. Like I said, he kept to himself." He shrugged.

I was quite sure all three men spoke the truth and didn't know about the peepholes. The question was, did Mr. Hardwick? I posed it to the others. "By all accounts, Mr. Hardwick and Mr. Rigg-Lyon were very close. Do you think Mr. Hardwick knew his friend was blackmailing Bert into doping Panther?"

Mr. Broadman scoffed. "He must have. It's only logical. Nobody is that vehement in their denial unless he's guilty."

"Major?" Harry prompted.

The major looked thoughtful, a welcome change from the angry look he'd sported earlier. "It's possible. Indeed, I'd say it's probable. They were good friends, both on and off the field. They went to university together, they socialized together, and they were even going into business together."

Harry and I stared at him. "Are you referring to the agency here in London?" Harry asked. "The one Hardwick was setting up to represent his father's breeding stables?"

The major shrugged one shoulder. "I don't know the particulars. Weeks ago, in the dining room, I overheard them joking about where they'd set up their office. They were laughing about it, making all kinds of silly suggestions, like near the club, or their favorite restaurant, or in Rigg-Lyon's mistress's flat."

"No wonder Mr. Hardwick was upset when Mr. Rigg-Lyon didn't tell him he wasn't going to retire," I said to Harry. "His change of mind could potentially halt their plans."

"Hardwick has decided to play on until the team appoints a new captain and vice," Mr. Broadman said. "As to Rigg-Lyon's intentions, I can't imagine him going into business with anyone. He just didn't seem to have the drive for it. Besides, he was obsessed with polo. He had a few good years left in him, so why give it up for something new, something he had no particular interest in?"

We stood there in silence, contemplating the question until Robbie departed, stating he had work to do in the tack room. Neither Mr. Broadman nor the major acknowledged him, and he slouched off, hands tucked into his pockets.

The major soon left, too, without a word. Mr. Broadman acknowledged Harry and me with nods then strode after him. "Major, I demand a re-match against the Polo and Gun Club. The cup final must be replayed, given they cheated."

We didn't hear the major's response.

"What do you think?" Harry asked me.

"I think Hardwick is a liar. He knew more about Rigg-Lyon's life than he let on. He was also upset with Rigg-Lyon for changing his mind about retiring."

"Upset enough to murder him? It seems unlikely."

He was right. It didn't feel like enough of a motive, although in the heat of an argument, Mr. Hardwick might have struck his friend in anger.

"Bert has a viable motive," I said. "He was terrified of his Peeping Tom secret coming out. He could not only lose his position here at the club, but the major was unlikely to give him a reference."

"We need to speak to him. Shall we find out where he lives?"

"Let's look around here first. I have an inkling where he might be." I set off with Harry on my heels.

"Where?" he asked as he fell into step beside me.

"Robbie told Broadman that Bert fled when he saw him. That was moments before we arrived, perhaps a few minutes. But we didn't see him in the vicinity. Aside from the tack room and stables, the area is open. There's nowhere for him to hide. I think he hid, planning to return to the tack room to get his kit after Broadman left. To do that, he'd need to keep an eye on the tack room."

"So he hid in the nearest building; the stables. But I looked in all the stalls and he wasn't there." He clicked his tongue as it dawned on him. "I didn't check the loft."

He quickened his pace, only to stop when he reached the stable entrance. He glanced at me over his shoulder. "Cleo, stay—"

The rest of his sentence was knocked out of him, along with his breath by Bert slamming into him. Harry lost his balance and fell, taking his assailant with him. They both ended up in the dirt, narrowly missing a pile of horse dung.

With his fall cushioned by Harry, Bert was the first to recover. He sprang up and would have fled again if Harry hadn't caught his foot. Bert fell onto his hands and knees in front of me.

"Are you both all right?" I asked.

Harry got up and hauled the groom to his feet. "I'm fine,

but this suit will need a thorough clean." Still clutching Bert's arm, he dusted himself off with his other hand.

Bert tried to shake himself free, but Harry held him tightly. Realizing it was hopeless, the groom lowered his head, all the fight gone out of him.

"You are in serious trouble," I began. "Not only have you been spying on the players in the changing room, but you doped Panther before last Saturday's match. What do you have to say for yourself?"

Bert had nothing to say. He stood there, sullen.

"Is that why you murdered Vernon Rigg-Lyon? To silence him?"

His head jerked up. "No! I didn't kill him."

"Were you worried he would tell the major?"

"It wasn't me!"

"Or did you kill him so he wouldn't force you to dope Panther a second time?"

He struggled against Harry, but Harry's grip was too firm.

"Answer her," he growled, giving Bert a shake.

Sweat beaded on Bert's brow and he looked like he wanted to cry. I felt sorry for him. All of his troubles could be traced back to a predilection that was taboo, one that he hadn't chosen. His breaths came hard and fast as panic set in.

We needed to banish the panic if we wanted the truth from him. If he thought we'd hand him over to the major, he'd not tell us anything. "I believe you," I assured him. "I don't think you killed Mr. Rigg-Lyon. If you trust us, and tell us what you know, we'll put in a good word with the major and ask him to keep your secret."

Bert swallowed hard.

Harry slowly released him but didn't step back in case Bert tried to run off again. "Did you dope Panther?"

Bert gave a slight nod. "Mr. Rigg-Lyon came up to me one day, a couple of weeks before he died, when they last played here. He told me he knew I was a Peeping Tom. He said he'd tell the major unless I injected Panther with a mixture he gave me. He didn't tell me what was in it, but I guessed. I used to be a groom at a racing stable, and they injected their horses with a cocaine and caffeine mixture. It's why I left and came here. I thought there'd be no doping in polo," he added with a bitter sneer. "I felt sick about it, but I did it. I had to. He gave me no choice."

"Was it just Panther?" Harry asked.

"And Leopard, Mr. Hardwick's horse."

"What about the rest of the Polo and Gun Club team's horses?"

Bert shook his head. "Just those two."

"Did Mr. Hardwick know?" I asked.

Bert snorted. "Course he bloody knew. He must have. Those two told each other everything."

I frowned as something occurred to me. "It wasn't Rigg-Lyon you were spying on, was it? It was Hardwick."

He scuffed the dirt with the toe of his shoe. "It was Rigg-Lyon," he muttered. "But it was Hardwick who caught me."

Harry and I exchanged glances. Mr. Hardwick was indeed a liar. What else had he lied about?

Bert looked up at Harry. "What happens now?"

Harry stepped aside to let him pass. "Now you return to work. We'll speak to the major on your behalf, if you like."

Bert gave a small nod then scurried away, arms folded and head down as if trying to make himself as small and inconspicuous as possible.

I sighed as I walked alongside Harry towards the clubhouse. "We need to confront Hardwick about all his lies. He has accumulated a number of them."

Harry checked his watch. "After lunch. We should find a teashop nearby, or we can return to the city, if you prefer."

We often didn't stop for lunch when we were in the middle of an investigation. I got the feeling from the expectant way Harry looked at me that he wanted to talk about things other than the murder.

"I can't today. I'm supposed to have a picnic with Flossy and some friends."

He gave me a flat smile and lengthened his strides, only to stop at the base of the front steps of the clubhouse. The major's assistant was coming down them, carrying a clipboard, and Harry asked if we could go inside and speak to Major Leavey.

"I'm sorry, he left," Watkins said.

"When will he return?"

"He didn't say. You could try again tomorrow. He'll be busy, it being Saturday, but he should be able to spare a few minutes. That's if he doesn't throw you out again."

Harry touched the brim of his hat in thanks and watched as Watkins passed us and walked off towards the lake and ground staff working there. "I suppose there's nothing more to do here now."

"We should plan our next course of action," I said.

"Why not come to my office after your picnic and we can talk at length then?"

"I'll have to get ready for a dinner party after the picnic. Harmony hates it when I don't give her enough time to do my hair. We can talk on our way home now."

"Right. Of course." He spoke stiffly. His shoulders were rigid too, and he stared straight ahead as we walked towards the gates.

"Is it really the case you want to discuss, Harry, or is it our earlier argument?"

For a moment, I thought he wouldn't answer. Then he suddenly turned to me. "I want to clear the air between us."

"It's clear."

"It's not. You're still cross with me."

"I didn't say that."

"You don't have to. I can tell."

He was intuitive, I'd give him that. "If anyone is still cross, it's you, Harry. Look at you. You're wound up tighter than a spinning top."

"That's not because I'm cross. It's because—" He cut himself off with a shake of his head. "Never mind. We'll talk again tomorrow. About the case."

"I have to go on a picnic in the countryside tomorrow. I'll try to see you before we leave. Or we can talk now."

We didn't talk. Not then and not on the drive back to the hotel, which felt interminably long. I wished the ice hadn't thickened between us, but it had, and I had no idea how to thaw it. The longer our silence stretched, the more worried I became that our easy friendship might never return, and the more I worried, the heavier the silence became.

It was a relief when we parted.

* * *

I WAS USED to Frank not smiling at me when he opened the front door of the hotel, but his complete silence was new. He didn't even respond when I greeted him. I passed through the doorway into the foyer, but waited by one of the large vases and watched. He didn't smile or speak to anyone who came or went from the hotel. It was one thing to ignore me, someone he thought of as an equal with my humble upbringing, but it was quite another for him to ignore the guests.

I rejoined him outside. "Is something the matter, Frank?"

"You could say that, Miss Fox."

I waited but he didn't go on. "What is it? Is it Cobbit's plight? Are you worried about him?"

"I am worried, yes, but that's not why I'm doing a go-slow."

"Go-slow?" I watched as he reached for the door to open it for a couple entering the hotel. "Your pace seems the same to me."

"It's a figure of speech. It means I'm doing the minimum I'm employed to do, no more. When a factory worker protests, they can work slowly and limit production. I can't do that, so I had to think of another way to get my point across to the Bainbridges. So I've stopped greeting folk and am merely opening the door for them."

"I see. Do you think your go-slow will have the desired effect?"

"We'll find out soon enough, won't we?"

"Has my uncle said anything to you? Given you a warning, or asked why you're doing it?"

He tugged on his cuff. "He hasn't noticed yet. He was in a hurry when he left this morning."

Considering Frank's entire plan hinged on my uncle noticing he wasn't greeting guests, it could all come to naught.

"He's an observant man, Sir Ronald," Frank went on. "He'll notice sooner or later."

That was true. Uncle Ronald was very observant when it came to the workings of the hotel. "Careful what you wish for, Frank. You're treading a thin line on behalf of someone else's losing battle."

"I appreciate the warning, Miss Fox, but if it's all the same, I'll continue with the fight." He held the door open for me. "Good day to you." Realizing he'd just broken his own go-slow rule, he clicked his tongue and berated himself under his breath.

Inside, Mr. Hobart beckoned me into his office with a tilt of his head. He closed the door behind us and asked me to sit. His usually sparkling blue eyes were dull, grim.

"Is this about Harry?" I asked.

"No? Why? Has something happened to him?"

"He's perfectly well. I was just with him, as it happens."

His gaze narrowed. "Is something the matter between the two of you?"

"Nothing that can't be resolved over a cup of Luigi's coffee." I attempted a smile and hoped it convinced him.

"Good, good. Miss Fox, I saw you speaking to Frank just now."

"Apparently he is doing the minimum and merely opening the door without offering greetings or smiles."

"So he warned me before his shift began this morning. Sir Ronald hasn't noticed, but I'm concerned that when he does, he'll dismiss Frank on the spot. As much as Frank is a curmudgeon, I'd miss him. He's been here a long time, and I can't imagine the front door of the hotel without him standing there."

"Yes, I agree."

"Cobbit's work is a little more specialized. There may be many other coachmen in London, but good ones don't grow on trees. Frank, however, is replaceable. Anyone can open a door, smile, and say 'good morning.' In fact, they'll probably do a better job of it. Frank can be a little curt, and he's famously rude to the staff or anyone he believes shouldn't be entering the Mayfair."

I remembered all too well the frosty reception I'd received from Frank on the day I arrived at the Mayfair in December. He took one look at my shabby clothes and luggage and couldn't believe I was related to the Bainbridges. He was as much a snob as any of my family's upper-class friends.

"I tried warning him not to anger my uncle just now, but he seemed determined to press on with his mission."

Mr. Hobart sighed. "He'll dig his own grave if he's not protected from his own folly."

"We need to do something. Convince him somehow that he can't win."

Mr. Hobart touched his tie to readjust it, even though it was perfectly straight.

"You've already got a plan, haven't you?" I said.

"You could say that."

I smiled. "You not only have a plan, but you've already enacted it. Tell me, Mr. Hobart. What is it?"

He gave me a smug look, something I'd never seen on the humble man's face before. "I told the front of house staff to inform the guests that Frank has lost his voice. I assured them he's otherwise well, but simply woke up this morning unable to talk."

I grinned. "That's an excellent plan. Does anyone in my family know the truth?"

"Only you. I'll make sure Sir Ronald and the others hear about Frank's laryngitis before they find out what he's really up to."

I breathed a sigh of relief as I stood. That was one crisis averted. Unfortunately it didn't lift my somber mood.

I worried about Harry for the rest of the day.

CHAPTER 13

*L*uncheon with my aunt, cousin and their friends was pleasant enough, and I wasn't lying to Harry when I said I wouldn't have time to meet him afterward. The event went late, as they often did, and by the time I returned to the hotel, there was only enough time for a cup of tea with Harmony in my suite, followed by a bath before I had to get ready for dinner. Considering I shared Harmony with Flossy, I had to have my hair done first to give her time to do both.

After stewing all afternoon, talking to someone was a relief. She listened to me babble on about Harry without interruption. When I finished, I watched her closely in the reflection of my dressing table mirror.

"Did I overreact?" I asked. "I mean, I did apologize for my mistake, but not for my reaction to his interference. Should I say sorry for that, too?"

She twisted my hair up and checked the effect in the mirror before releasing it. She watched the honey-brown tresses tumble past my shoulders. "I can see you're still cross with him."

"I suppose I am. It was condescending of him to think I couldn't take care of myself, but to go behind my back was devious."

"He explained why he did it."

"Yes. And he apologized."

"Then it comes down to one thing." She twisted my hair

up again and dug a comb into it to hold it in place. "Do you want this to come between you?"

"No. Definitely not."

"Then you have to make a conscious decision to accept his apology. It's the only way to move on."

She was right, as always. "Very well, I *will* accept it. I'm quite sure he won't do something like this again, anyway. He seemed genuinely sorry." I reached up and patted her hand. "Thank you, Harmony. You've been a great help."

But it wasn't the answer to every facet of the issue standing between Harry and me and she could see I wasn't completely satisfied. "And yet?" she prompted.

"And yet *he's* cross with *me* now, because I falsely accused him of going to Uncle Ronald. He says he accepts my apology, but I don't think he does, deep down."

Harmony tapped another comb against her cheek as she thought. "Is he cross, or just disappointed?"

I whipped around to face her. "Why would he be disappointed?"

"Because you leapt to the wrong conclusion. It means you misjudged him, Cleo. He probably thought you knew him better by now, and is disappointed that you don't." She clasped my chin and faced me forward again. "To be quite honest, I'm surprised you jumped to that conclusion too. You're an intelligent woman and I think you do know him well enough to know he wouldn't go to your uncle. So the question is, why did you accuse him?"

I stared at her reflection in the mirror, my head suddenly feeling as though it was stuffed with wool. "I... I don't know."

She thrust the comb into my hair, followed by hairpin after hairpin. "Were you sabotaging something, perhaps?"

"Sabotaging what?"

Her gaze met mine. "What do you think?"

"I don't know," I said again.

She pinned a silk bow in the same shade of blue as my gown to the back of my head to complete the arrangement. "I meant about your hair. I think it looks very fetching."

* * *

With my mind preoccupied, I wanted to enjoy an evening with simple conversation that I didn't need to follow too carefully. Unfortunately, the one person I needed to be most careful with my comments was there, and he made a point of talking to me the moment I found myself on my own.

I smiled politely. "Good evening, Mr. Miller."

He bowed. "Good evening, Miss Fox. You look well. Very well, in fact."

"Thank you." I looked around the drawing room for one of my cousins or a friend, but they were deep in conversation with other guests. I caught sight of our hostess watching us, clearly unaware that my family didn't want me associating with Mr. Miller. She seemed to think we'd make a good match, if her secretive little smile had anything to do with it.

Oh dear. I hoped she hadn't seated us together.

"I see from the panic in your eyes that you believe them." It was to Mr. Miller's credit that he didn't shy away from the reason for the awkwardness between us.

"You're brave speaking to me with my uncle nearby."

"And your cousin." He nodded at Floyd, his back to us as he chatted with a young lady. "Do you think they'll intervene here or is the famous British politeness too ingrained?"

"If I told you, it would take all the fun out of finding out. Fun for me, that is."

He flashed a grin, but it quickly faded. "Since we only have a few moments to ourselves, I'll get straight to the point. I'd like the opportunity to explain."

"Please, Mr. Miller. It's not necessary."

"It is. I don't want you forming an opinion of me based on rumor."

"I haven't. I make up my own mind about people."

His face lifted. "Oh. That is a relief to hear. Then…may I ask, what opinion do you have—"

"I should stop you there."

"—of Walt Whitman?"

I laughed, relieved. Then I stopped as I realized his question meant he didn't know I'd returned the book. Either it had got lost among the parcels at the post desk or he hadn't checked his mail since I left it with Terry.

He leaned closer and lowered his voice to an earnest whisper. "I don't really care what you think about Whitman. What I really want is the opportunity to explain. May I take you to lunch tomorrow?"

"I can't, sorry. I have to continue with my investigation. It's at a crucial juncture and I've spent enough time away from it today."

The look on his face told me everything I needed to know. He was miffed that I'd placed the investigation higher than him in the pecking order. His reaction made me feel less guilt over my decision to reject him.

Uncle Ronald spotted Mr. Miller speaking to me and broke away from his companions. He advanced across the room, collecting Floyd as he passed him. I'd never thought they looked alike, but with their flared nostrils and matching bullish frowns, the family resemblance was clear.

The dinner gong saved us. Mr. Miller moved off to find the lady he was assigned to escort into the dining room, and I turned on a bright smile for my uncle and cousin.

"Ah, the cavalry has arrived. You're a little late, but never mind. You can scowl at him from across the table all night, if you like. I'm sure he'll get the message."

My uncle gave me a baffled look before going to find my aunt.

Floyd put out his arm to me. "Apparently I'm escorting you."

I took his arm and we waited in the queue to enter the dining room.

"What were you and Miller discussing just now?" he asked.

"Walt Whitman."

He huffed. "If you're planning on running away with him, I advise you to think seriously first. My father will cut you off completely."

I turned to face him properly. "Do you honestly think I'd elope with Mr. Miller?"

He sighed deeply, and I could feel the rigidity leave his body. "No. I know if you're going to run off with someone inappropriate, it won't be him."

* * *

Saturday's weather was perfect for a picnic—sunny and calm. Unfortunately, the picnic went ahead without us. The hotel was in chaos. Cobbit and the other coachman and grooms had gone on strike, meaning cabs needed to be found for those guests leaving the hotel. That wouldn't have been a particularly difficult task ordinarily, but the striking staff had sat down on the road, blocking it. Traffic was at a standstill and no cabs could stop close to the hotel entrance. Not only that, Frank was still not speaking to guests, and he refused to signal to cab drivers that they were needed. He'd also managed to enlist the other doorman in his protest, so it was left to the porters to manage the luggage as well as hail taxis, whose drivers were not inclined to stop and cause even more congestion.

Mr. Hobart and Peter did their best to soothe anxious guests who were worried about missing their trains, while the angriest guests were left to members of the Bainbridge family to placate. Since Aunt Lilian, Flossy and Floyd were all still in their rooms, Uncle Ronald and I were kept busy.

I didn't even have a chance to telephone Harry. I filled the single momentary lull in the chaos by speaking to Frank and the other doorman, but neither would give in. They opened the front door, but that was the sum total of their tasks.

"Frank, you are not going to sway my uncle this way," I told him after one of the cab drivers ordered me to get out of his way.

"You don't reckon, Miss Fox?" He nodded at Uncle Ronald attempting to calm an irate guest in the foyer. "I give it fifteen minutes before he gives in."

"This isn't fair on the other staff." I indicated Goliath, attempting to hail a taxi while clutching three hat boxes by their straps, a small bag wedged under each arm.

"You're right. It isn't fair. I reckon they can go on strike too. Support your fellow worker, that's what I say." He opened the door for a guest then waited until they were inside before turning to me. "I think the cooks will join in. They're a radical lot."

"Not since Mrs. Poole took over as *chef de cuisine*. They like her."

"The maids? Harmony's a supporter of good causes for

the working man, or woman. She's a good organizer, too. The other girls will follow her."

"Don't drag Harmony into this. It's not her fight, and it's certainly not a winnable one."

The door was pushed open from the other side and a frustrated guest marched out. He stepped onto the road to hail his own taxi, but there were none in the vicinity.

"Frank, what will you do if my uncle dismisses you?"

"He won't dismiss me. I've been here a long time. Besides, I'm doing the job I was hired to do. I'm opening doors for guests." He stepped up to the door and opened it. He indicated I should return inside.

I spent most of the morning helping my uncle in the foyer. I didn't notice the time until my aunt and Flossy came downstairs carrying parasols and gloves. Aunt Lilian frowned at my uncle and he gave her a grim nod in response. They didn't need to exchange words to communicate. Like many couples who'd been together for years, they often knew what the other meant with a mere look.

Flossy took my hand and squeezed. "Is it true, Cleo? Everyone is on strike?"

"Not everyone. Just the doormen and mews staff. I'm afraid some are blocking the street and it's quite impossible to get a cab."

She sighed. "That's that, then."

"What's what?"

"Mother wasn't particularly interested in going on this picnic. She'll use this as an excuse."

Poor Flossy. She'd been looking forward to the outing. I, however, would rather spend the rest of the day investigating. I put out my hand to my aunt.

"What shall we do?" I asked her. "Cobbit won't take us, and any taxis that get through must be allocated to guests." There was quite a queue forming outside, waiting for the taxis that managed to get through the traffic. "Would you like to walk to Hyde Park and see if the traffic improves there? We could carry the picnic basket between us. The porters are a little busy to help." I watched as Goliath spoke to a guest who'd been waiting several minutes for Mr. Hobart to be free. Giving up, he'd stopped the first staff member to pass by, which happened to be Goliath, pushing a luggage trolley.

Aunt Lilian sighed. "We can't possibly manage a basket, as well as our parasols, a picnic blanket and chairs. Besides, this entire experience has put me in a gloomy mood. I feel a headache coming on."

"You retire, Mother," Flossy said gently. "I'll stay down here and help Father."

Aunt Lilian gratefully returned to the lift, while Flossy and I turned on smiles for Mrs. and Miss Hessing, who emerged from it.

A few minutes later, I slipped into Mr. Hobart's office and telephoned Harry. "My day suddenly became free. I think we should try to speak to Hardwick."

He agreed. "There are matches being played at the Polo and Gun Club today. Do you think you can get vouchers at the last minute?"

"No, but I have a better way of getting through the gate. Meet me there. Wear working men's clothes."

I hung up, then sent a message to the staff's residence hall before returning to my suite to change outfits.

* * *

VICTOR MET me outside the residence hall, and together we traveled to the Polo and Gun Club, a mere ten miles from the Elms. The enormous popularity of polo meant two clubs could not only survive within close proximity to each other, but thrive.

Victor approved of my plain black dress and modest hat. It was the most inconspicuous ensemble in my wardrobe. We found Harry waiting behind a tree near the service entrance. He also wore the simple clothes of a working man along with a cap and ill-fitting jacket with patches on the elbows. He and Victor acknowledged one another with nods then we entered the estate via the gate. It stood open to allow for deliveries. With luncheon being served for special guests in the club-house and refreshments in the pavilion for other spectators, there was much activity with carts and staff coming and going through the gate.

In his cook's uniform, Victor was waved through by the security staff, but Harry and I were stopped.

"They're with me," Victor said. "Kitchen's short-staffed. I was asked to bring friends to help for the day."

They gave us a disinterested glance then signaled that we could continue.

We followed Victor to the rear of the clubhouse and crossed the courtyard to the kitchen entrance. No one paid us any attention. They were too busy carrying crates laden with vegetables inside, or rolling barrels. Sturdy women in aprons and mob caps hefted baskets filled with bread on their hips, while youths trailed behind carrying eggs.

We followed the smell of roasting meat to the kitchen, where Victor sought out his friend. He found him at one of the long benches chopping potatoes. After a quiet word, the friend escorted us to a small storeroom filled with brooms, mops and other cleaning equipment.

Harry picked up a mop and bucket while I found a cleaning cloth, dustpan and brush. We listened as Victor's friend outlined the layout of all the buildings on the estate. At this hour, Barnaby Hardwick would most likely be changing into his playing uniform, so Harry and I headed to the changing rooms while Victor and his friend returned to the kitchen. I wasn't sure what Victor would do in our absence, but he knew how to blend in.

I waited outside the changing room while Harry entered. It galled me that I couldn't go in, but staff weren't entirely invisible. A maid would be noticed in an all-male changing room.

As it happened, being outside was the best place to be. It gave me the perfect spot to see Mr. Hardwick as he ambled in my direction, clutching a piece of paper in one hand and a brown leather bag in the other. With his head lowered to read, he didn't see me.

Harry emerged from the changing room and was about to speak when I put a hand up to hush him. I indicated the slowly approaching Mr. Hardwick. We watched as he stopped suddenly and pressed his fingertips to his forehead. With a twist of his lips, he scrunched the paper into a ball and tossed it into a nearby hedge. He strode towards us.

"I want to see that note before we speak to him," Harry whispered as he turned away. He inspected his bucket while I crouched to sweep dust into my pan.

Mr. Hardwick entered the changing rooms without so much as a glance in our direction.

Harry reached the hedge before me and fished out the ball of paper. He flattened it and read. "'You knew what Rigg-Lyon did and did not try to stop him. You should shoulder just as much of the blame. Gentlemen who lack honor face pistols at dawn.'"

"Pistols at dawn!" I repeated. "The writer of this letter is in the wrong century."

Harry turned the paper over but it was blank. "It's unsigned, but the writing is masculine, as is the style of the threat."

"Whoever wrote it clearly blames Rigg-Lyon for something and thinks Hardwick is complicit. His life may be in danger."

Harry glanced at the entrance to the changing room. "The writer of this note might not wait for a duel, particularly if Hardwick doesn't comply."

"Given that he threw the note away, I'd say he has no intention of complying."

Harry inspected the note again. "There are no identifying details on here. No way Hardwick can contact the author and organize a duel."

I gasped. "Hardwick must know who sent it. Or the author *thinks* Hardwick knows, or will work it out, and so didn't bother with his name."

Voices echoed off the tiled walls in the changing room, and soon the players spilled out. The forest-green jersey of the Polo and Gun Club team emerged first, led by their interim captain, Barnaby Hardwick. Harry and I pretended to work as they passed us, quietly discussing tactics.

Once all the players rounded the corner and were out of sight, Harry and I wordlessly entered the changing room. We were of one mind: search Mr. Hardwick's belongings.

There were several brown leather bags lined up on the changing room benches with hats on hooks above and polished shoes slipped under the bench, but only one sported the stamped initials BH. Harry pulled out clothing items from Barnaby Hardwick's bag and handed them to me. I rifled through pockets but found only a single handkerchief. The only other items in the bag were a Tattersalls catalog and the cap Mr. Hardwick should be wearing.

We realized too late that it meant he would be returning to retrieve it.

"What the devil?" Mr. Hardwick strode up to Harry and snatched the cap out of his grip. He shook it at the exit. "How dare you! Get out!"

"We will," Harry assured him. "But first you need to explain why you lied to us."

Mr. Hardwick bristled. "I did no such thing."

"You told us Rigg-Lyon never ruined high-born girls, that his mistresses were all entertainers. We have it on good authority that's not the case, and you knew."

He sniffed. "Perhaps he strayed once or twice into green pastures. I can't recall. I wasn't his keeper. Anyway, they may have been high born, but they weren't well-bred if they allowed themselves to be ruined."

The sheer force of my anger was like a punch to my gut, knocking the wind out of me. I couldn't speak, it was so over-whelming. All I could do was stare at him and shake my head in disbelief. Was this what passed as a gentleman?

I may not have been able to utter my horror at his words, but Mr. Hardwick certainly felt the force of my anger. He backed away, eyeing me closely as if I were a bomb.

Harry subtly closed his hand around my fist in an attempt to calm me down before I scared off our quarry. "We also know Rigg-Lyon was doping Panther," he said.

Mr. Hardwick stepped forward, baring his teeth and pointing his finger at Harry. He was more upset about this accusation than the one about Rigg-Lyon ruining young ladies. "You can't go around accusing him without proof!"

"We have proof. The groom he blackmailed into injecting Panther admitted it."

"He's lying!"

"Considering that you and Rigg-Lyon were so close, it stands to reason you knew about it."

"I did not! You need proof, Armitage, and I don't think you have any. The word of an idiot groom means nothing."

"Why so vehement in your denial?" I asked, finally finding my voice. "Not just now, but also at the cricketer's party? Your reaction is excessive if you truly didn't know."

He barked a laugh. "That's it? Your proof is that I strongly denied the accusations? Good grief, Miss Fox, you need to do better than that."

Harry held the note up between two fingers. "Who is this from?"

It took a moment for Mr. Hardwick to register that we'd picked up the discarded paper. When he did, he snatched it out of Harry's hand. "I don't know. It's not signed."

"But you have a suspicion as to the identity of the author."

Mr. Hardwick's only response was to glare at Harry.

"You should alert the police."

Mr. Hardwick snorted. "Don't be absurd." He waved the note in the air. "This is ridiculous."

"I would take it more seriously, if I were you. If the murderer sent it, your life could be in danger, too."

"If the killer wanted me to pay for something he thinks I did, then I'd already be dead." He tucked the note into the pocket of his riding breeches. "He wouldn't challenge me to a duel, of all things. Anyway, Vernon didn't receive any threatening letters before his death, so I don't think this has anything to do with it."

A teammate arrived and urged his captain to hurry along. "Everyone's waiting for you, Hardwick. Come on."

Mr. Hardwick pointed at Harry and me. "These two aren't staff. They're private investigators and they're going through our things. Help me throw them out, will you?"

The teammate looked at me. "Both of them?"

Harry edged closer to Mr. Hardwick. With mere inches separating them, Harry's superior height and build were obvious. "Do not lay a hand on Miss Fox." The words were barely audible, but the menace in his tone was loud and clear.

Mr. Hardwick lifted his chin in defiance, but his hard swallow gave him away.

His teammate stepped aside and indicated the exit. "Sir, miss, if you don't mind."

I took Harry's hand and we left. I didn't let go or look back until we reached the service courtyard behind the clubhouse. "He was lying about not knowing who wrote the letter," I said.

Harry nodded. "And probably about not knowing Rigg-Lyon doped the horses. But we only have instinct, not proof."

"How do we get proof?"

Neither of us had the answer to that, but Harry had a suggestion for how to move forward. "Hardwick mentioned that Rigg-Lyon didn't receive a threatening letter before his death. He seemed certain, but I think it's worth checking with Mrs. Rigg-Lyon." He blew out a breath, releasing the final vestiges of his anger. "I'll fetch Victor and tell him we're leaving."

He went to move off, but I caught his arm, only to quickly release it. I folded my arms over my chest, tucking my hands away. "You didn't have to stand up for me as you did."

His jaw firmed. "Right. You can take care of yourself and don't need me. I understand perfectly."

"Let me finish," I chided. "I was going to say you didn't have to stand up for me, but thank you for doing so. I appreciate it."

Since he merely stood there, staring at me without moving, I offered to fetch Victor. I headed into the clubhouse with Harry's gaze burning into my back. I'd admitted my appreciation as a peace offering for incorrectly assuming he'd told my uncle about Mr. Miller. Hopefully we could now put the tension that incident had caused behind us.

Hopefully, I hadn't made everything even more awkward.

CHAPTER 14

$\mathcal{V}$ictor returned to the hotel while Harry and I traveled to Marylebone to speak to Mrs. Rigg-Lyon. We told her housekeeper that we had news about her husband's murder and she showed us through to the drawing room. It wasn't a lie. We did have news. Just not answers.

Mrs. Rigg-Lyon's face was unreadable when we explained that we had more questions. It was difficult to know from her icy stiffness whether she was upset that we hadn't found her husband's killer, or relieved that we weren't accusing her.

I began by telling her about the threatening letter Mr. Hardwick received. "The anonymous author of the note stated that Mr. Hardwick knew something your husband did, the implication being that he'd done something heinous. Do you know what that might be?"

Her pale face did show a measure of relief, finally. "No, Miss Fox. Vernon didn't make a habit of confiding in me."

"But he did confide in Mr. Hardwick?"

"They were as thick as thieves, so you can draw your own conclusions."

"Can you hazard a guess what the author might be referring to?"

"It could be any number of sins."

"There are many?" Harry asked.

She gave him a cool look. "That's something Mr. Hardwick could answer better than me. As I said, Vernon didn't confide in me. Marriage didn't make us close. It merely tied us together...until death."

A chill crept across my scalp and down my spine.

"Did your husband receive any threatening letters before his death?" Harry asked.

"Have I not made it clear that I wouldn't know, Mr. Armitage?"

"Forgive me. I thought you might have come across something when you cleared out his study."

She twisted the wedding ring on her thin finger, around and around. "I haven't had the strength for the task yet. You may look for yourselves, if you like."

Her offer was unexpected, given her curt responses so far, but most welcome.

She rang the bell, and the housekeeper entered the drawing room. Mrs. Rigg-Lyon asked her to show us to the master's study. I wondered why she didn't join us to oversee our search, until I saw her slump into the sofa when she thought we were no longer looking. It was as if she was keeping herself upright through sheer force of will, but that no longer became necessary when we left. I admired her strength.

Mrs. Rigg-Lyon may not have overseen our search, but the housekeeper didn't leave the room. She didn't get in the way or disturb us, but stood guard by the door. I wasn't sure if she was doing so to report back to her mistress, or to make sure we didn't steal anything.

I checked the desk and drawers while Harry searched the bookshelves. I didn't find a threatening letter, or any correspondence. It occurred to me that Mrs. Rigg-Lyon had lied to us and had already removed incriminating evidence. It would explain her acquiescence to our request. The study was certainly filled with the sorts of things a polo-loving gentleman might have, including the same Tattersalls catalog that we'd found in Mr. Hardwick's possession.

I stared at it. Why *did* Mr. Rigg-Lyon have the horse auctioneer's catalog? Panther wasn't retiring. He'd said so in his celebratory speech on the day of his murder. He didn't need to buy another polo horse.

There was something I wasn't quite seeing, dots I couldn't quite connect. It was frustrating, like an itch I couldn't reach.

I was about to show the catalog to Harry when he asked the housekeeper to open the safe he'd found behind a painting. She hesitated before complying and allowing him to withdraw the contents.

He set aside jewelry boxes and removed documents. He flipped through them, stopping when one caught his attention. He showed it to me.

It was a contract for the auction of Panther at Tattersalls. Across the top, someone had written WITHDRAWN in black ink.

This was the connection, the one that tied together several of the disparate threads we'd uncovered. But I needed a little more information. I needed to be sure.

Harry replaced the contents back into the safe, including the contract, and the housekeeper locked it.

We returned to the drawing room where we thanked Mrs. Rigg-Lyon for her assistance. She gave us a tight, brief smile. It was the first time I understood the curtness behind her responses. It wasn't poor manners. It was pain. Years of good breeding had instilled in her to be the perfect hostess, to greet guests with smiles and invite them to tea. But the cancer that ravaged her body turned her smiles into grimaces and left her unable to entertain guests.

The kindest thing we could do was leave her in peace.

Harry and I were of like mind about our next steps. We headed to Tattersalls on the western edge of Knightsbridge Green. It wasn't auction day, but it was busy nonetheless with a regal thoroughbred being put through its paces in the enclosed internal yard. One of the staff there directed us to the manager's office, located in one of the two buildings flanking the arched entrance. The manager was too busy to speak to us, but his assistant was keen to help when we explained who we were and why we were there. I suspected he fancied himself as an amateur detective.

He searched through the large ledger of upcoming auctions for polo horses and found the entry for Panther. Beside the entry were the letters WD.

"It's code for withdrawn," the assistant explained.

"Is a reason given?" I asked.

"No, but there is a note to say the owner withdrew it. The other one wasn't withdrawn, though."

"Other one?"

The assistant pointed to an entry for Leopard, Mr. Hardwick's horse. "They were sired by the same horse, a champion polo mount in his day," he said as he read. "Hardwicks is listed as the breeder of both horses, as well as the owner of Leopard. The owner of Panther is Rigg-Lyon. It's he who withdrew it from sale."

"Why would he do that?" Harry asked.

The assistant shrugged. "It could be any number of reasons, ranging from the horse being ill to the owner deciding he wanted to keep it for himself. I heard Rigg-Lyon decided not to retire, so I think the latter is your answer."

It explained why Mr. Rigg-Lyon withdrew the horse from sale, but it didn't explain why Mr. Hardwick would be angry about it. The profit wouldn't go to him.

"I wonder what will happen to Panther now," the assistant murmured.

"What do you know about Hardwicks, the breeder?" I asked.

"Almost nothing. They're still establishing themselves. Barnaby Hardwick's father was a legendary polo player in his day, and one of his horses sired Panther and Leopard. Both are champion polo ponies. Their speed and stamina are quite something to behold, so I hear. Panther is the best of the two, but Leopard also has an excellent reputation. There was a lot of interest in them both, but more for Panther. Still, Leopard will fetch a nice sum for the Hardwicks. There are still two seasons left in him, perhaps three, then he can be used for breeding."

I considered asking how doping would affect a horse's price, but the answer to that was obvious and I didn't want to start a rumor that could ruin the Hardwick family's business. I didn't like Mr. Hardwick, but his parents could be good people and unaware of their son's scheme.

Harry thanked the assistant and indicated I should leave the office ahead of him. "Hardwick knew about the doping," he said once we were outside. "I'm certain of it now. He probably even encouraged it to drive up the price at auction."

I agreed. The doping of Panther and Leopard had led to their superior performance on the polo field, and their rising status among that set. Fast horses fetched more money at auction. "I don't think financial gain was Rigg-Lyon's motive for doping Panther," I said. "I think it was purely about winning for him. He loved everything that came with it, the fame and attention. It was like an addiction. That's why he couldn't face retiring yet. And to keep winning, he needed Panther, and Panther needed cocaine." The poor animal was merely an instrument to be cruelly used by Rigg-Lyon and Hardwick. "Hardwick is trying to establish himself as an agent here in London for his parents' breeding business," I went on. "The sale of Panther and Leopard was going to help establish his reputation. He didn't own Panther, and wouldn't get any money from the sale, but he was the higher profile of the two horses and withdrawing him from the auction would diminish interest overall. That's why Hardwick was angry when Rigg-Lyon withdrew Panther from sale by back flipping on his retirement plans."

"Angry enough to kill?"

It was a question we contemplated as we walked towards Hyde Park Corner. We could confront Hardwick, but he wouldn't admit anything. He would probably refuse to even speak to us. We needed further evidence, and neither of us was sure how to get it.

We walked up Piccadilly in silence and stopped outside the hotel. The traffic flowed better than it had this morning, thanks to the constable monitoring the situation. Taxis deposited guests who were greeted by perspiring porters. Frank and the other doorman merely opened the hotel door for them, neither smiling nor speaking. Goliath and his cohort of porters did their best to fill the silence, but the doormen's protest was noticed.

"Where are Cobbit and the rest of the mews staff who were blocking the traffic?" I asked.

Frank turned away from me so I posed my question to Goliath.

"The police ordered them to move or face arrest," he said.

"Did they return to work?" Harry asked.

Goliath shook his head. "I don't know if they're going to. Cobbit's riled them all up, and Sir Ronald isn't backing down. The guests are angry, the hotel's reputation is getting smeared all over the city, and no one is talking to anyone." He indicated Frank's stiff back. "We porters can't take on half of the doormen's work forever. The stalemate has to end soon, but I can't see how if the two sides aren't willing to negotiate."

Frank proved he was listening by turning his head into profile and grunting in response to Goliath's remarks.

I said goodbye to Harry and suggested we meet again in the morning after contemplating the case overnight.

He murmured agreement as he watched Frank.

Frank didn't move when I approached the door. He'd opened it for me this morning, but it would seem I was now being lumped in with the rest of the family.

Harry stepped forward and opened the door for me. I smiled as I passed him. He smiled back and released the door once I was through. "She's a Fox, not a Bainbridge," I heard him tell Frank. "She's also a lady. Next time open the door for her."

My smile widened.

I didn't stop to speak to anyone in the foyer. I didn't want to be dragged into the dispute and forced to choose sides, although it seemed Frank had already chosen for me. I headed upstairs and sat at the desk by the window. It was warm on the fourth floor, even with the windows open, and I was glad when Harmony arrived with strawberry-flavored ices in glass bowls. We enjoyed them on the balcony overlooking the park before they melted, while I told her what we'd learned today.

I thought she'd have something to say about the scheme of doping horses before matches, but her only comment on that was to shake her head sadly and say, "Horrible men, both Hardwick and Rigg-Lyon. I have no sympathy for either." She was more interested in the note Mr. Hardwick had discarded at the polo club, however. "It sounds like something from a book."

"What do you mean?"

"Lately I've been reading old novels set in the Georgian

period. Gentlemen were always going on about challenging one another to duels when the reputations of ladies were ruined. Perhaps the author of that note had a wife or sister who was ruined by Rigg-Lyon."

"And Hardwick knew? It's possible, I suppose, but a big leap to make."

Even so, Harmony continued to make it. The more she talked, the more she warmed to her theory. "You need to find out whose wife, sister or other female family member was ruined by Rigg-Lyon. Even though you think a man wrote the note, don't discount a female author. She could have deliberately disguised her style to make it more masculine." She gasped. "What if it was Mrs. Rigg-Lyon? We know her husband kept mistresses. What if that made her angry? Then she learned he seduced someone innocent, someone close to her, and it tipped her over the edge. She has nothing to lose if she's already dying."

The theory was as sound as any other. I promised to bring it up with Harry in the morning.

"How are things between you?" she asked.

I licked my spoon, determined to get every last morsel of the cool iced confection. "Strange."

"Is he still disappointed that you misjudged him?"

"I feel as though we've moved past disappointment, but I don't know what we've moved on to. Whatever it is, it's not the same. I miss him. His friendship, I mean."

"And I'm sure he misses you."

"You mean my friendship."

"That too."

* * *

THE DINNER PARTY that night was a more intimate affair than the recent ones we'd attended. It was hosted by the Digbys, good friends of my aunt and uncle, and included other mutual family friends. Although the adult children were approximately the same age as Flossy, Floyd and me, no one was attempting to pair us off in marriage, although they'd once tried to match me to Edward Caldicott. They'd failed and not tried again. Without that pressure, we were able to enjoy a more relaxed dinner.

Even so, Aunt Lilian must have taken some of her tonic before we left. She was bright-eyed and alert, her conversation free-flowing, her laughter infectious. Small things gave away her overuse, however—the busy fingers toying with her pearls, the twitch of facial muscles, the dilated pupils.

The alertness didn't last long. By the time the women retired to the drawing room, she was listless, her energy waning, and the smiles were nowhere in sight. She refused to entertain an early departure, however, dismissing my suggestion with an irritated click of her tongue.

I joined Flossy and some of the younger women. Now that we were alone, without the hovering mothers and aunts, and after wine had loosened tongues, they were more inclined to gossip about girls they knew, and the gentlemen they liked.

Since they'd all liked Vernon Rigg-Lyon, and had begun to hear the stories whispered about him now that he was gone, the conversation soon gravitated in that direction. Flossy, bless her, encouraged it.

"I heard Miss Rivera, his mistress, showed up at the funeral," she said with the self-important air of someone with knowledge of a good secret.

Cora Druitt-Poore gasped. "How terribly gauche."

"Perhaps she remained outside." Flossy shrugged. "The point is, she was there."

Felicity Digby lifted a teacup to lips tilted with a sly smile, drawing everyone's attention. "I heard several girls were there, crying as if they'd lost their one true love." She lowered her voice. "Some were girls from good families; girls we know."

I found myself leaning closer, along with the rest of the group.

"Who else was crying?" whispered Cora. "Don't keep it to yourself, Felicity. Tell us."

Cora's younger sister, Mary, looked like she'd stopped breathing, she was so keen to know. "Yes, you *must* say, Felicity."

"Victoria Canning," Felicity said. "Harriet Winterbottom, and Anne Dunkley."

A collective gasp from the group drew the attention of the mothers and aunts. All remained seated on the other side of the drawing room, however, except for Mrs. Mannering, eldest daughter of Lady Caldicott. Being married, she tended to gravitate towards her mother's group of friends, but she was only a few years older than me, and sometimes she joined the younger set. Of all the daughters of Aunt Lilian's friends, I found her the most sensible.

She wanted to know what we were gossiping about, so Flossy told her.

She promptly sat on the sofa, her grave face a contrast to those of the giggling girls around us.

"What is it?" I asked her.

She glanced at the group of older women, but they'd resumed their own discussion and paid us no mind. "Vernon Rigg-Lyon was an awful man. I was as guilty as anyone of placing him on a pedestal when he was alive, but now I've learned a few truths and I've changed my opinion of him."

"What truths?" Cora asked.

Mrs. Mannering spread her fingers across her lap. "He took advantage of young ladies."

"Who?" Flossy blurted out.

"It's not my place to say."

Mary gasped. "It was those girls who were crying at the funeral, wasn't it?"

Cora screwed her nose up at her little sister. "Don't be silly. If he took advantage of them, they wouldn't be crying with sorrow. They'd be rejoicing over his death."

Mrs. Mannering nodded. "Those girls at the funeral were clearly silly innocents. The girls I'm referring to were thoroughly ruined by him. So much so that they haven't reappeared in society since their downfall."

Mary frowned. "I don't understand. What happened to them? Why can't they attend balls and the like?"

Everyone looked to her older sister. Cora sighed and turned to Mary. "He got them…in the family way."

Mary's frown deepened. "How? They weren't married."

"Cora will explain later," Flossy said impatiently. To Mrs. Mannering, she said, "How do you know that was the reason for their disappearance from society?"

"I can't be certain. It's all merely gossip, but now that he's gone, it's surprising how many people want to talk about his wicked ways. I've considered all the facts, the timing, and I think most of the gossip is true."

"Anyone we know?" Felicity asked with a gleam in her eye.

"Not personally. Don't look so bloodthirsty," Mrs. Mannering chided. "It's awful what he did to them. Particularly if one believes the rumor that one of the ruined girls was so distressed that she took her own life."

The news doused everyone's enthusiasm and put an end to the giggles and gossip.

Mrs. Mannering rose. "Let it be a lesson to you all. Even handsome paragons like Vernon Rigg-Lyon can have a sinister side. You must always be on your guard, and never meet with a gentleman in private, no matter how much you want to."

She walked off and rejoined the older women, just as the gentlemen returned to the drawing room smelling of cigar smoke and port.

I spent the rest of the night wondering if Mrs. Mannering's reason for imparting gossip was to frighten the young ladies enough that they'd discourage the advances of over-eager gentlemen. Perhaps she'd even made up the stories about Rigg-Lyon's string of ruined girls for the purpose of warning them against his kind.

Even as the thought occurred to me, I knew in the pit of my stomach she told the truth about the girl who'd taken her own life. I suspected I knew who, although I fervently hoped I was wrong.

There was only one way to find out.

When it came time to say goodnight, I took Mrs. Mannering's hand and separated her from the others. "The girl you spoke of earlier...was it Major Leavey's daughter?"

Her eyes widened. "How did you know?"

"Are you sure she took her own life? She didn't die of illness?"

"I'm as sure as anyone can be when the source of information is third-hand rumor." She glanced past me, then drew me even further away from the others. "No one knows whether she killed herself because he didn't love her or because she fell pregnant to him. I'm not sure it really matters. Either way, she discovered he was horrid."

"Are you sure Vernon Rigg-Lyon was the gentleman involved?"

"That I am certain about. Apparently she confided in her best friend in the weeks leading up to her death." She sighed. "The poor girl, to feel as though the only way out was to take her own life, and the man responsible gets away without so much as a smear on his character."

Not quite. He'd been murdered. Was he killed because he ruined Major Leavey's daughter's reputation, driving her to her death?

I couldn't be entirely certain if the major was the murderer, but I did know one thing now—he'd written the threatening note to Hardwick, because he assumed Hardwick knew what Rigg-Lyon had done. In his mind, Hardwick was complicit in his daughter's downfall.

He was probably right.

CHAPTER 15

$\mathcal{A}$ glance into the hotel foyer when I reached the base of the stairs the following morning showed that little had improved from the day before. My uncle and Mr. Hobart were trying to placate frustrated guests who needed transportation, but it seemed to be doing little good. I overheard one gentleman say this wouldn't happen at the Savoy. After Uncle Ronald had a quiet word, the guest seemed to calm down a little. I wondered if he'd been offered a discount on his next stay.

When the front door opened, I was surprised to see Peter was the one opening it. Frank and the other doorman were nowhere in sight, and the porters were too busy moving luggage.

If I went that way, I was in danger of being enlisted to help, so I avoided the foyer altogether by slipping out of the hotel via the staff entrance that led to the lane. I sidestepped a lettuce that had fallen off a delivery cart and been left for the stray cats to nibble and made my way to Piccadilly where I dodged traffic to cross to the other side.

It was a warm day with dark clouds on the horizon, hinting at an afternoon thunderstorm. It was the sort of day where my hair would turn wild if not tightly arranged, and my skin would feel sticky in a few hours. Having failed to look out of the window before leaving my suite, I'd not taken a fan or umbrella with me, and the parasol was pointless, given the sun was hiding behind a bank of clouds.

I slotted it into Harry's umbrella stand when I arrived at his office. "I know who wrote the note to Hardwick, and why."

He seemed not to be listening. He stood and rounded the desk to pull the chair out for me. "Do you need water? You look flushed." He picked up a newspaper and flapped it in front of my face.

I removed my gloves—it was too hot to wear them anyway—and touched my cheek with the back of my hand. "It's humid outside." I took the newspaper from him and fanned myself. "Did you hear what I said?"

"You know who wrote the note to Hardwick. Go on then, who is it?"

"Major Leavey." I waited for that to sink in then added, "His daughter took her own life after Rigg-Lyon ruined her."

He sat on the edge of the desk. "Bloody hell. Are you sure?"

"Almost positive."

He tilted his head to the side. "Gossip?"

I nodded. "I think the major realized Hardwick knew what his best friend had done. He thinks he's somewhat to blame because he didn't stop Rigg-Lyon."

"It fits with the style of the threat. I can see the major challenging a scoundrel to a duel. It also fits with the timing. When we brought up the doping issue the other day at the club, the major was there. He would have heard us suggest that Hardwick knew everything Rigg-Lyon did. He must have decided then and there that Hardwick also knew Rigg-Lyon seduced his daughter."

"Then he sent the note to Hardwick yesterday," I added. "Do you think Hardwick knew who sent it?"

"There's only one way to find out. Let's ask him."

* * *

Unfortunately, Mr. Hardwick wasn't at home and his landlady didn't know when he'd return. Instead of waiting, we decided to call on the other man in the equation. Knowing

Major Leavey's work ethic, we suspected we'd find him at the Elms Polo Club, even though it was Sunday.

Harry hailed a cab and we traveled there in silence. Although the tension between us wasn't as fraught as it had been, it was still there, as ominous as the gray clouds overhead. Relief would only come when it burst, but I dreaded being caught in the downpour.

As we crossed the lawn, we heard a shout coming from the clubhouse, followed by another in response. The angry voices were familiar, and not unexpected.

"You knew!" I heard the major shout. "You knew and did nothing to stop him!"

"I wasn't his keeper!" Mr. Hardwick shouted back.

"Sir," added a third voice, that of Watkins, the major's assistant. "Please leave!"

We both started to run, but Harry's long strides meant he easily outpaced me. He took the steps three at a time and rushed inside. By the time I entered the clubhouse foyer, he'd stepped between the two men, arms outstretched to keep them apart. Watkins stood to one side, looking relieved that the role of mediator had been filled by someone else.

Major Leavey may have been the older of the two, but he looked formidable with veins bulging on his neck and his fists raised to fight. If he decided to charge at Hardwick, I wasn't sure Harry could hold him back. The situation needed defusing, and quickly.

"Mr. Hardwick, why are you here?" I asked.

He pointed a finger at the major. "He invited me. I think he's going to shoot me."

"He's unarmed," Harry growled.

I turned to the major. "Why did you invite him? To have it out with him?"

The major lowered his fists but kept them balled. "He knew what Rigg-Lyon did, and that makes him just as evil."

Mr. Hardwick made a scoffing sound.

"He needs to be held accountable for my...my..." All of a sudden, the major's face crumpled. He turned away, a hand pressed to his mouth, eyes screwed shut.

I touched his arm, but he shook me off.

Mr. Hardwick sniffed. "What happened to your daughter

was not my fault. But clearly you believe Vernon was responsible. Did you challenge him to a duel, too? Or did you ambush him in the stables like a coward?"

The major spun around and swung his fist. Harry caught his arm and they tussled, until Harry wrestled him back, out of reach of Hardwick. Watkins was no help. He took another step farther away.

The major's chest heaved and the veins in his neck throbbed. His glare drilled into Hardwick, but Hardwick merely tugged on his cuffs as if he didn't have a care.

"If anyone had a reason to kill him, it was probably you," the major snarled.

"Me? We were best friends!"

"You were jealous of him. He was better than you at everything. You were always in his shadow, always playing second fiddle, and it ate at you, didn't it? *Didn't it?*"

Mr. Hardwick's chuckle sounded forced. "You know nothing about us."

"But *we* do," I said.

Both men turned to me. "I suppose you're going to accuse me of doping the horses again?" Mr. Hardwick sneered.

"Yes, and this time we have a motive, as well as a motive for you killing Rigg-Lyon, and it's not jealousy."

Mr. Hardwick planted his hands on his hips and arched his brows, challenging me to present evidence.

"As agent to your father's business, you wanted to make a name for yourself. You decided to put Panther and Leopard up for sale. You were considering retiring anyway. You talked Rigg-Lyon into following suit and selling his horse alongside yours. You needed Panther to make a splash. As the better horse, he'd be the one to garner all the attention. But first, you needed to make them the best polo horses on the market. So you decided on one last season in which Panther and Leopard would be the stars. You achieved success by doping them before matches."

"Vernon doped Panther. Not me, and not Leopard."

The major snorted. "Everyone knows you two were joined at the hip. Where he went, you followed."

"At the end of the season, Rigg-Lyon decided he wasn't retiring, and nor was Panther," I went on. "I saw you on the day he announced it, the day of his murder. You were angry, because it put an end to a scheme you'd been planning for some time, and would result in much less money for you."

"I didn't own Panther. He did. *He* would get the money for the sale of Panther, not me."

"Panther came from your father's stables. He was sired by your father's own horse, and would probably attract a record sale price for a polo horse. Leopard wouldn't. He was in his brother's shadow."

"Just as you were in Rigg-Lyon's," the major sneered.

"The attention the sale would bring to your family's business was potentially enormous. As agent, you would reap the rewards too, of course, but it would bring worldwide acknowledgement for your parents' stud farm. Withdrawing Panther from the auction was devastating. It made you angry when you heard. Were you angry enough to kill your best friend, Mr. Hardwick?"

"No! Good Lord, it wasn't me! I was here, in the privy." He waved at the door that led to the restaurant. "I told you that."

"No one saw you leave," Harry said. "You don't have an alibi."

I frowned. "Where is the privy?"

"Through the restaurant," Watkins said.

"Not here, off the foyer?"

He shook his head.

"But in the minutes before the murder, the restaurant was busy. Everyone was cleaning up. When you told us you were in the privy and saw no one when you left, I thought it was located off the foyer since this area was empty at the time. But if you came out of the privy at the back of the restaurant, then you needed to walk through the restaurant to leave. Is that so?"

Watkins' sharp intake of breath was the only sound. "He would have been seen."

Mr. Hardwick swallowed.

"You claimed you saw no one, so no one could have seen you and given you an alibi," I said.

Mr. Hardwick glanced at the exit. I moved to stand in the way of his escape.

"Where were you really?" Harry asked.

"I can't recall," Mr. Hardwick said with a sniff.

The major stabbed a finger in his direction. "You murdered Rigg-Lyon. You must have, otherwise why lie? Arrest him, Armitage. Watkins, telephone the police."

Watkins moved to his desk, but Mr. Hardwick stepped in front of him. He grabbed Watkins' jacket and scrunched it in his fist. Watkins tried to smack the hand away, but Mr. Hardwick was bigger and stronger.

"It wasn't me!" Mr. Hardwick shouted. "I didn't kill him. I admit I lied about being in the privy, but that doesn't mean I murdered Vernon. He was my friend. My very good, dear friend...I would never hurt him. I loved him." His voice cracked and tears welled in his eyes. He let Watkins go and rubbed the back of his neck while he struggled to regain his composure.

"Tell us where you were really," I said. "Do you have an alibi?"

He closed his eyes and nodded. "I was ensuring one of the grooms kept quiet about the doping. I didn't tell you because I didn't want you thinking I was involved. If it gets out, it'll ruin me."

"Bert?" Harry asked.

Mr. Hardwick nodded. "All the grooms knew, but he was being the most difficult about it."

"*All* the grooms?" I asked.

"They had to know. We had to enlist their help to inject the horses. They'd known all season. If any of them tell you they didn't, they're lying. They all happily took our money. Except Bert. Money wasn't enough for him. Vernon had to resort to blackmail."

"He threatened to tell the major about the peepholes."

Mr. Hardwick nodded. "But Bert was wavering again that day."

"It was the final," the major said. "He's an Elms lad and wanted a fair match."

"He doesn't care about the club," Mr. Hardwick snapped. "He didn't care who won. He cared about the horses. On the day of the final, Panther was put in his care. He found the animal frothing at the mouth, listless, anxious. He didn't want to inject him again and refused. So I went to talk to him. I offered him money, but he wouldn't take it. I had to reiterate the threat Vernon already held over his head. If he didn't inject Panther, we'd tell the major about the peepholes."

"That was *before* the match," I pointed out. "Where were you afterwards, at the time of death?"

Mr. Hardwick cleared his throat. "I went to make sure Bert understood the consequences of telling anyone about the doping."

"The entire time? There was a twenty-minute window."

He looked away, his cheeks pink. "Ask him."

"We will."

The major's whiskers twitched with his bitter smile. "Your alibi will be thoroughly questioned. Your word can't be trusted. You're a liar, Hardwick, as well as a cheat. I will make sure the world knows it."

Mr. Hardwick dragged his hand through his hair. He didn't appeal to the major, he didn't attempt to talk him out of spreading the truth. He must have known it was hopeless. "My father's going to disown me. He had no part in this. He didn't know about the doping." He passed his hand over his face. When it came away, he looked ashen and close to tears. "He was always telling me to *do* something, to be better, like him. I was never good enough. I never made captain of the team, never won a championship until this year."

Now I could see what drove him. He wasn't in Rigg-Lyon's shadow; he was in his father's.

"My fortunes would have turned around after the auction. Not just mine, but the entire family's. He would have been proud."

"Until he found out you doped the horses in order to win," the major said. "Did you think no one would know? What excuse would you give when the horses failed to perform after they were sold?"

Mr. Hardwick shrugged. "They were pining for us?"

The major's bitter laugh echoed around the foyer. "You fool. You deserve everything that's coming to you when word of this spreads."

"Don't tell anyone." Mr. Hardwick pressed his palms together. "I beg you, Major. Don't ruin me. I didn't know anything about your daughter, I swear. She was just one of many girls he—"

Mr. Hardwick didn't see the major's fist until it was too late and it hit him square in the jaw. He stumbled, clutching the side of his face, but wisely kept his mouth shut.

The major shook out his hand, then strode up to Mr. Hardwick. The younger man cowered. "Get out or I will have you thrown out!"

I suspected Harry was the one who was supposed to play security guard, but he simply stood by and watched, just as he'd done nothing to stop the major punching Mr. Hardwick. He'd been close enough to intervene, and his reflexes were quick, but he'd kept his hands at his sides.

Mr. Hardwick lowered his head and left the clubhouse of his own accord.

Watkins returned to the reception desk while the major headed to his office. Harry and I followed. Harry closed the door behind us for privacy.

The major stood behind his desk and stared out of the window into the distance. "How did you find out about my daughter and Rigg-Lyon?"

"A sympathetic source told me," I said. "I don't think many know."

He picked up the framed photograph of his family, the one in which his daughter was a young woman. "This was taken six months before she..." He drew in a shuddery breath. "She drowned. Fell out of a boat on a lake. She couldn't swim."

"We're so sorry," I said.

"The coroner's report stated it was an accident, that it was no one's fault. My wife agrees with the verdict. It's better than the alternative, that she deliberately..." He cleared his throat. "The thing is, she took the dinghy out on her own. Her shoes were found in the boat, placed together beside her folded jacket with her hat on top."

The coroner had been kind to record the verdict as accidental for Mrs. Leavey's sake.

The major returned the photograph to the table. "I know what you're thinking. That I killed Rigg-Lyon when I learned about his relationship with my daughter. But I didn't. God knows I thought about it, but I'm no murderer."

"Did you send him a threatening letter too?" Harry asked.

"No. I thought he might retaliate by spreading lies about her, so I refrained. After he died, I wished I had. That's why, when I realized Hardwick must have known, I sent one to him."

I believed him. Yet there was one thing still troubling me. "Why did you take the ribbon from Rigg-Lyon's pocket?"

He didn't try to deny it this time. "I suspected it belonged to a girl who gave it to him as a love token. It was such a distinctive color that I worried she'd be easily identified if the details were leaked to the press. I didn't want her honor besmirched. The police investigation struck me as incompetent from day one, so I never regretted my hasty decision. Whoever she is, she didn't deserve to pay the price for trusting Rigg-Lyon's lies."

Neither I nor Harry informed the major that the woman who gave the ribbon to Mr. Rigg-Lyon was his mistress, and she was aware of his fickle nature. We didn't want to diminish the good deed he thought he'd done for her.

We thanked him and went in search of Bert to confirm Mr. Hardwick's alibi. Outside, we waded through the darkly brooding air towards the stables and tack room. Lightning brightened the horizon and moments later, thunder rolled in, bringing with it a sense of inevitability.

We were on the cusp of solving the case. I could feel it as clearly as I could feel the sweat dampening my back.

We found Bert in the tack room, rubbing polish into a saddle. He was alone. His cheeks pinked before we'd even asked a question. I suppose having his secret exposed was embarrassing enough, but to have it exposed in such a public fashion was even worse. I suspected he also knew we were about to bring it up again.

I left the questioning to Harry this time. "Hardwick claims he was with you between three-fifty and four-ten on the day of the murder. Is that true?"

Bert's eyes widened. "He told you? Am I going to prison?"

"Was he with you?" Harry pressed.

Bert nodded quickly. "We were in the woods, behind a tree."

I frowned. "The entire twenty minutes? That seems longer than necessary."

Bert choked and his face flamed. It was then that I realized what Harry had already guessed. That Mr. Hardwick hadn't met with Bert to remind him what would happen if he told anyone about the doping. They'd met to be intimate.

"Did you see a brown-coated man there?" Harry asked.

"I saw Mr. Broadman's cousin," Bert said. "And a woman."

Harry and I exchanged glances. Then my heart sank. There could only be one reason Mr. Liddicoat met with a woman in the woods.

"Was she tall?" I asked hopefully.

Bert shook his head.

My heart plunged further. Poor Miss Hessing.

Harry thanked him and we trudged to the gate, neither of us speaking. We were lost in our own thoughts. So much so that we'd forgotten about the impending storm until a streak of lightning and a thunderclap signaled its unleashing.

A few fat drops of rain fell as a warning then, as if the clouds could no longer carry the heavy load, it came down in a torrent. Even if we'd brought umbrellas, they wouldn't have helped. We were soaked within seconds.

Harry grabbed my hand and we ran towards the gate where a taxi that had just deposited passengers was about to pull away from the curb. The driver saw our frantic signaling and stopped. Harry assisted me on board and sat beside me as the coach lurched forward.

He removed his hat and shook it. It had provided no protection. Water dripped off his hair, down his face, and into his collar. I resisted the urge to stroke the strands plastered to his forehead, and plucked at my wet skirts, stuck to my legs. My hat felt off-kilter and some of my hair had come loose from the arrangement and fell past my shoulders, becoming conduits for drips to soak my back. I must look a sight.

Harry clearly thought so, too, because when I suddenly looked at him, I caught him about to fix my hat. He changed course and instead removed a handkerchief from his breast pocket. He offered it to me.

I unfolded it and held up the sodden square of material. It was too wet to be of use. For some inexplicable reason, we both thought it was the most ridiculous thing. We laughed. We laughed harder than the silly situation warranted.

And it felt wonderful.

When I arrived at the hotel, I felt lighter than I had in days. Seeing the harried staff and frustrated guests no longer worried me. Not even my uncle's scowl at my sorry state bothered me. I smiled, gave him a cheerful wave, and continued on my way, leaving a trail of drips on the foyer's tiles.

I removed my wet clothes in my suite and dried off. My hair wasn't so easily or quickly dried, so I left it loose and dressed in a simple skirt and white cotton blouse. I had a few hours to spare before my afternoon tea engagement with Flossy and Aunt Lilian.

Harry and I hadn't discussed our next steps in the investigation, so I was about to settle down at the desk to write notes when there was a brisk knock on the door. I opened it to see Harmony standing there.

"Thank goodness you're here, Cleo! Goliath said he saw you return, but I wasn't sure if you'd left again." She spoke rapidly and could barely contain her smile.

"You look like you have interesting gossip to impart. Dare I hope it's regarding the investigation?"

She dug into her apron pocket. "I think I've found the clue that will solve it." She pulled out a coral ribbon and dangled it in front of my face. "Is this the same color ribbon you found on the victim's body?"

I fingered the silk material. It was the same shade and texture as Rosa Rivera's ribbons. If it was in Harmony's possession, it meant she'd found it here in the hotel when she was cleaning rooms.

But why would one of Rosa's ribbons be here? Who had she given the love token to? And what did it mean for our investigation?

"Where did you get it?"

"I found it tied around one of the room's door handles. I'll show you."

She led me along the corridor and down the service stairs to the second floor. The guest rooms on this level were just single rooms and not all of them had *en suites* attached. The rate was cheaper than the larger rooms, but it was still too expensive for most people.

They were too expensive for Rosa Rivera, but not if someone paid for it on her behalf.

Harmony's housekeeping cart was parked outside room 221. She retied the ribbon around the handle and pointed to the DO NOT DISTURB sign hanging there. Her discreet but rather rude hand gesture made it clear what she thought was going on behind the closed door. Knowing what I knew about the hotel's comings and goings, I suspected she was right. While it was never discussed by members of my family, it was obvious that the hotel was sometimes used as a place for clandestine rendezvous between a gentleman guest and his mistress. Inviting a common whore to one's room was never condoned, but mistresses were a different matter, as long as discretion was maintained.

"Whose room is this?" I whispered.

She shrugged. With her finger to her lips, she indicated I should hide behind the large potted plant at the end of the corridor while she continued her cleaning rounds.

I waited and watched. Most guests were out during the day so few people came and went. I began to wonder if room 221 was occupied at all, but finally, the door opened. A middle-aged man's head poked through the gap.

He looked left and right along the corridor then, thinking no one was in the vicinity, emerged from the room. He turned and smiled to the person still inside then walked off, away from me.

I recognized him.

Suddenly, everything began to click into place.

CHAPTER 16

I watched from the safety of my hiding spot behind the potted palm as a woman's hand snaked around the door of room 221 and untied the ribbon from the handle. I didn't need to see her to know it was Rosa. I had no doubt the ribbon belonged to her. She was using it as a signal to tell her lover where to meet her.

Her current lover being Lord Dunmere, owner of a fast automobile.

I went in search of Harmony and found her cleaning the last room on level two. "Rosa Rivera is having a relationship with Lord Dunmere," I said as I helped her make the bed.

She straightened, frowning. "Is he the murderer? It would be a shame if he is."

"Why?"

"I hear he's a nice man. Very wealthy, too. No wonder Rosa went from Rigg-Lyon to him."

"I think their relationship started before Rigg-Lyon died. Or perhaps soon afterward. Either way, I don't think he's the murderer. I don't think he played a part at all." I lowered my voice, even though we were alone. "*She* killed Rigg-Lyon."

Harmony gasped. "She used his automobile to transport her from the theater to the Elms and back again!" She frowned and shook her head. "That can't be right. *You* borrowed his automobile that day."

"That's why we never considered that vehicle. But while

206

we enjoyed our picnic and the polo, it was available for a few hours. I think the driver returned to London and collected Rosa from the Royal Albert Hall after her fitting, then sped to the Elms. By then, the match was over, or almost over. She waited for the initial flurry of activity at the stables to be completed then lured Rigg-Lyon to the stables by tying her ribbon somewhere visible. It's her signal to her lovers, to show where she is and that she's available."

"A nice touch, and discreet too."

"Then she murdered him and departed in a cab. She couldn't have gone back to London in Dunmere's automobile because we needed it. It had broken down and we were waiting for the mechanic to fix it when we heard Mr. Broadman's shout upon discovering the body. The reason it broke down in the first place is because the engine overheated when the mechanic sped back to the Elms with Rosa in the passenger seat. It needed time to cool down before it would work again."

"Is the driver guilty, too?"

I hesitated, thinking it through. Finally, I shook my head. "I don't think so, but I do think he holds the key to solving this. We need to speak to him."

While Harmony took her cleaning cart back to the basement storeroom, I asked the clerk at the front desk who was paying for room 221. His answer confirmed my suspicion—Lord Dunmere. He was currently paying for two rooms, one for himself where he could come and go at will, and room 221 which he'd paid in advance for two nights.

I rejoined Harmony in the service corridor and we left the hotel via the exit near the kitchen. It was no longer raining, but puddles had formed on the road and a rivulet trickled in the gutter. We dodged the water and mud, and were careful to hide our faces as we passed the hotel's front door on the way to the mews.

There was a risk that Lord Dunmere was using his automobile, but we found the mechanic in the stables, asleep in the front seat, his feet on the dashboard, ankles and arms crossed. He was alone, aside from the horses. The stables and adjoining coach house were otherwise empty, with Cobbit and the rest of the staff on strike.

I cleared my throat. "Excuse me. May we have a word?"

The mechanic's eyes flew open and he quickly got out of the automobile. "My apologies, Miss Fox. I didn't see you there. I was busy inspecting the, um…"

"Backs of your eyelids?" I smiled to put him at ease. "This is Miss Cotton. Do you mind if we ask you some questions?"

"Are you still investigating the murder? I thought you might have given up."

"We're still investigating."

"Right you are. How may I help?"

"Do you recall the day of the murder, when you had to fix the automobile before you could drive us home?"

He removed his cap and scratched the side of his head. "I remember. The engine overheated."

"Why did it overheat?"

"It does that sometimes, if it's a warm day and it's been on a long drive. The water needed to keep it cool dries up." He jerked his thumb at the rear of the vehicle, where the engine was housed under the back seat. "Do you want me to show you?"

"It's all right. I wouldn't know what I was looking at."

He shrugged. "Once it cooled down, it was fine."

"Why had it overheated? It was some hours since you'd driven us to the Elms. Did you go somewhere else?"

"Aye. I had to collect a passenger in London and take her to the Elms. His lordship asked me to drive his, er, friend to the polo. She had to deliver something."

"Do you know her name?"

"Miss Rivera. She's a singer. I collected her from the Royal Albert Hall."

"Do you know what she was delivering to the Elms?"

He shook his head. "She didn't say. We didn't talk much. You know what it's like, with the wind whipping past your ears. It's real hard to have a conversation. All I know is, she carried a bag with her but when I saw her again later, it looked empty."

"You saw her again as she was leaving?"

"She caught a cab." He frowned. "Why all these questions about Miss Rivera? What's she got to do with the murder?"

I wasn't going to respond, but Harmony spoke up. "Did you know who her lover was before Lord Dunmere?"

He feigned shock at her question, but neither Harmony nor I showed any coquettishness, so he stopped pretending to be offended. "No, miss. I know these London singers have certain reputations, but I don't keep up with the gossip. I don't know who folk are unless they're a close acquaintance of his lordship, so it means nothing to me. Why? Who was he? And what's all this got to do with the murder?"

Harmony and I exchanged what I thought were subtle glances, but the mechanic was observant.

His frown deepened. "Blimey. Is she involved somehow? She's not the murderer, though. She can't be."

"Why not?" I asked.

He looked at us askance. "Because she's a woman."

Harmony bristled. "You don't think women are capable of murder?"

"You misunderstand. The police reckon a man killed that polo player. It's been all over the papers. They're looking for witnesses who saw a *man* leave the Elms that afternoon. He was wearing a brown coat and hat. They have a witness who saw him there but want to find the cab driver who picked him up."

I sighed. The police truly had been incompetent. Not only were they still hoping to find a cab driver who collected a man wearing a brown coat and hat, they hadn't even considered the fact the hat and coat could have been discarded or that a woman wore them.

"You mentioned seeing Miss Rivera leave the polo club," I said. "Are you sure her bag was empty?"

He nodded. "When she got out of my motor, she used two hands and it was bulging." He indicated the size of the bag with his hands. It wasn't overly big, but big enough to carrying a coat and hat. "When she walked through the gate to leave, she carried it in one hand while she dusted it off with the other. There was no bulge."

The reason the police couldn't find a cab driver who'd picked up the coat-wearing murderer was because the murderer had discarded the coat at the crime scene. But we'd not found it in the stables. The police might be incompetent, but even they would have found a brown coat if there was one there to be found.

"What time exactly did you collect Miss Rivera from Royal Albert Hall?" Harmony asked.

The mechanic scratched his head. "It was supposed to be three-thirty. I was on time but had to wait five minutes. We arrived at the Elms a little before four."

I thanked him and we made to leave, but I doubled back. The mechanic hadn't moved. He still stood by the automobile, frowning. "Don't mention this to anyone," I told him. "Not even Lord Dunmere."

He gave me a lazy salute. "Right you are, Miss Fox."

"And one other thing. Do you know where Miss Rivera lives?"

"I do. I collected her from there yesterday, and I'm to take her back there in an hour, before driving her to the Royal Albert later for her performance."

"May I have the address?"

A few minutes later, Harmony and I exited the mews onto Piccadilly. Instead of returning to the hotel, we walked to the address the mechanic had given us. Rosa Rivera lived on the ground floor of a modern block of flats overlooking a small grassy common. I wondered if Mr. Rigg-Lyon paid for it, but dismissed the notion. If he did, she was unlikely to have murdered him.

I was now almost positive she was the murderer. I still lacked a motive, however, as well as evidence that would convince both the police and a jury.

The door to the flat was locked and I didn't want to be seen attempting to pick the lock in broad daylight. Harmony suggested we try the window around the side. It was hidden by a tree and, as it turned out, the lock was flimsier. I used the slender tools I always carried with me nowadays and picked it in a matter of minutes.

Getting through the window was not quite as easy, and much less elegant. Both Harmony and I were too short to simply climb in, so she suggested giving me a boost. She linked her fingers together and formed a cradle for me to step into. With a grunt, she lifted me up and pushed me through the open window.

She shoved with such force that I sailed right through, knocked over a lamp on the table beneath the window, and tumbled onto the floor. Both the lamp base and I made loud thuds.

"Cleo? Are you all right?" Harmony loudly whispered.

I rubbed my elbow as I stood. "Yes."

Her face appeared at the window. "Grab my arms and haul me in."

I picked up a stool and passed it out to her. "Or you could step on this."

We knew from the mechanic that we had time before Rosa returned, so we were able to make a thorough inspection of the flat. We searched the bedroom first, looking through the wardrobe for a brown coat, in case she had brought it back with her, after all. We didn't find it, but did discover more coral ribbons in her dressing table drawer. There were no signs that she brought gentlemen to the flat, and there were no photographs of men either. There was some expensive jewelry and a box full of money, but no letters or tokens from lovers. There were no personal items that she'd kept to remind her of Mr. Rigg-Lyon. She'd told the truth when she said she didn't love him. She hadn't cared enough to keep even a single photograph of him. Jealousy wasn't a motive, then. One had to care about a man to be jealous of his other lovers.

Harmony and I moved into the only other room in the flat. It was larger than the bedroom. At one end was a small kitchen, while at the other was the sitting room where we'd entered via the window. It contained only a sofa, no armchairs, and a cabinet with books and a shelf of trinket boxes of various sizes. While I inspected the boxes, Harmony looked around the kitchen.

"Cleo, I've found something."

I joined her at the bench where she held a small bottle made of purple glass. She held it out to me. "Smell it."

I sniffed. "Is it mint?"

She tipped a little of the oil on her finger and rubbed it with her thumb. "Pennyroyal. You know what that means."

"No. What?"

"Oil of pennyroyal is used to get rid of an unborn child."

I gasped. "She was pregnant to Rigg-Lyon."

She replaced the stopper in the neck of the bottle. "It can be dangerous for the woman if taken in large doses. Even in small doses, it can leave her feeling quite unwell. She must have been desperate to take this."

"That's if she has taken it at all. She didn't seem unwell when we saw her, and she wouldn't have met with Lord Dunmere today if she was sick." I took the bottle from her and held it up to the light. "Perhaps she decided to keep the baby. That explains why the dressmaker at the Royal Albert Hall was altering her outfits. Her waistline was expanding."

Harmony took back the bottle and returned it to the cupboard shelf where she found it. "If she decided to keep it, and Rigg-Lyon was the father, why kill him? She'd need him to help financially. She couldn't do it alone. She'd have to give up performing when she started to show. So why murder her best source of income?"

"Because he wasn't a source of income. He refused to support her."

It was a tragic story, but it was the motive we'd been searching for. Now we needed to find the proof.

I climbed onto the table near the window and peered out to make sure no one was watching. I got the fright of my life when Harry peered back at me.

He grinned that wicked grin of his. He somehow knew I was in here and had been waiting for me to re-emerge. "Need assistance?"

"No." I put one leg out through the window, but the stool was too low for me to reach. Drat. Either I backed out through the window, both feet first and lowered myself, or I accepted his help. The first option was unladylike and had great potential for embarrassment. The second option required him to touch me. "Yes, please."

I sat on the windowsill, legs dangling outside, and placed my hands on his shoulders. He reached up and clasped my waist, lifting me off the sill. He slowly lowered me to the ground, holding me closer than necessary and taking his time. A thrill shot through me when my chest pressed against his. The heat in his eyes warmed my own when our gazes connected.

Harmony cleared her throat, and Harry released me to assist her.

"How did you know we'd be here?" she asked him.

"The mechanic told me. He said you discovered Rosa Rivera had become Lord Dunmere's mistress, but he didn't say how you knew. He told me what he'd told you about collecting her from the Royal Albert Hall and driving her to the Elms, then mentioned he gave you Rosa's address." He glanced over his shoulder at the block of flats as we crossed the grassy common. "It was a risk coming here in broad daylight. What if she was home?"

"We knew she wouldn't be here," I said. "She's at the hotel."

"Ah. That's how you knew she was Dunmere's mistress."

"How did you know to go to the mews in the first place?"

"Never mind that. You've found something. I can tell by the gleam in your eyes."

Harmony explained about the oil of pennyroyal and what it was used for. Neither Harry nor I asked how she knew. Harmony had been raised in a slum, and the girls brought up in that environment had a wisdom that was beyond book-learning. Experience had taught her things I would never know.

"We think she killed Rigg-Lyon because he wouldn't support her and the baby," I said. "But we won't know for certain unless she admits it."

He removed his watch from his waistcoat pocket. "She'll be back at the flat soon before she heads off to the Royal Albert. We could wait and confront her."

"She'll only deny it. We need proof. We need to find the coat in her possession."

Harmony sighed. "But we looked everywhere."

"It won't be in the flat. The mechanic says he saw her leaving the Elms with the same bag she brought with her, but it was empty. She lifted it with two hands when she climbed out of his vehicle, but carried it with only one when she left." I stopped suddenly as something the mechanic had said occurred to me. "Her other hand was dusting it off. She would only need to dust it off if it were dirty."

Harmony shrugged. "So?"

Harry, who knew all the clues, came to the same conclusion as me. "She buried the coat and hat. She placed the bag on the ground as she dug the hole and it got dirty. She probably took a garden spade with her, then brought it home in the bag."

"She must have discarded it," I said, absently. "We didn't see one in the flat."

Harmony sighed. "Then you'll never find the hat and coat. The Elms estate is big, isn't it?"

"Enormous." I smiled. "But we have an area to focus on. Mr. Liddicoat told us he saw a man dressed in a brown coat and hat in the vicinity of the stables, but changed his story when we realized he couldn't see the stables from there. He then told us the truth—that he saw the man in the woods where he was walking. I worried he was lying about the whole thing, but he wasn't. He was wrong about it being a man, however. It was Rosa, dressed in a man's clothing. Then this morning, Bert mentioned seeing a woman and Mr. Liddicoat when he was in the woods around the time of the murder. I assumed he meant the woman was *with* Mr. Liddicoat, but I recall now he said he saw Mr. Liddicoat *and* a woman."

Harry nodded slowly as he followed along. "I worried about that, too, thinking I'd missed something in my investigation of him. He seemed so decent, so honest, and there'd been no hint of a woman in his life other than Miss Hessing. Then Bert said he saw him with a woman, so I thought I was wrong. But I wasn't. It's as you say, Cleo, Bert never said he saw Liddicoat *with* a woman, just that he saw them both in the woods. He must have meant he saw them separately."

"Why didn't you clarify with him this morning?" Harmony asked.

I bit my lip and lowered my gaze. "I was distracted by what he'd just told us."

"Oh?"

"I'll explain later," I whispered.

Harry started walking again, his strides long and purposeful, leaving Harmony and me behind. "We have to find the coat and hat. I'll return to the Elms now."

I picked up my skirts and raced to catch up. "You're not going without me."

"You told me you have an afternoon tea."

"I have a dreadful headache that means I can't get out of bed. Harmony?"

"No need to ask," she said. "I'm already thinking up a reason to stop Miss Bainbridge from checking on you."

I looped my arm with hers and hugged it. "You are a good friend."

"Because I lie for you?"

"Because you protect me."

Beside me, Harry loudly cleared his throat.

While the situation wasn't entirely parallel to the way he protected me from Mr. Miller, I saw his point. I couldn't take his arm and hug it, so instead I cast him the ghost of a smile so that he knew everything was all right between us.

Where a lesser man might respond with a gloating smirk, he did not. He merely gave me the wisp of a relieved smile in return.

* * *

HARRY and I returned to his office to telephone Detective Forrester at Scotland Yard and brief him on our evidence. Although he wasn't in charge of this investigation, he was our best chance of convincing the incompetent detective who was that we ought to be taken seriously.

We met the police at the front gate of the Elms Polo Club. The detective, Fanning, insisted on speaking to the manager before we looked for the coat, so we went in search of Major Leavey, only to see him striding towards us, Watkins in tow. At first, I wondered how they knew we were there, then I realized they were leaving. It was nearing five o'clock.

"What is the meaning of this?" the major bellowed.

Detective Fanning did a poor job of explaining why his men carried shovels, so it was left to Harry and me to fill in the gaps.

"We'll need to speak to Bert," I finished. "He can tell us precisely where he saw the woman."

Watkins went to fetch him from the stables and returned with both Bert and Robbie.

"Why didn't you tell the police you were in the woods at the time of the murder?" the major asked him as we walked.

Detective Fanning growled in agreement. "You could have saved us time if we knew we were looking for a woman."

Bert's face paled. "I, uh…"

"He never saw anyone wearing the coat," Harry pointed out. "So he didn't connect the woman he saw to the person Liddicoat saw. No one did."

"Not until we realized Rosa Rivera was a viable suspect," I added.

Bert quickened his pace, then stopped near a large beech tree. He waved in the general vicinity of some smaller trees. "Around there. She was heading in that direction." He pointed to the right. "Then she looked over her shoulder before leaving the woods altogether."

We all spread out across the area Bert indicated, and it wasn't long before Harry called out that he'd found something. We crowded around, the constables ready with their shovels. They weren't needed. The heavy rain had washed away the leaves and soil to reveal a corner of fabric. Detective Fanning tugged on it and pulled out the entire coat, dislodging more soil in the process and revealing the crown of a bowler hat.

The front of the coat was splattered with blood.

It was a satisfying outcome, and proved that not only did Mr. Liddicoat tell the truth, but the police had wasted their time by looking for a cab driver. It didn't prove that Rosa Rivera killed Vernon Rigg-Lyon, but thankfully Detective Fanning was willing to interrogate her, given the mechanic's account proved she'd lied about where she was at the time of the murder.

As we left the Elms Polo Club estate, Detective Fanning turned to Harry. "You're Hobart's son?"

"That's right."

"Good detective, Hobart. Shame he was forced out of the Yard like that." He was kinder about D.I. Hobart than D.I. Hobart had been about him. "Travel with me to the Royal

Albert Hall and tell me again why you think Rosa Rivera is the killer."

"This is Miss Fox's investigation. She'll tell you everything you need to know."

"It's your investigation, too," I said.

"I was only involved because of my investigation into Liddicoat, and his link to Broadman. The murder was yours."

I stared at him. "But…are you at least coming to see Rosa arrested?"

"No need. You have it in hand. But I will accept a ride back into the city, thank you."

Nothing I said on the way back to London convinced him to come with us to the Royal Albert. He continued to insist it was my case and that I ought to be there, not him. It was infuriating. He'd been with me almost every step of the way, so why not see the investigation through to its conclusion?

We drove Harry to his office then continued on to the Hall. As we alighted from the carriage, Detective Fanning asked me to reiterate why I thought Rosa did it. "As Rigg-Lyon was her benefactor, didn't she need him alive, particularly if she was carrying his child?" He wasn't particularly bright, but at least he was willing to listen. Not every man in his position believed a lady detective could solve a murder.

"Let me do the talking and you'll find out," I told him.

It was still early. Rosa's performance wasn't due to begin for another two hours, but she and the other singers were there preparing. We found her alone in her dressing room, humming as she brushed her hair. The room was too small for all of us, so both constables remained outside while Detective Fanning and I spoke to her.

Rosa slowly lowered her brush to the dressing table. Her gaze met mine in the mirror's reflection then shifted to Detective Fanning at my side. He was too busy looking around at the clothing strewn about to notice. When he spotted the corset hanging over the privacy screen, he tugged on his collar and quickly looked away.

"Miss Fox. Detective. To what do I owe the pleasure this time?"

Detective Fanning cleared his throat. "You're under arrest for the murder of Vernon Rigg-Lyon. Come with me, please."

She rolled her eyes. "Don't be absurd. What proof do you have?"

Detective Fanning looked to me.

"You weren't here at the time of the murder," I said. "Lord Dunmere's mechanic drove you to the Elms."

"Ah. So you know about that. It's not what you think. I lied because I was worried you would assume I murdered Vernon. As his mistress, I was an obvious suspect. And clearly you do suspect me, so I was right to lie. Was I not, Detective?"

"We found the coat and hat you buried in the woods," he blurted out.

She hesitated ever so slightly before responding. "Did someone *see* me bury them?"

"No-o."

"Is that all your evidence?" She clicked her tongue. "I'm sorry you've come here for nothing, but you're welcome to stay for my performance. Speaking of which, I have a rehearsal on stage."

She rose and rested her hand on his arm, smiling gently. She was very beautiful, but there was something about her that transcended beauty. It was the regal tilt of her chin, the air of composure, coupled with a smoldering sensuality and a hint of vulnerability. The combination was compelling, alluring.

"May I rehearse?" She directed the question entirely to Detective Fanning. She knew I wouldn't fall under her spell.

It was clear from the way he stared at her, unblinking, that the detective had. He stepped aside to let her pass, earning a grateful smile from Rosa.

I moved to block her exit. "I felt sorry for you."

"Please, Miss Fox. I only want to perform for my audience. Performing is all I have, now that Vernon is gone."

"I felt sorry for you when you were in tears that day we came to question you. But you weren't crying for Rigg-Lyon. You were crying because you had to make a choice about the baby you carried. Keep it and raise it alone, without his financial help, or abort it."

Her lips parted in a gasp. "I didn't murder him, Miss Fox. I merely went to the polo that day to talk to him and tell him about the baby. I lied about going, and I shouldn't have. I know that now. But I was so ashamed."

"You didn't go there with the intention of telling him you were with child. He already knew. You told him when you called at his house after his wife went out. He was angry. Angry that you'd dared to show up there, and angry that you'd fallen pregnant. He didn't want the child, and he didn't want to marry you, even though he would be free to marry soon, given his wife was so ill."

She pressed a hand to her stomach. "You can't know any of that."

"The staff overheard you arguing." It wasn't quite the truth. The staff claimed they were arguing, but couldn't hear their words. Rosa didn't need to know that I was guessing, however. "His wife was dying, and he was childless. You could step into her shoes and raise the child together. But he didn't want that."

"This is pure speculation. It was merely a lovers' quarrel. I can't even recall what it was about now."

"It wasn't insignificant. You'd never called at his house before, so something important warranted your visit that time."

Rosa clasped Detective Fanning's arm and blinked back tears. "You can't believe her wild stories, sir. I'm innocent and I can prove it. But I must rehearse now and then prepare for the performance. Stay. Your men can keep watch over me to make sure I don't leave. Then afterwards, I'll prove to you I didn't kill Vernon."

The detective's gaze shifted to me.

She touched his cheek, gently forcing him to look only at her. "I admit I was at the polo club, but did anyone see me with a brown coat and man's hat? Did someone see me bury them?" When he didn't respond, she released him. "There is no proof that the coat and hat you found belong to me. Let me rehearse, Detective. Then I will prove that I didn't do it."

"Prove it now," I said. "If you can."

She ignored me and blinked at Detective Fanning. She still looked close to tears, but I suspected that was because she didn't have any proof, and she knew it.

But there was still hope for her. She was right about that.

We couldn't link the coat and hat to her. Without that proof, this performance could see her released if Detective Fanning believed her.

He moved aside. "We'll be watching you, Miss Rivera. Straight onto the stage and straight off afterward. Understood?"

"Understood. Thank you, Detective. You are a good man."

She grabbed a jacket off the back of her chair and put it on then left. The detective and constables followed her.

I sat on the chair at the dressing table and swore at my reflection. Rosa was going to get away with it.

CHAPTER 17

I looked around the dressing room at the wigs and elegant gown Rosa wore on stage and fingered the sticks of stage makeup she used. She didn't need makeup. She was beautiful without it, but I supposed it was necessary underneath the bright lights. The wigs, too, were for the shows. She had lovely natural black hair, but sometimes she had to play a character, hence the blonde wig or red-haired one.

She was good at playing characters. Detective Fanning believed her act of the innocent, vulnerable girl taken advantage of by Rigg-Lyon, a cad. A judge and jury might believe the act, too.

The dressmaker, Mrs. Warden, entered carrying a corset identical to the one hanging over the privacy screen. She hesitated upon seeing me. "Aren't you the private detective?"

"I am. Are you looking for Miss Rivera? She's rehearsing on stage."

"Now? But I have her costume ready. She was supposed to try it on before approving it."

"She said it's time for her final rehearsal."

She frowned. "She doesn't need a final rehearsal. She has performed this same show so many times, she knows it by heart."

I rose slowly. "That corset...did you have to let it out to accommodate her expanding waistline?"

She bit the inside of her lip.

"Never mind," I said. "I know she's with child." I indicated the clothing around the room. "Have any costume items gone missing lately?"

"A hat and coat. Why?"

My pulse quickened. "A brown coat?"

She nodded. "It hasn't been used for years, but I was looking for it recently to cut it up and use the material for wood nymph costumes." She looked around. "Is it in here?"

"No, but I know how you can get it back."

Rosa must have known we would realize Mrs. Warden was the key to linking her to the brown coat, and that it was only a matter of time before we talked to her. She must be desperate to delay her arrest by pretending to rehearse. Arrest was inevitable, however.

Unless she planned to escape

I grasped Mrs. Warden's shoulders. "Is there a trapdoor in the stage floor?"

"Yes. The performers emerge through it as if by magic during some shows."

"Can you show me the room underneath the stage, where the trapdoor leads to?"

I followed her along the corridor, down a set of stairs, along another, narrower corridor and through a door. The room was small and windowless, the only light coming from the electric globe in the corridor outside. I didn't want to turn on the light in the room itself. I didn't want anyone to know we were there.

Props painted to look like waves and a boat had been pushed to one side, but the only other structure in the room was a set of steps leading up to a raised platform that reached three feet below the trapdoor in the ceiling.

We were just in time. The trapdoor was flung open from above and Rosa jumped onto the platform, landing softly.

Detective Fanning shouted in the distance. "Where did she go?"

Rosa descended the steps without looking, only to stop when she came face to face with me.

"You're under arrest," I said.

She shoved me in the chest, but I'd been ready for the

attack and braced myself. I went to grab her, but Rosa stepped backward, tripping over the bottom step and landing on her bottom. She held on to the balustrade with one hand and the other clutched at her jacket.

I went to haul her to her feet. At the same time, she lashed out with a small knife. It must have been hidden in the jacket pocket. She struck the palm of my hand.

I hissed and drew my hand against my body to protect it, while kicking with my right foot. I connected with the blade, knocking it away, then I grabbed her wrist to stop her reaching for the knife.

Mrs. Warden grabbed Rosa's other wrist. Together, we hauled her to her feet.

Detective Fanning's face appeared through the trapdoor. "Ah, good, you stopped her."

His face disappeared, to be replaced by one constable dropping onto the platform then the other. They seized Rosa. She struggled and shouted at them in Spanish, then kicked one constable's shin. He hissed in pain, but held her firmly until she finally stopped struggling.

Detective Fanning joined us. "So you're guilty, after all, Miss Rivera. You almost had me fooled, but I outsmarted you by letting you think you could escape."

Mrs. Warden rolled her eyes, saving me from doing it.

"I am innocent!" Rosa spat.

"If you didn't run, I might have thought so, but now…"

I introduced him to Mrs. Warden, and she told him about the missing coat and hat from the costume department. Their description matched the items uncovered in the woods at the Elms Polo Club.

"Take Miss Rivera away," he ordered. Once Rosa and the constables were gone, he turned to me. "You're injured, Miss Fox."

I inspected the wound. It had already stopped bleeding, but it stung. "It's just a scratch."

He touched the brim of his hat. "I'll need a statement from you both before you leave." He indicated we should walk ahead of him out of the room. "Clever of you to realize she'd try to escape through the trapdoor. Clever indeed. You have a good brain on you, Miss Fox. I'll be sure to tell my superiors that you helped. You and Armitage."

"I think we did a little more than help, Detective Fanning."

"And I'll be sure you get the credit you deserve."

Somehow I doubted that. At least the murderer was caught, and Vernon Rigg-Lyon would receive justice. Even he deserved it.

* * *

COBBIT SAT on the driver's perch of the black carriage parked out the front of the hotel, his shoulders back and his gaze direct. He touched the brim of his hat as the guests climbed into the cabin and held the reins steady while Goliath strapped luggage to the roof. The coachman had never looked prouder to be in charge of one of the hotel's official vehicles.

I patted the nearest horse's flank. "I'm so glad you've ended your strike."

"We got our point across." From his smile, I suspected he'd achieved more than that.

"And?"

"And Sir Ronald agreed to our terms an hour ago."

I wasn't aware Cobbit had terms, just grievances.

"We wrote 'em up and presented 'em to him, and he agreed to employ us until such time as automobiles replace carriages here at the Mayfair. Then he'll pay to retrain the grooms and other coachmen as mechanics, and I'll be given a payment to tide me over while I find work elsewhere. Or maybe I'll retire."

"You won't retrain as a mechanic, too?"

"I'm too old, Miss Fox, too set in my ways. A retirement fund will do me just fine, I reckon."

"That seems like a good compromise to me." One he'd not entertained when I suggested it to him, yet now he thought it a good idea. "What made you decide to take that course?"

"Someone gave us good advice. Someone with no irons in this fire, just our interests at heart."

"Who?"

He tapped the side of his nose. "A friend of both the hotel and the staff, but not the Bainbridge family."

I stood there trying to work it out as Frank stepped closer. He wiped his gloved thumb over one of the points of the capital M inside the circle, painted on the carriage door. Goliath thumped the back of the carriage to signal the luggage was secure, and Cobbit drove off.

"Do either of you know who helped the mews staff with their negotiation?" I asked.

"Can you not guess?" Goliath asked with an arch of his brows. "A friend of the staff, but not the family. Who has had run-ins with Sir Ronald, but used to work here?"

"It was Armitage," Frank said, in case I couldn't work it out. "I s'pose he's not a bad sort, after all."

I smiled. "I suppose not. I see your voice came back."

"Louder than ever. A very good afternoon to you, Miss Fox."

Inside, the relief was palpable. There was a calmness in the foyer that had been absent recently. Guests engaged in amiable conversation with one another, Mr. Hobart was smiling again, and Peter was an enthusiastic tour guide as he gave directions to an American couple wanting to know where the best shopping could be found.

My mood improved even further when I met Mrs. and Miss Hessing as they stepped out of the lift into the foyer. Miss Hessing greeted me by clasping both my hands and firmly squeezing. She could barely contain her smile.

"You look lovely," I said. "Are you dining in the restaurant this evening?"

"We have an early reservation. We're dining with Mr. Liddicoat." She bounced on her toes, as if she couldn't stand still. "Mother has given her approval."

Mrs. Hessing was near enough to overhear, but her daughter didn't seem to care. "Clare, see if we have any mail, will you?"

Miss Hessing gave my hands one last squeeze, then crossed the foyer to the post desk, none the wiser to her mother's reason for sending her away.

Mrs. Hessing watched her daughter go. She looked odd to

me, but then I realized it was because I'd never seen her give a genuine smile before. "I've never seen her so happy."

"I'm pleased everything has worked out," I said.

"Has it? I haven't met him properly yet. I might not like him."

I could have told her he was an agreeable gentleman, but decided saying nothing was best. I wouldn't put it past her to decide to dislike him merely to be contrary.

"Your advice about investigating him was sound, Miss Fox. Mr. Armitage did a thorough job. He's satisfied that Mr. Liddicoat isn't a fortune hunter, and if he's satisfied, then so am I. So I am keeping my end of our bargain and will allow nature to take its course. If Liddicoat wishes to court her, then he may, and good luck to him."

There was no time to say anything more as Miss Hessing rejoined us. "There was no post, Mother."

Peter strode up, his watch in hand. "Don't you have to get ready, Miss Fox?"

He was right. It was growing late. Mr. Hobart was leaving for the day, passing Mr. Chapman the steward as he headed for the restaurant entrance, reservation book in hand. The Hessings followed him.

Peter watched them go. "You looked like you needed rescuing."

"Thank you, Peter. It seems you're now accomplished in the most difficult skill of the assistant manager's position."

"Which is?"

"Anticipating one's needs."

He smiled. "In this instance, it wasn't difficult to anticipate." He showed me his watch. "Besides, knowing Harmony is busy at this time, I suspected you really do need to go."

"Good Lord, yes I do. Thank you." I picked up my skirts and raced up the stairs to the fourth floor.

Instead of heading directly to my suite, I diverted to my uncle and aunt's rooms to have a quiet word with Aunt Lilian before we went out. I had hoped Uncle Ronald would be in his office, but he was in the sitting room with Floyd, enjoying a glass of sherry. Aunt Lilian was lying down in the bedroom. Warning her about the cocaine tonic would have to wait. It was a conversation best left to when we were alone, anyway.

Since I had to give a reason for my visit to their suite, I brought up the strike. "What a relief it's over."

"Cobbit finally came to his senses," Uncle Ronald agreed.

"Thanks to some intervention, so I hear."

"Is that so? I did wonder. The terms were fair to both parties and well thought out. It didn't seem like something Cobbit would write." He watched the liquid stick to the inside of his glass as he swirled it. "It must have been Hobart."

"It was Harry Armitage, actually."

Uncle Ronald's head snapped up. "How do *you* know that? Have you seen him lately?"

"It was the staff who told me. They all seemed to know that Harry provided a guiding hand to Cobbit."

Uncle Ronald grunted. "Why would he care?"

"Because his uncle is still employed here. Because he cares for the other staff, too, and wants to see the hotel succeed, for everyone's sakes."

He sipped his sherry, pretending he hadn't heard a word I'd said. He was too stubborn to admit out loud that he'd been wrong about Harry, but if he could at least admit it to himself, that would be something.

It was Floyd's reaction that interested me more. He simply sat silently in the armchair, his expression thoughtful as he studied me. Floyd wasn't a deep thinker, and he usually wore his emotions on his sleeve, but this time I couldn't read him.

* * *

I WAS STOPPED in the foyer by Mr. Miller as I went to leave the hotel the following morning. He and his uncle were checking out, their London business having reached its conclusion. I briefly thought about making up an excuse that I was in a hurry, but decided against it. I didn't want to part on bad terms.

He drew me aside while his uncle dealt with the checking out process. We stood by one of the vases of flowers where we could still be seen, but were afforded some privacy from eavesdroppers. There were several who took an interest in us, from Mr. Hobart and Peter, to Uncle Ronald and the Hessings.

227

All looked as though they were involved in their own conversations, but close scrutiny proved they were watching us surreptitiously.

Mr. Miller saw them, too, but forged on as if they weren't there. "I wanted to ask you about the book."

"Oh? I see. Uh, well, I didn't have the chance to read it."

"My question isn't about the contents. It's about why you returned it to me. Were you forced to?" His gaze flicked to Uncle Ronald, pretending to read a newspaper at the post desk.

I didn't need to follow the direction of his gaze to understand what he was really asking. My thoughts on the Walt Whitman book were of no interest to him. I chose my next words carefully, to get my point across without offending. "I returned it of my own volition when I realized Whitman wasn't for me. That's not to say he wasn't a talented writer. I'm sure many readers find something to their taste in his work."

"But you don't?"

"I do not. I am sorry."

He looked towards Mrs. Hessing, standing silently to one side, observing us through the ostrich feathers drooping over the brim of her hat. "Miss Fox, may I speak plainly?"

"Please do."

"It's come to my attention that someone has spread a rumor about me, and I want to be sure you know the correct version." When I didn't comment, he went on. "I was supposed to marry a young lady by the name of Grace. We were very happy, but she came from a wealthy family. The more I grew to know her, the more I loved her and she me. But I also came to realize that she was accustomed to her family's wealth. They lived lavishly, and she enjoyed all the trappings of that life. As you've discovered, I am an employee of my uncle's, not an heir. I live comfortably and can support a family, but it wouldn't be at the same level that Grace was used to." He rocked on his heels and stretched his neck out of his collar. This was obviously difficult for him, but he was swallowing his pride for me. "When her father lost his fortune in the depression of '93, I was unconcerned. My own situation was unaffected. But Grace minded. Although she claimed my wages would suffice, I didn't quite believe her. As the day of our wedding drew closer, she became more and more withdrawn until, finally, I suggested we go our separate ways. She agreed, and that was that. We've hardly seen one another since."

"That must have been very hard for you. I'm sorry you went through that."

"Thank you. It was hard." Again, his gaze shifted to Uncle Ronald then Mrs. Hessing. "A gentleman must protect his family and Sir Ronald couldn't afford not to believe the rumors. But I had hoped you would give me the benefit of the doubt and come to me for the truth."

I bristled. "The rumor has nothing to do with my decision, Mr. Miller. I realized the night you learned that I was a private detective that you and I couldn't be anything more than acquaintances."

He frowned. "I don't understand."

"You spoke of my detecting as if it were a hobby, an acceptable, if unusual, pastime to occupy my days until I become a wife and mother, at which point I would give it up."

He waited for more. When he realized there was none, he said, "You disagree?"

"I do."

"I see." From the way his brow furrowed further, I suspected he didn't understand at all. "Is this because you don't plan to marry?"

I sighed and extended my hand to him. "Goodbye, Mr. Miller, and good luck."

He shook my hand, still frowning.

I left, glad I'd never fallen for his good looks and charming ways. He would make someone a wonderful husband one day. But not me.

* * *

I STOPPED at the Roma Café and purchased two coffees from Luigi. Before leaving, I pecked the cheeks of the two elderly men, then I hummed as I headed upstairs and pushed open Harry's office door.

He accepted one of the cups from me with a smile. "You seem happy this morning. The arrest went well?"

"It did. Better than expected, in fact." I told him about the dressmaker's search for the missing brown coat and bowler hat from the costume department. "It's the final piece we needed to convince Rosa Rivera she couldn't get away with it. She tried to escape, which will only make her look guilty in the eyes of the jury."

"Well done, Cleo. It's a pity you won't get paid for this one."

"Consider it a community service. I do feel some sympathy for Rosa, though. Rigg-Lyon was cruel to abandon her when she needed him most. But resorting to murder is never the answer, not even when one's life is about to change."

"Did you find out if she's still with child?"

"No, but I suspect she is. The dressmaker had adjusted another outfit for her."

"They won't hang her then, but the baby will be born in prison and adopted out."

"Pregnant or not, she couldn't be allowed to get away with it," I said.

"Nor would she, with you on the case." He drained his coffee cup and set it down.

"With *both* of us on it."

He smiled.

"Speaking of being paid, have you sent Mrs. Hessing your bill? Make sure she doesn't delay paying your fee. I get the sense that she will put it off as long as possible."

He picked up the cup again. Even though it was empty, he gave it his full attention.

"Harry? Why are you avoiding answering my question?"

"I'm not."

"Then answer it."

"I waived my fee. It wasn't right to take money for ensuring Miss Hessing's future happiness."

I narrowed my gaze. I didn't believe him for a moment. He'd put a great deal of time and effort into his investigation of Mr. Liddicoat. So why waive his fee? Either Miss or Mrs.

Hessing must have done something for Harry in return. There was one obvious thing that sprang to mind.

"That was her price, wasn't it? You wanted information from her about Mr. Miller and she gave it in exchange for you waiving her fee."

Head bowed, he peered up at me through his long, dark lashes. "She offered the information to me freely. I was unsuspecting before that. She thought you ought to know, so that you could make up your own mind about him."

"If she thought I could make up my own mind, then why did she go to Uncle Ronald and inform him?"

He stood and opened the window. "It's warm in here."

"Ah. I see. *You* asked her to go to Uncle Ronald. She wasn't keen, but you said you'd waive your fee if she did. You knew he wouldn't receive you, so you needed another way to feed the information about Mr. Miller to him."

"That's not why I did it."

"It also meant you were able to deny it when I accused you of interfering."

He looked sheepish. "That's why."

I huffed out a breath. "Harry..." I shook my head, at a loss.

He perched on the edge of the desk near me. "You're angry with me again." The tone of his voice matched the quietness in my heart.

This could drive a wedge between us, if I let it. The fact he left it up to me to make that decision was both powerful and a little overwhelming. He was giving me a choice—forgive him or not.

It was not a difficult choice to make. I smiled up at him. "I'm not angry, Harry. I believe you acted out of concern for a friend."

"You think I did it because you're my *friend*?"

The warmth in his eyes reminded me of something Harmony had said, that Harry was jealous of Mr. Miller. "I would have done the same thing." Too late, I realized I'd just admitted I would have behaved the same way out of jealousy, if the roles were reversed.

His smile spread slowly, starting as a mere twitch, and becoming a lop-sided, deliciously wicked grin. "Is that so?"

I quickly changed the subject, settling on the first thing that came to mind that couldn't be misconstrued. "You spoke to Cobbit. You gave him a way to end the strike with his pride intact. Thank you."

He leaned down to my level. Those warm eyes of his sucked me in, trapping me in their velvet depths. "I don't want to talk about the strike."

My quiet heart became a raging storm, throwing itself against my ribcage. "What do you want to talk about?"

"Nothing." He reached out and cupped my jaw. His thumb lightly stroked the contour of my cheek. "I want to do this."

He closed the gap between us and kissed me.

Available 4th June 2024 :
MURDER AT THE DINNER PARTY
The 8th Cleopatra Fox Mystery

A MESSAGE FROM THE AUTHOR

I hope you enjoyed reading MURDER AT THE POLO CLUB as much as I enjoyed writing it. As an independent author, getting the word out about my book is vital to its success, so if you liked this book please consider telling your friends and writing a review at the store where you purchased it. If you would like to be contacted when I release a new book, subscribe to my newsletter at http://cjarcher.com/contact-cj/newsletter/. You will only be contacted when I have a new book out.

ALSO BY C.J. ARCHER

SERIES WITH 2 OR MORE BOOKS

The Glass Library

Cleopatra Fox Mysteries

After The Rift

Glass and Steele

The Ministry of Curiosities Series

The Emily Chambers Spirit Medium Trilogy

The 1st Freak House Trilogy

The 2nd Freak House Trilogy

The 3rd Freak House Trilogy

The Assassins Guild Series

Lord Hawkesbury's Players Series

Witch Born

SINGLE TITLES NOT IN A SERIES

Courting His Countess

Surrender

Redemption

The Mercenary's Price

ABOUT THE AUTHOR

C.J. Archer has loved history and books for as long as she can remember and feels fortunate that she found a way to combine the two. She spent her early childhood in the dramatic beauty of outback Queensland, Australia, but now lives in suburban Melbourne with her husband, two children and a mischievous black & white cat named Coco.

Subscribe to C.J.'s newsletter through her website to be notified when she releases a new book, as well as get access to exclusive content and subscriber-only giveaways. Her website also contains up to date details on all her books: http://cjarcher.com She loves to hear from readers. You can contact her through email cj@cjarcher.com or follow her on social media to get the latest updates on her books:

facebook.com/CJArcherAuthorPage

twitter.com/cj_archer

instagram.com/authorcjarcher

www.ingramcontent.com/pod-product-compliance
Lightning Source LLC
Chambersburg PA
CBHW010541170726
48285CB00008B/2707